To: Bill Sanders
Chief Bill Sanders
You have been an
inspiration to many a
new Lt. in Oakland and
beyond. Thanks for being my
friend!
Steve Davis #6012

"22E ... Officer Down!"

Steve Davis

This is my first novel.
Steve

D1571544

Third Printing, 2018; Create Space Publishing
ISBN# 97806157988-2-0.

Cover Art by Fred Christensen, Lakeport, CA.

The author wishes to thank and acknowledge the assistance
and encouragement provided by Erica Dyal in reviewing and
editing an early version of the story.

This book is dedicated to my grandfather,
James Thomas Davis*, who inspired me
long after he passed;
To my father,* **Gerard G. Davis***, whose
honor and integrity served as a beacon
throughout my life; and to my mother,*
Arline Thursby Davis*, who encouraged me to
"always take the path that will give you 'the story'
to laugh about when you are old."*

And to my wife, **Elizabeth Dittmar Davis***,
for her love and support.*

Section One

Arcata, California.

Thursday, October 15, 1970; 05:41 a.m.

It had been almost fifty years since a cop had been killed on California's North Coast. In fact, only the oldest of the old timers that met for breakfast at Fernbridge every day could even recall that spring morning in April, 1921, when Constable Purvis McKenzie was gunned down by an armed assailant near Klamath. The shooter, who was captured four hours later attempting to flee from a roadblock set up in Orick, had long since died in San Quentin prison of natural causes.

Of course, that incident was not even on the mind of California Highway Patrol Officer Dean Brennan as he turned his older blue Datsun pickup off the freeway. In fact, he was only thinking about football, Pop Warner peewee football to be exact.

All of that was about to change in the next few minutes. History has a habit of repeating itself in small, remote communities that time and progress seem to have forgotten, and Humboldt County was just such a community in 1970. Brennan made the two quick right turns that led him back toward the CHP Office, a lonely cinderblock building that sat alone at the edge of the huge open wetlands on the southern outskirts of the small bayside city of Arcata.

The remnants of a crescent moon hung just over the western horizon, creeping in and out of the gray-black clouds that told of a pending storm coming in over the ocean. An early morning fog hung low, touching the ground, low enough to see over it as he drove up to the closed office.

The nondescript office was 'ground zero' for the 25 Traffic Officers who patrolled the highways in rural Humboldt County. Nestled against the background of the vast Giant Redwood forests as they meet the Pacific Ocean, Humboldt remains one of California's almost forgotten northern coastal counties.

From the outside, at that time of the morning, the building didn't appear to be inhabited, but then, it was supposed to look that way. The CHP, for safety purposes, would prefer that no one knew that inside the building, CHP Dispatcher Sylvia Santos sat alone all night in the

Dispatch Center, a one-room cubicle set aside in one corner of the CHP Office.

The Dispatch Center was manned 24 hours per day, seven days per week, to answer public calls for help and to dispatch Officers via radio to such calls. Sylvia was working alone tonight on the "all-nighter" shift, which began at midnight. She was the sole communication link for radio calls to and from the two-man graveyard unit, which went off-duty at 4:30 a.m., and for unit "16-22-E"[1], the solo Officer on the early morning "E" shift, which covers the two hour gap until the regular morning shift, including Brennan and three other Officers, began.

Officer Brennan pulled up to the locked gate, which opens to the back parking lot. The gate was always locked, except when there was a uniformed Officer present in the building. The fact that the gate was locked as he approached meant his closest friend on the CHP, Officer Sonny Tyler, who was working 16-22-E, must have gotten a call and had "hit the road."

---

[1] CHP Radio Call Sign; '16-' signifies Humboldt CHP Area; '22-' refers to the Officer's assigned beat for the day; and 'E' signifies the Officer's assigned Shift that day.

"Damn," thought Brennan as he got out, entered the four-digit security code, and rolled the big gate open.

He parked in the first empty stall, and a few moments later, he unlocked the back door of the office and went inside. He made his way through the locker room and walked briskly to the front corner of the building where Sylvia was sitting at the dispatch console, illuminated by a single reading light in the mostly unlighted room, engrossed in what appeared to be a romance novel.

Sylvia was by far the prettiest of the eight dispatchers at the office, the 28-year-old granddaughter of Enrico Santos, one of the many Portuguese dairy farmers in the community of Ferndale, 18 miles south of Eureka. Her jet black hair fairly framed her striking features, and her alluring dark eyes complimented her naturally tanned complexion.

"Morning, Sylvia," he said, "I guess Sonny is already out on a call?"

She looked up and smiled as she closed the book on her index finger between the pages. "Yes, Dean, he left just a few minutes ago for an accident out in the Freshwater area. You're in here early."

"I hoped to catch Sonny before he left and talk some football. I want to go over some football plays with him before we got busy. How bad is the accident, do I need to get out there to help?"

"Just a reported non-injury accident. Football, huh?" she said, "You guys still coaching football together?"

Brennan pulled out the only other chair in the room and sat down across from the desk. A big man, he could barely fit his 1958 University-of-Oregon-starting-left-tackle body into the chair. Sylvia finished closing the book and set it on the table, marking her place with a blank dispatch card.

"Yeah. Pop Warner Football; and this is the big game this weekend. Fortuna versus Eureka."

"Which side are you guys on?"

"Eureka, of course. We coach the Eureka Pirates, the 9 to 12-year-olds. We play in Fortuna this week, and I got this great draw play I wanted to show him. I'll have to catch up with him on the road later."

"Men and football," she said with a slight shake of her head. "Of course, my family is all about High School football. No, make that Ferndale High School football."

"We'll be there soon. Watch out for Eureka High in 1976, when our kids get there."

Their conversation was interrupted by the arrival of Wayne Coughlin and Russ Gibson, two other day shift Officers coming on duty. Coughlin, the older and shorter of the two by two inches, was smiling proudly under his thick black mustache. He fancied himself quite a ladies man, and everyone could see he was proud of something he had to share with them as he maneuvered his way into the now-crowded room. Gibson, quieter by nature, stood slightly behind him in the doorway in anticipation. Without hesitation, Coughlin broke into the conversation. "Hey, Sylvia," he said seductively, "I had a dream about you and me last night…"

"That'll be the day!" she said, rolling her eyes and looking down at the desk.

"No, really," Coughlin continued, now a little louder and cockier, "We were together and you said I was the biggest you'd ever had!" He paused, gloating over the thought that he'd caught her off guard with his crude innuendo.

"Coughlin." Sylvia paused. She slowly and deliberately rotated her head and eyes from the desk to look directly at him. "Didn't anyone ever tell you that being told you're the biggest prick they've ever seen is NOT a compliment?"

"Whoohoo," Officer Brennan shouted as he and Gibson burst into laughter. Coughlin turned red and looked at them and said, "That's not funny!" He pressed backwards past Gibson and walked away muttering to himself.

"That is the first time I've ever heard Coughlin speechless," Gibson laughed. "What a hit for his giant ego."

"We gotta tell the Sergeant about this, he'll love it." Brennan chuckled as they made their way down the hall toward the briefing room. Sylvia smiled proudly to herself, as she re-opened the novel and began to read again.

Brennan and Gibson were still chuckling about the incident in the briefing room a few minutes later, when Sergeant George Anderson walked into the room, walked past the podium at the front of the room, and sat with his right leg on the corner of the front desk, just as he always did. Three minutes till 6:00 a.m., just like every other day. He was punctual, if nothing else.

Anderson was one of three Sergeants assigned to the Area. He was not highly respected by any of the Officers, since they saw him as a man who commanded attention by virtue of the stripes on his sleeve, rather than through his actions. Four years previously, when the CHP was doubling in size statewide, he had taken the Sergeant's test and came near at the bottom of the 320 who took the test. Normally about 100 Officers would be promoted on a list, but as fate would have it, new Sergeants were needed throughout the state, and every person on the list was promoted. So there he was, a Sergeant, even if in name only, and the Officers were stuck with him.

He looked over at the two men assembled in the room and smirked with anticipation. Officer Coughlin was not there yet, but he could hear him in the adjacent locker room. Coughlin was always the last one in the room, and the Sergeant knew he would come breezing in, half dressed, and usually with seconds to spare before the clock struck 6:00 a.m. Once in a while, he'd be a few seconds late, and the Sergeant hoped today would be one of those days. He looked up at the clock again, ready to catch Officer Coughlin late, so he could call out to him in the locker room, "Coughlin, get in here!" It was a little ritual they played out every morning. It was Officer Coughlin's way of showing his lack of respect for the Sergeant, and it was Sergeant Anderson's way of reminding Coughlin who was in charge.

"Hey Serge," Brennan said, "You'll love this. Wait'll you hear what Sylvia just did to Coughlin." But before he could continue, Coughlin shouted, "Shut up, you guys," from the adjacent locker room. Again, Brennan and Gibson burst into laughter.

As he watched the clock and waited, Sergeant Anderson didn't attempt to get involved in the conversation, but quietly waited for the second hand of the clock to point exactly to the 12, at which time he would be officially in charge once again. His silent sentinel was interrupted by the voice of Sylvia, on the intercom. "Sergeant Anderson, please come up to dispatch immediately. Please hurry!"

The collective heartbeat of everyone in the room stopped in its tracks. That certain pitch in a dispatcher's voice was reserved only for a singular type of emergency; that involving one of their own. An Officer was in great danger!

Officer Brennan was closest to the door, and was the first to react to the call, with Officer Gibson right behind. After a moment's delay to realize what he just heard, Sergeant Anderson caught his breath and raced up the short hallway to the dispatcher's office, pushing his way into the small, crowded, room. "What's up?" he gulped. Officer Coughlin came up from the locker room, his shirt out and his pants half zipped, yelling, "What's going on, guys."

"Shut up, Coughlin!" the Sergeant said. Then, turning to the ashen-faced dispatcher, "What's wrong?" he asked breathlessly.

"I got a faint call a few minutes ago. I couldn't make it out, but it sounded urgent. The only unit we have out is Officer Tyler, and now he doesn't answer." I pulled the master tape and put it on the spare reel, but this is all I can get from it." She pushed the PLAY button and out of the quiet they heard a short, faint utterance. The entire transmission was very short, just the keying of the microphone, followed by a few labored, breathless words, but it was clearly from Unit 22E, Officer Tyler. "Play it back! ... Play it back!" someone yelled from the rear, "and turn it up!"

Once again, the dispatcher backed up the tape, turned up the volume, and clicked the PLAY button. A chill ran down the neck of everyone in the room, when they heard Officer Tyler, in obvious anguish, take a deep breath and groan, "22E, ... Officer Down!" For a few short seconds, there was silence, another labored breath, and then the mike went dead. Officer Gibson said, "Holy Shit!"

Officer Brennan shouted, "Where is he?"

Sergeant Anderson asked excitedly, "When did you talk to him last?"

Without waiting for an answer, Officer Brennan sprinted from the room. From the dispatch center, his footsteps could be heard as he ran down the hallway to the locker room. Moments later, a locker door slammed, and he was out the door to the carport. Behind him, you could hear other lockers and doors slamming, and the jangling of keys, as Gibson also prepared to respond to a location neither had yet determined.

Back in the dispatch center, Sylvia turned to Sergeant Anderson and Officer Coughlin, "Just a few minutes before the call, he radioed he was clear from the accident call on the east side. Grabbing the log, she said, "Here it is! Dispatched at 5:49 a.m. Citizen report of a non-injury accident, Myrtle Avenue at Freshwater Road. It was GOA, gone on arrival. Then, a few minutes later, he called in a traffic stop for a registration violation on a California plate, but didn't give a location. It has to be close to Myrtle and Freshwater."

Officer Coughlin moved quickly through the doorway to respond to the call. At that moment, Officer Brennan came over the radio, "Humboldt, 16-18.[2] I'm en-route. What was Tyler's last location?"

Switching to the countywide radio frequencies, Sylvia alerted all available units of the situation, "16-18 and all units, Emergency Traffic! 11-99![3] Repeat, 11-99! Officer Needs Help! Last reported making a traffic stop on a white late-model Chevy, expired California license

---

[2] CHP Radio Codes; 'Humboldt' refers to the CHP Dispatch Center call sign, '16-18' is the Officer's assigned beat for the day.

[3] Radio code '11-99'; Officer Needs Help! Emergency response needed.

ARM601, about three minutes after clearing a call at Myrtle Avenue and Freshwater Road."

Brennan responded, "16-18 is en-route; run that license plate and get the vehicle and Registered Owner information to me as soon as possible."

Minutes later, first Gibson, and then Coughlin, also called in to report they, too, were en-route to the area from which Tyler was last heard.

In the dispatch center, Sylvia went over the details again with the Sergeant. "Tyler is working E watch alone. He responded at 5:19 a.m. to a non-injury accident call at Myrtle and Freshwater. At 5:49 a.m., he calls it in as GOA. A few minutes later he made a traffic stop on a white late-model Chevrolet; California license ARM601, for expired registration, but didn't give a location. The last radio traffic was me advising him there was no record on the plate; it shows unregistered for at least five years. That's as far as DMV records are available."

"No record in five years?" Sergeant Anderson asked. "Run it again, there has to be something! Call DMV in Sacramento. Get the old owner, new owner, anything!"

"That plate number means it is a very old plate, Sarge," Sylvia declared, "But I'll see what I can find out. In the meantime, I could use some help with notifications and getting the All Points Bulletin out to other agencies to be on the lookout for a white late-model Chevy." Pausing, her voice dropped, "It sounds bad … don't you think we should let the Commander know what's happening?"

Sergeant Anderson nodded.

Moments later, while they waited for the Officers to arrive at the last known location of Officer Tyler, the phone rang. "CHP dispatch. Is this an emergency?" Sylvia answered. After eight years at the same console, she instinctively drew the correct dispatch card from the slot without looking, punched it in the time stamp machine, and began to make notes on the card.

"What? I'm having a hard time hearing you, sir. There's some traffic noise in the background. Can you speak a little louder? That's better, it went away. No sir. What is the location?" She then repeated the information she was being given so that the Sergeant could follow along, "CHP unit with its emergency lights on and no-one appears to be around. Where? Greenwood Heights Drive one-half mile north of Freshwater? Can I get your name, sir?" There was a short pause, and then she said, "He hung up."

"That's less than a mile from Myrtle and Freshwater." Sergeant Anderson said.

Back on the radio, Sylvia said, "Attention 16-18 and all units; Citizen's report of a CHP vehicle with its lights flashing and no-one around on Greenwood Heights Drive one-half mile north of Freshwater."

"10-4. En route," answered Brennan.

It seemed like an eternity as she and the Sergeant waited for the call they didn't want to hear. While they waited, anticipating the worst, Sylvia picked up the phone and dialed the ambulance 'hot line'. "Morning, Verna. I want you to start an ambulance, with EMT's and Paramedics, everything, as soon as you can, Code 3[4], to Greenwood Heights Drive one-half mile north of Freshwater. No, it isn't an accident, but I think we may need all the help we can get for an Officer down at that location, and I want to get help started."

---

[4] CHP Radio Code; 'Respond with siren and emergency lights'.

As she waited, she went over in her mind what she would do if this was really the "worst case scenario" every dispatcher dreads. She grabbed the Emergency Procedures Manual from the shelf, but before she could open it, they heard Officer Brennan say, in an obviously excited voice, loud enough to be heard above the siren in the background, "16-18 is on the scene with the unit on Greenwood Heights; it appears no-one is around. Advise other units for backup. I'll be looking around."

"This isn't good," Sergeant Anderson said. "This is NOT good!"

Within seconds, the silence was again broken by the now-panicked voice of Officer Brennan, "Humboldt, 16-18," he said breathlessly, "Officer Down! Send an ambulance, supervisor, and Sheriff for … he paused to force the words out of his mouth … possible 11-44[5], Officer Down!"

"11-44 Officer?" Sergeant Anderson grimaced as if someone had just punched him in the stomach. He sank back in distress into the empty chair at his side. A half-hour

---

[5] CHP Radio Code; 'Fatal, Coroner requested at scene.'

ago, he relished being "in charge." Now, the thought that an Officer had been killed on his watch made him want to throw down his badge and run away. "This can't be true," he muttered to himself. "I'd better get out there," he said, as he walked from the room.

"10-4, 16-18," Sylvia responded to Officer Brennan, tears already streaming down her face. She took a deep breath to compose herself, and said slowly into the microphone, "Ambulance is already en-route. I'll make the notifications." She looked at the timestamp on the dispatch card she held; it was 6:21 a.m.

Back at the scene, Officer Brennan hung up the microphone and stared out through the windshield at Officer Tyler's unit in front of him. He took a deep breath and slowly let it out as he took in the enormity of the situation. He swallowed hard and hesitated a moment in shock and disbelief.

He knew what to do next; he had done it a thousand times on lesser cases than this over the last 16 years. He had to preserve the crime scene, and protect potential evidence. But this was his closest friend on the CHP, and he couldn't just let him lie there, dead, while he waited helplessly. What if he weren't really dead?

Brennan got out of the unit and walked quickly between the vehicles and along the right side of Tyler's car, approaching the still, lifeless form on the ground near the right front fender.

He winced as he kneeled down near his friend, who was slouched against the right front wheel and fender, his head cocked to the left staring eerily into the adjacent forest. A medium caliber bullet hole was visible in the Officer's blood-soaked shirt just to the left of the top button. A second hole was in the throat area, and everything below it was drenched in deep red blood.

There was no blood coming from the wounds now; it appeared that it had all drained down his shirt and into his lap, forming a large puddle on the ground around the Officer. The smell of fresh blood filled his senses, and as his heart held out hope for his fallen comrade, reality kept reminding him that he'd seen and smelled death before, and this was exactly what it looked and smelled like.

By now the last remnants of the moon had vanished beyond the western horizon, and the first rays of daylight were yet to appear from the east. Lost somewhere between night and day, reality and denial, Officer Brennan knelt down, supported Officer Tyler's head, held it in his arms and, in a broken voice, begged his friend not to die.

Steve Davis

Notification of Commander
6:25 a.m.

Brrring!!!

Across town, CHP Captain Kurt Richards, was suddenly awakened by the phone next to the bed. He raised his arm and stabbed at the alarm clock on the nightstand, before he even opened his eyes.

Brrring!!!

The second ring jolted him further out of his deep sleep, but he was not yet awake. His heart was pounding as he tried to differentiate between the dreams he left behind and the reality that had so rudely pulled him away from them.

As he scooped up the phone awkwardly, he had no idea what time it was; he only knew that it was sometime in the middle of the night, and he had been fast asleep when the phone shook him to his senses.

He took a moment to shake the sleep out of his head, and glanced at the clock on the nightstand. Exactly 6:25a.m. He sat up stiffly before speaking to the caller. His nine years as a CHP Area Commander had taught him that any call after 9:00 p.m. and before 7:30 a.m. was cause for immediate alarm. He used to say, *"No-one has ever called me in the middle of the night with good news."* Even that knowledge, however, could not prepare him for this call.

"Hello," he said tentatively into the phone. As the Humboldt Area Commander, he was on call every night of the year, and he always thought that he must be the only person in the world who actually hoped to get a wrong number in the middle of the night.

"Captain," said the anguished voice he recognized immediately as that of Sylvia Santos, "We need you as soon as possible. I have terrible news." She paused awkwardly, and the Captain listened for an equally awkward time. Then, she continued, her voice breaking, "Officer Tyler … has been killed."

"Killed?" he repeated, in an effort to buy a few seconds time. Now fully shaken from any lingering thoughts of peaceful rest, he said, "How? An accident?"

"No, Sir," she said, the tears welling up again as she struggled with the words, "He was shot. Murdered."

"Murdered? Holy Shit! Did they get the asshole that did it? Please tell me that he's dead, too."

"No, Sir. We don't know who did it. They found him with no one around on Greenwood Heights Drive. The Sheriff's Homicide team is en-route at this time. Sergeant Anderson is asking for you to get here as soon as you can."

"I'll be right there. Tell me again where it happened. I want to go there on the way."

"Yes, Sir," she said, "but I thought I'd better warn you; the Officer's wife isn't aware of it yet, and she is known to listen to the scanner early in the morning."

"Good point," he said, "What's her name, again?"

"Bonnie. And they have a young son, Casey."

"Bonnie. Right, I remember her, now. I'd better handle that first. Let me think a minute. Anderson's the Sergeant, huh. That's not much help." After a moment's pause, he said, "Who is his best friend among the Officers? Fulton, isn't it?"

"I think so, sir," said Sylvia, "Fulton or Brennan, and Brennan found him, and he's pretty shook up."

"OK," said Richards, "Call Fulton and get him into ⁻the office ASAP. I'll meet him there in fifteen minutes, and we'll go out to Tyler's house together. Be sure and tell him fifteen minutes. Okay? Goodbye."

As he sat on the edge of the bed, he wished he'd taken the time to know Tyler and his family better. Tyler usually worked the early and late shifts, because of his youth sports activities, so he hadn't gotten to know him as well as the officers who worked the day and afternoon shifts. Now he pondered how it could be that he knew so little about an officer who worked for him for over four years and was now dead.

Emergency Response
6:30 a.m.

Back at the scene, the whole event seemed surreal to Officer Brennan. The flashing emergency lights from Officer Tyler's unit, thrust into the still darkness of the early morning, cast an eerie glow on the horror he had found. Red, amber and white lights, rejected by the low hanging fog, dispersed back onto the scene in a mystic blur of colors. The contrast of the fog, the lights and the blackness of the thick forest along both sides of the road made him feel alone and vulnerable. Suddenly, he didn't feel like the hardened veteran Officer that he was.

Was that fear that was causing the hair on the back of his neck to stand up? Was the shooter, or shooters, still around, perhaps watching him even now? He shined his flashlight out into the darkness, hunkered down a little, and waited for help to arrive.

"Is this how life is supposed to end," he questioned. *"You give your heart and soul to unselfishly protect the lives of people you don't even know, and who often don't care, only to die, alone, along a lonely highway?"*

Brennan wasn't the kind of guy who made friends easily, and Sonny Tyler was the closest thing he had to a 'best friend'. His mind raced through the details of the past few years: how he and Tyler had become close friends, although their friendship didn't start easily.

When Tyler first transferred to the squad in 1966, he brought a level of enthusiasm to the job that hadn't been seen for years in rural Humboldt County. Although Tyler had eight years on the CHP when he arrived in the squad, he was still considered a rookie in Humboldt by the established officers, like Brennan, who had a dozen or more years of experience at the time. Like the other 'veterans', Brennan felt that Tyler was trying to show them up by working harder than he needed to. In time, however, he grew to respect Tyler's eagerness and love of the job, which had even begun to wear off on himself and some of the other officers.

Over the last four years, they bonded by virtue of their mutual involvement in their children's sports activities. They shared a love of family and sports, and eventually found themselves coaching alongside each other on the youth sports fields in football and baseball, where both were coaches for their sons' teams.

"*Why?*" he thought to himself. He hoped the answers would be unraveled later, but he didn't know how much later.

Jostled from a sense of subconsciousness, Officer Brennan was relieved to hear sirens, lots of them, converging on the scene from all directions. The next thing he knew, there were voices running toward him, and a young Paramedic took him by the arm and led him away from the fallen Officer, while other ambulance personnel began their lifesaving efforts.

Brennan sat on the push bumper of his unit and watched as ambulance and fire personnel, most of whom he knew only by sight from scores of accident scenes, worked feverishly over the motionless Officer. They all knew their efforts were in vain, for he was hopelessly lost, and they could only go through the motions for so long, before declaring the Officer legally deceased.

An older Paramedic with whom he was familiar walked over to him and whispered, "I'm sorry, Dean, he's gone." Brennan took a deep breath and exhaled slowly through pursed lips, as he struggled to grasp the full measure of the loss. As he choked back his emotions, he nodded knowingly and whispered, "Thanks," to the Paramedic, who turned and walked away. Brennan covered his eyes with his right hand, and sobbed quietly for a few seconds, but only a few seconds. Then he took another deep breath and drew upon the strength to compose himself; he could grieve privately later.

The ambulance personnel quietly picked up their gear and carried it back to their vehicle. Someone had already placed a bright yellow plastic DMB, or 'dead man blanket', as the officers called it, over the fallen Officer.

Officer Gibson arrived next, looked around at the gravity of the situation and, after quickly pausing to look at the covered body of his deceased comrade, began to take charge of the scene. That's what cops do, when they really just want to cry, they take a deep breath and take charge. Keeping busy kept him from thinking about the horrific drama being played out in front of him.

Since a homicide at this location fell under the scope of responsibility of the Humboldt County Sheriff's Office, he began preparing the scene for the Sheriff's

Homicide Investigation Team, which had been called out, and would be en-route to the scene from the city of Eureka, 5 miles away. He directed Officer Coughlin, as he was approaching the scene, to close the entire highway for at least one-half mile in both directions. Officer Gibson took some photos of the scene from the highway, while the first uniformed Sheriff's Deputy, who arrived moments earlier, silently marked off the area with crime scene tape.

Brennan could see Sergeant Anderson's patrol car rapidly approaching from the west. Suddenly feeling wet and cold, Brennan glanced down for the first time and saw that his shirt and pants were covered with Officer Tyler's blood. He looked at his watch and saw it was already 6:40 a.m., and the first light of dawn was starting to light up the scene.

Sergeant Anderson pulled up at the scene, got out and glanced at the covered body of Officer Tyler, then immediately approached Brennan, still seated on the push bumper of his unit. He leaned down and put his hand on Brennan's shoulder. "You OK, Dean? I know you and Tyler were close."

"Yeah, I'll make it. I just need a minute for it to sink in. Who is going to tell his family?"

"Sylvia called the Commander, and they called out Officer Fulton, who will go with him to Tyler's place to break the news to the wife. I'm glad it's not me. You need to go back to the office and change clothes. I'll have Coughlin drive you there."

"OK, Sarge," Brennan replied softly. His patrol car was in the middle of the crime scene, so he knew that it couldn't be removed from the crime scene for hours, and he was relieved to get a ride. "I'm OK. Don't worry. I'll just go back and wait for the Sheriff's investigators."

"Remember," Anderson added, "Since you were in contact with Tyler, they'll need your uniform for trace evidence, so just put each item in a separate paper bag, nothing else. Change into your civvies, and wait there. The Sheriff's investigators will need to talk to you, so just stand by at the office until they get there. You should make notes of everything you saw, smelled, heard, etc. I'll see you back there as soon as we get cleared up here."

Brennan nodded toward the Sergeant. He had never heard Anderson actually act like a Sergeant before, and he was a little surprised as he slowly walked toward Officer Coughlin's unit.

Steve Davis

En-route back to the office, Officer Brennan sat quietly and stared out the window. Familiar sights, landscapes, and features were as though he'd never laid eyes on them before. Nothing seemed familiar to him anymore. It was as if his whole world, everything he knew and had come to believe in, had suddenly turned on him.

He thought about Officer Tyler's family. He had personally always considered Bonnie Tyler to be a little 'different', but then, he thought his own wife was even stranger, so he never gave it much thought. He had been around her enough to know that Bonnie was more interested in her husband's work than most cop wives, and would not take this very well. He thought to himself, "*She's going to have a hard time handling this; the worst nightmare of every cop's wife.*" He hoped that whoever broke the news to her and little Casey would be up to the task.

Notification of Bonnie Tyler
6:45 HRS

When Captain Richards arrived at the Office, he was relieved to find Officer Abe Fulton waiting just inside the door, in uniform. He was standing tall and ready, but anyone who knew him could see through the military-tough exterior, and knew that he was badly shaken. Standing next to the Officer was his wife, Katie. Katie was not nearly as pretty this morning as Richards had seen her in the past, but that was always at parties and social events where she was dressed to the nines. Appreciative of the ladies, he always took a second look at Katie, but this morning she was … well … a little haggard. Her hair was barely combed into place, her face was puffy, and her eyes were red from tears that were still streaming down her cheeks. He silently scolded himself for thinking about women at this moment.

"Captain," Fulton said, "I brought Katie, because she's as close to Bonnie as anyone, and we are going to need her to deal with Bonnie and little Casey."

"Good thinking," he said. Then, turning to Katie, he said half seriously, "But you have got to stop that," pointing to her tears, "or none of us will get through this."

"I'll ... try," she said.

Captain Richards excused himself and walked over to the dispatch center. Sylvia was talking to the Sheriff's Dispatcher on the phone. In front of her, on the console, was the Emergency Operations Manual. Captain Richards could see that the pages were wet with tears, although Sylvia appeared under control at the moment, as she worked. "You OK?" he asked.

"Yes, for now. I'll fall apart later," she said. "I've got overtime help coming in and I've prepared a teletype for Division and Headquarters. We'll get through this. I just hope they catch the asshole that did it."

"We'll do everything possible; he won't get away. I won't rest until he's dead or behind bars. Tell me what's going on at this moment."

"Well," Sylvia said, as she reached for a stack of radio cards, "Officer Brennan found him and is en-route back to the office to wait for the Sheriff's Homicide Team to be interviewed. The team has just begun to arrive at the scene, so it'll be awhile before they get around to Brennan. I'm worried about him. Until they get here, I don't think he should be alone."

"I'm not sure what we can do for him right now, but we'll do what we can, when we can. Great job, Sylvia. As soon as your backup arrives, send the teletype to Division and Headquarters. I'll talk to the Chief as soon as I get back from breaking the news to Bonnie Tyler."

Then he and the Fultons walked outside and got into the Commander's unmarked unit.

"Humboldt, 16-C, 10-8[6] and en-route." He said into the radio, as he steered the new Dodge toward the Cutten area, south of Eureka.

"16-C, Humboldt, 10-4," Sylvia replied.

He looked at the clock on the dashboard; 6:54 a.m. Today was a school day, so he knew Officer Tyler's wife might already be up, and they hoped they could get to her house before she turned on the police scanner. He began to go over the Departmental Procedures for events such as this

---

[6] CHP Radio Codes: Humboldt is the radio code for the CHP Dispatch Center; '16-C' is the radio code for the CHP Area Commander; '10-8' means 'on the air and available by radio'

in his mind, and he wished he'd looked at them more recently than when he was studying for Captain 10 years ago.

"Tell me about Tyler, Abe."

"Remember, Captain? Tyler and I reported in to this office together about four years ago," Fulton reminisced. "There hadn't been any new Officers transfer in for several years, and we took the place of two Officers who got fired. We were younger than the other Officers, and the two guys who got fired were pretty popular. That didn't help. For a while we weren't exactly accepted."

"Yeah, I remember," said the Captain softly.

It appeared the Captain was scarcely listening and was lost in some parallel thought, but Fulton continued, "We both liked to work hard and arrest drunks, and that made the older Officers look bad. We were outcasts for the first few months. But we helped most of them over time; even took their crashes just to have something to do. Once we started doing their work for them, they came around quick. Over time they accepted us, and today there is no problem. But Tyler and I always felt like the two musketeers."

Captain Richards didn't say anything, but continued to stare blankly out the windshield.

"What happens when we get there?" asked Katie. "Bonnie is going to know as soon as she sees us."

"Yes. I know," said the Captain, as he rejoined the conversation. "We always try to break it gently, but wives know that when a Sergeant or Captain comes calling, it is bad news. We'll just do the best we can. I don't really know Bonnie that well. Tell me about her; anything I need to know?"

"Well, let's see," Katie began, "She has a reputation as a bit of a drama queen, but I like her a lot."

"Drama queen?" he interrupted. "What do you mean by that?"

"Well, it seems like there's always some issue going on in her life, or there's someone who she isn't -getting along with."

"Some of the wives don't like her," she continued, "but there are a lot of others, like me, who think she's nice. I guess maybe it depends …"

"Really? Depends on what?"

Steve Davis

"Jealousy, I guess. She is very active in the local youth sports; football, baseball. She has had problems with some other parents, usually women. It seems with Bonnie, most of the men like her, but some of the wives don't. I like her."

Abe continued where his wife left off. "For some reason, she seems to relate better with guys, she likes police work, and relates well with cops. She clashes with some wives who seem to be jealous of her ability to understand their husband's jobs better than they do. From what Tyler told me through the years, I think she was working as a clerk for a Sheriff's Department down in the Bay Area when they met, and she really enjoys being around police work. She probably would have been a cop herself, if they allowed women."

"It's going to happen, someday," Richards said resignedly. "Even the CHP is gearing up for it. It is inevitable. They'll probably do fine, but it's going to be awkward for a while. I hope I'm gone before they get this far north."

Fulton continued, "She likes to talk cop stuff with Sonny and other cops, and she has all the radio codes and call signs memorized. I probably shouldn't tell you this, but she has ridden with Sonny on nights quite a few times."

"Really? Sounds like a unique person. Let me ask you this, are you saying between the lines that she likes to play around with other guys ... cops?"

"Oh, no!" said Katie, as Abe shook his head in agreement. "She just relates better to the guys than to women," Katie continued. "I get along great with her because I grew up in a home with four older brothers, so I kind of think like a guy, too."

Captain Richards was known to drive fast, but this morning he drove notably much slower than usual, as he headed south on H Street toward the Cutten area, a rural wooded community just south of the Eureka city limits. Cutten was sparsely populated, surrounded by redwood forests owned by the Louisiana Pacific and Pacific Lumber Companies, with some Bureau of Land Management land thrown in.

Everyone in the car seemed deep in their own thoughts, and there was no further conversation as they turned south on Walnut Drive and approached the Tyler family home.

Inside the Tyler's home, Bonnie Tyler stood in the kitchen facing the street and quietly stirred the pan of oatmeal cooking on the stove. She opened the curtains, and looking out the window, she said to no one, "Beautiful! It is going to be a nice day."

She and Sonny had bought the "fixer-upper" house when they moved to Eureka four years ago, and they were slowly renovating it to their liking. The old house sat back from the road, nestled in among tall redwood trees. Two ancient redwood trees near the road partially hid the structure from the highway. The circular gravel driveway arched in front of the house and culminated at the walkway leading to the front porch.

Inside the house, already dressed, Bonnie walked into Casey's bedroom and gently woke him up. Her voice was dripping with sweetness, the way she always talked when she was in a good mood, "Casey, honey, it's ten 'til seven; time to get up and get ready for school. I'm cooking breakfast, so come out and eat right away."

Returning to the kitchen, she stirred the oatmeal and called over her shoulder, "Casey. Honey, it's ready. Come in now, Sweetie."

Nine-year-old Casey Tyler walked into the room in his pajamas, wiping the sleep from his eyes. He was small for his age, and most people thought he was younger than he was. His blond hair still showed the effects of a long night's sleep, accentuated by his natural cowlick that stuck straight into the air. He didn't wake up easily, and he still hadn't uttered a word. She said to him, "You don't need to hurry too much today, honey. I've got some errands to run, and I'll drive you to school, today."

Then she turned back towards the cabinet in the corner and flipped the switch on the police radio scanner, which she kept in the corner of the kitchen counter. *"I wonder what is going on this morning?"*

"S-2, Control 1.[7]" The voice of the Humboldt County Sheriff's Dispatcher said on the scanner. "Your Homicide Team members have all reported in and are en-route to the scene on Greenwood Heights."

"Control 1, S-2. 10-4."

---

[7] Humboldt County Sheriff Radio Codes; Control 1 is the Sheriffs Department's Dispatch Center; S-2 is the radio call sign for the Sheriff's Sergeant; in this case, the #2 sergeant in departmental seniority.

"S-2, Control 1. Also, be advised, Unit 23 is responding to another shooting, possible second 187[8], in Sequoia Park. No further details at this time."

"Control 1, S-2. 10-4. Keep me advised. I'll assign another team if it turns out to be another homicide."

"Oh, my," Bonnie said aloud. "The SO has two murders at the same time. And one is in Sequoia Park." She turned up the volume on the scanner.

Back when she was Bonnie Montague, and a civilian records clerk for the Alameda County Sheriff's Office, Bonnie always worked the graveyard shift at the records desk in the jail, where occasionally she would be pressed into service as an assistant jail matron by the booking desk whenever a particularly obnoxious female prisoner was being booked. She never actually handled any prisoners, but she was there to serve as a witness that the Officers and Deputies acted appropriately in processing the female booking. She lived for these opportunities, when she could almost feel like a real cop. To fulfill her fantasy, she had memorized the common criminal Penal Code sections and police radio codes.

---

[8] 187 refers to Calif. Penal Code 187; homicide or murder.

It was on one such occasion that she had met Sonny Tyler, when he brought in a combative female drunk driver. The woman later made allegations of impropriety against Sonny at the jail, and the CHP had interviewed Bonnie in their investigation before exonerating Sonny of the allegations. After that, Bonnie would listen for Sonny's call number and when she heard he was en-route to the jail, she would conveniently show up in the break room when he came in after booking his prisoner. They hit it off immediately, and after a year or so, they were married, and Casey was born the following year.

Now, nine years later, after Sonny got a transfer from the urban San Francisco East Bay to rural Humboldt County, she continued to live her cop fantasy vicariously through Sonny, and occasionally talked him into letting her ride along with him on patrol. Accustomed to the tales of the streets, she was not easily shocked or even mildly surprised by crimes and the actions of criminals.

In the kitchen, the CHP radio channel came to life on the scanner, "Humboldt, 16-C is 10-97[9]."

"16-C, Humboldt, 10-4." The radio acknowledged.

---

[9] CHP Radio Code: 10-97 is 'Arrived on the scene.'

"16-C?" Bonnie questioned to no one in particular. "I wonder why the Captain is out this early?"

Captain Richards turned the car into the gravel driveway and pulled up near the front door of the Tyler house. Taking a deep breath, he said to the Fultons, "Well, here we go."

Bonnie heard the sound of the wheels of the car on the gravel driveway outside. She turned off the stove, and, wiping her hands on a dish towel, walked to the window and looked out. As the Commander's car came into view, she recognized it as an unmarked CHP vehicle and recognized Captain Richards.

She dropped the towel she was holding, and ran to the front door and threw it open. By now she could see Abe and Katie Fulton getting out of the car, and she screamed, "Oh, no! Not Sonny! Please, No!" Then, as they approached her in silence, she knew her fears were true, and, sensing the gravity of their visit, she bargained, "He's … He's just hurt, right?"

Captain Richards walked briskly to her side, and shaking his head slowly side to side, said, "I'm sorry, Bonnie. It's worse than that." She screamed, and stepped forward and buried her face and lightly pounded her fists

on his chest and sobbed hysterically, repeating, "No! …
No! Not Sonny!" Helplessly, Captain Richards just held her
and fought back his own tears.

Seeing his mother crying hysterically frightened
Casey, and he also ran to the door crying, "What's wrong,
mommy?" Katie Fulton scooped him up into her arms and
said, "She'll be OK, Casey … we'll all be OK!" Captain
Richards and Abe Fulton half-walked, half-carried Bonnie
into the kitchen and sat her down at the table.

Katie took Casey into the front room and turned on
cartoons on TV. She stayed with him and asked him
questions about the cartoon characters to distract him from
the conversations in the kitchen. Undeterred, he kept
looking back toward the kitchen and asking, "What's
wrong? Is Mommy alright? Where's Daddy? What
happened?"

"It'll be OK, Casey," Katie answered, "Mommy
will come in here in a minute."

At the kitchen table, composing herself to a degree,
Bonnie continued to sob as she wiped at the tears streaming
down her cheeks and pleaded, "What … happened?"

"Sonny was shot on a traffic stop out in the Greenwood Heights area about 6:00 a.m."

"You'd better tell me that the bastard who shot him is dead, or I'll go out and kill him myself."

"No, we haven't identified or caught him yet. The SO is working on the case right now and I'm sure we will locate the killer. Whether he is alive or dead depends on who catches him, and how stupid he is when he gets caught."

"How did it happen?" she pleaded, her voice several octaves higher.

"Someone appears to have caught him off guard and shot him right after the stop was made, and all we know at this time is they were driving a white late-model Chevy."

"I can't imagine Sonny would get caught off guard and not get a shot off, are you …" Her sentence tailed off as she interrupted herself, "Wait a minute, did you say a white Chevy?"

"Yes. Why?" asked the Captain.

"That son-of-a-bitch! Alden Snider. I'll bet he did it. That son-of-a-bitch." she screamed.

"Who is Alden Snider, and why do you think he did it?"

"I remember that name," Fulton interrupted, "Sonny told me about him. He is a neighbor, isn't he? Didn't you and Sonny have some trouble with him last year? I think Sonny even arrested him once after that."

"Yes," she said, "He lives just down the street on Redwood Trail. He drives a white Chevy Malibu. He's had it in for Sonny for two years. We've reported him twice in the last year, and Sonny has arrested him once. In fact, early this morning, he stopped on the road in front of the house in his white Chevy. He revved up the motor until it woke me up. When I looked out through the curtains, he took off south toward his house. I didn't think anything about it, because he always does that kind of stuff in the daytime, when he doesn't see Sonny's car out front, but he usually doesn't do it when it's still dark. I just know he had something to do with it. If he did, I'll kill him if you don't get to him first!"

"That's very important. We'll follow up on Snider. I'm sure the SO knows him well." Richards said.

"The office has at least one arrest report on file," Abe Fulton said.

"If you don't get to him first, I will kill him, I swear it." Then, reflecting on the situation, she lost her bravado and sobbed into her hands, "Oh my God. Sonny is dead? What am I going to do?"

"We will take care of all the arrangements for now, so you can just worry about yourself and Casey, OK? Someone will be here with you as much as you want for a couple of days to assist you with anything you need, OK? Trust me, Bonnie, the SO and the CHP will do everything we can in the investigation and I promise we will find the killer."

"Casey! He must be scared to death. I need to talk to Casey," she said, as she got up and left the room.

Abe and Captain Richards looked at each other in silence across the table. Finally, Captain Richards said, "Abe, can you and Katie stay with her for a while, while I go to the office and do what I've got to do?"

"Sure, Captain. Don't forget to tell the S.O. about Alden Snyder."

"I'll be doing that right away. I'll send a car for you when you are ready, and I'll be available on the radio if you need me. We've got to get this guy. I'll keep you posted, and you do the same."

"Yes, sir."

The two men walked into the living room where the two women and Casey were huddled, crying; the women in pain, and Casey in fear and confusion. Captain Richards quietly excused himself, and let himself out the door.

Steve Davis

The On-Scene Investigation
7:05 a.m.

When the Sheriff's Homicide Investigation Team began arriving on the scene, the area was now awash in the reddish glow of dawn, even though the sun itself would not be visible for some time yet. Each man on the well-practiced team moved right into his assignment with little conversation, securing the scene and searching for evidence, inch by inch.

The Homicide Investigation Team was headed up by Sheriff's Detective Sergeant Don Regan, a young, but highly regarded ex-Marine. Only 28 years old, he had served a tour of duty in Viet Nam before joining the Sheriff's Office just over five years ago.

He was raised in Eureka, mostly by his mother, since his father was a commercial fisherman who had a serious drinking problem and worked long stretches at sea. As a teenager, he excelled at sports through his junior year, earning All-County honors in football and baseball. A professional sports career certainly seemed within his grasp.

That dream, and his life changed in 1958, when, at 17 years old, he came home and found his mother crying and nursing a black eye given to her by his drunken father. He left the home without a word, hunted his father down at a local bar and beat the man severely, leaving him unconscious on the bar room floor.

Juvenile authorities agreed to not prosecute him if he joined the military, and so, two weeks after graduation from high school, and a few weeks after his 18th birthday, young Don Regan joined the Marine Corps and eventually found himself in Viet Nam. The Corp seemed just what he needed, and he re-upped once. For a time, everyone expected him to be a career Marine, but when he came home from Nam in 1965, he left the Corp when his time was up.

Less than six months later, he was a Deputy on the Humboldt Sheriff's Department, and began to build a reputation as a tenacious cop, an informal leader, and an exceptional investigator. He had been promoted from Deputy to Sergeant on the first promotional list he took, and then he was given the choice assignment of Detective

Sergeant shortly after that. Everyone around him believed he was destined to be the future of the Sheriff's Department not too many years down the road.

He was a tall, husky man, with a demeanor as commanding as his appearance. He stood 6-4 with his hair cropped short, just like he wore it in the Marine Corp. He had added a deep black mustache, darker than his hair, and though many wondered, no-one dared to ask if he colored it.

As a Detective, he could opt to wear a sport coat and tie, but he preferred to wear a full uniform, which still fit smartly. He had a booming voice that stopped any other conversation within earshot, and his demeanor demanded that you listen to whatever he had to say. His ruddy complexion was accentuated by a scar on the side of his neck from breaking up a bar fight his first month on the job, which almost got him killed.

Regan was just the type of man you would want on this kind of case; tough, highly qualified, a competent investigator, and he had already earned an excellent record for solving major crimes.

The last to arrive was Evidence Technician Melvin Graham, in his unmarked Sheriff's evidence van. Although he wasn't a sworn Deputy, Graham had a cop mentality, and after Sergeant Regan, he was the key player on the team. He had prepared for a career in law enforcement, but he was $1/8^{th}$ of an inch too short to pass the physical in 1959. A quick vocation change, and now he was a career Evidence Tech.

Regan assembled the homicide team in the headlights of his unmarked police vehicle, and he had just begun to go over their investigative assignments, when he received a radio call from Sheriff's dispatch. "S-2, Control 1."

"Control 1, S-2, go ahead."

"Will you be there long? We have another confirmed 187, unit standing by, no suspects present, south of Eureka, at Sequoia Park," the radio blared.

"Well, Hell!" he said to no one in particular. "Two homicides in one night, at pretty much the same time, no less. We don't have 3 in a year, and now during the most important case I've ever handled, here comes another murder."

"Shit," he said aloud, then, speaking into the radio, he said, "Control 1, S-2. Do you have any details?"

"Deputy on scene reports that it appears to be gang-related, one deceased, from an apparent drug deal gone bad."

"That'll have to wait." Regan said on the air. Then turning to his assistant, he said, "This is a hell of a lot more important than some gang banger offing another!" Pausing for a few seconds, he pushed the radio mike button and said, "Control 1, S-2. Tell the Deputy on-scene to stand by, locate any witnesses, and secure the area. Call out Detective Landon and tell him to assemble a back-up team and respond to the Sequoia Park 187."

Returning to his team, they began the task at hand. Under his direction, the team methodically began the arduous task of plotting, photographing, documenting, and collecting everything within the crime scene. Since they didn't know what would and would not have a bearing on the findings of their investigation, each potential piece of "evidence" had to be meticulously preserved, bagged, and catalogued by the team, and placed in the custody of the Evidence Tech.

As the investigation was fully underway, it was again interrupted, this time by the sound of a vehicle approaching from the south. Since the roads were closed a half-mile in both directions, and there were no driveways in between, they assumed it was another police vehicle. But as it approached, the engine noise and headlight out of adjustment attracted their attention. This was a small car, and its deteriorated condition indicated that it was not much of a car at that.

Regan and the others watched as a small lime green Chevy Vega hatchback pulled up to the crime scene tape and stopped. The young driver, maybe 22-years-old at the most, got out and walked briskly up to the crime scene tape barrier.

He was very young, cleanly shaven, and his short hair was neatly parted. Small in stature, he was wearing an oversized trench coat, from which he pulled a pencil and pad. He had what appeared to be a brand new, medium quality Nikon camera draped over his shoulder with a thin leather strap. Leaning over the tape barrier, he started calling out to anyone, "Excuse me … Excuse me."

"Go see what that idiot wants," Regan said to a nearby Deputy in a voice loud enough for the young man to hear.

A few moments later, the Deputy came back over to Sergeant Regan and whispered, "The 'idiot' is a reporter for the Eureka Times-Standard, and he's demanding access to the crime scene."

"Oh, he is, is he?" Regan said with more than a hint of sarcasm. "Tell him 'Sure thing'. Tell him to stand right there and I'll be with him right away."

Several minutes passed as the young man stood patiently, but no one approached and they all appeared to be ignoring him. Finally, he made eye contact with another investigator and said again, "Excuse me…." The investigator looked over at Sergeant Regan, who stopped his task and slowly walked over to the young reporter. Drawing himself up in a manner reminiscent of John Wayne, he looked the kid up and down and exclaimed, "You're the new press guy, huh?"

"Yes, sir," said the kid. "My name is Jeffrey Olson. I'm new at the Times-Standard, and I need access to the crime scene to cover the story."

"You want access to the crime scene, huh?"

"Yes, sir."

"I don't think you really want to see this, son," suggested Sergeant Regan.

"Yes, sir. I insist, sir."

"Oh, you insist, do you? Okay, Sonny. If you insist." said the Sergeant, "Leave your camera there, and come with me." Raising the crime scene tape, he motioned to the kid to follow. Olson put his camera down, and ducked quickly under the yellow tape and followed Sergeant Regan over to the blanket-covered body.

"Oh, Shit. Here we go again," one Deputy whispered to another in anticipation of what was to follow.

Leaning down, the Sergeant motioned for him to bend down for a close look. "Take a good look, kid, because I doubt if you've ever seen a dead man before. And this is one I don't want you to ever forget."

With that, he ripped the blanket away from the body, which by then was showing the first effects of rigor mortis; pale, clammy, and colorless on the topside, and dark blue closer to the ground. The Officer's shirt and "bullet-proof" vest had been cut away and partially removed by the paramedics, revealing the bullet wounds, just above where the protective vest would have been, now revealing huge gaps where flesh had once been, and thick dried blood covered the Officer's body, uniform, badge, and gun belt, in which the gun was still holstered.

Everyone stopped what they were doing because they knew what was going to happen next, and they waited out of morbid curiosity. Olson stared closely at the body and winced. He started to dry heave, and the Sergeant pointed to a nearby embankment and said, "Puke over there, kid, and don't contaminate my crime scene."

The young reporter ran over to the location indicated by Sergeant Regan and emptied his stomach unmercifully. When he was finished, the Sergeant took his arm and escorted him out of the crime scene.

When he was again safely outside the crime scene tape, Regan said to him, "Jeffrey, a good man died here tonight, a family man, a cop who protected you while you slept, right up until you got this call. That is your story. Now go write it. I'll call you later with all the information you need to know. That's how it works best around here."

"Yes, sir," Olson said meekly and obediently, still shaken and unsteady from vomiting profusely. He picked up his camera and slowly walked to his Vega, got in, and drove away.

Regan turned back to the team. "Get back to work you guys, we've got another one waiting for us when we get done here." Then, walking back to where he had left off, he said to no one in particular, "God, I hate breaking in new reporters."

Section Two

The Gang Banger Murder
7:50 a.m.

Within forty-five minutes, about ten miles away, on the south side of Eureka, Sheriff's Detective Mark Landon, in charge of the backup homicide investigation team, arrived at the second murder scene. The scene of the second murder was in Sequoia Park, a seventy-acre old-growth redwood grove within which the Sequoia Park Zoo is located. A local elementary school and youth baseball and football sports complex are located across the street from the park and zoo.

The park was still pretty deserted except for a couple of joggers on the road that encircles the ball fields, and a man walking his dog in the grass near the children's playground. The zoo itself was actually located several hundred yards away, nestled among the ancient redwood trees, but the snack bar was conveniently located by the park entrance, where it served the zoo, the picnic tables around the park, the children's playground, and the ball fields across the street.

The overcast remnants of the morning fog brought a fresh piney, redwood smell to the park. Although the morning daylight was illuminating the tops of the majestic evergreens for which the park was named, the area behind the cinderblock building which housed the snack bar was still dark as it lay in the shadows of the giant trees framing the entrance.

Off to his right, Landon spotted a marked Sheriff's patrol car and drove toward it. As he got closer, he could see Deputy Mike Egan seated on a picnic table with his feet up on the bench near the side of the snack bar. *"Great! Egan! Just my freaking luck. I get a leftover murder call and I get the biggest prick on our department."* he thought to himself.

The area behind the snack bar was secured with bright yellow crime scene tape. Behind Egan, another man, disheveled and dirty, appearing to be homeless, was seated wrapped up in a tattered blanket, facing away from Egan at another bench about fifteen feet away

Landon got out of the car and walked toward Egan, who got up and walked across the entry to meet him. Looking at his watch, Egan said, "7:50 a.m.! It's about damn time. I've been sitting here since 6:45 a.m. waiting for your team to get here."

"I'd like to hear you say that to Sergeant Regan if it were him instead of me," said Landon. He intentionally looked toward the crime scene instead of at Egan as he continued. "He'd stick it up your ass, so don't give me any grief, or I'll tell him you said so. He's a little busy right now, so you got me. Live with it. What have you got?"

"Yeah, I heard about the Chippie getting wasted. Shame. Probably stopped a car for a taillight out, and the guy just went postal on him."

"What are you saying, Egan?"

"Well it's not like it was one of us; I mean, a real cop. He was just a taillight chaser. One of us, and we'd probably have shot the bastard first, right?"

"You're an asshole, Egan. I should have expected something like that from you. You've had a hard-on for the CHP since they rejected you years ago. I guess they weren't as desperate as we were."

There was a pause of maybe ten seconds, and then Landon interrupted the silence, "Let me tell you something. I knew Tyler. He was a nice guy, a family man, and a better cop than you'll ever be." Waving the back of his hand towards Egan, as if to dismiss him, he said disgustedly, "Now shut up before you really piss me off. Now just tell me; what have you got here."

"Not much of a loss. Just a gang-banger; a drug deal gone bad. That guy over there saw it happen," he said, gesturing toward the man in the blanket. "Dead guy met some other guy behind the snack bar and the dead guy sold him some drugs, but instead of paying like an honorable dirtbag, the guy shoots him dead and takes the drugs AND the money. I tell you, what is the world coming to when you can't even buy drugs in the middle of the night behind a deserted snack bar at a city park without getting whacked?"

"I'll take it from here; just have your report on my desk before you go off shift."

"I'm way ahead of you. It took you so long to get here, I wrote it while I waited." Handing him a single sheet of paper, he motioned toward the witness and said, "Oh, and this guy is really scared. Thinks the killer might come back for him. Fat chance. He's homeless; where's the killer going to find him?"

Looking at the single sheet of paper in his hand, Landon sneered, "A one page murder report. You sure outdid yourself again, Sherlock. Why don't you show me the crime scene, so you can get going. I'm sure you're very tired from all this writing, and would like to get home."

Egan didn't protest, or even take particular offense to Landon's derogatory comments. He was used to hearing that kind of contempt; possibly even relishing the negative attention. He walked Landon over to the back of the building. Behind the snack bar was an open area about 25 feet by 15 feet, smelling of years of old grease and trash accumulation having come and gone. Against the east wall was a huge dumpster and alongside that were accumulated overflow items; boxes and packages used at the snack bar, and even a couple trash bags thrown there by residents attempting to evade trash pickup fees.

Opposite that, along the west wall, the shape of a body could be seen under yet another bright yellow dead man blanket.

Removing the blanket, he observed a young Hispanic adult male sitting with his head, or what remained of it, against the cinder blocks. He was a small man, but his shaved head and the prison tattoos that covered his neck made him look formidable. They also stood as evidence of a life of crime and violence. He was covered in blood and appeared to have been shot several times in the body, neck, and from close range in the face.

At that time, Assistant Evidence Tech Eddie Williams walked up to the scene and approached Detective Landon. Deputy Egan took that opportunity to slip from view and walk quietly to the patrol unit before he could be given an assignment. As he drove by with his window up, he gave a sarcastic wave and nod, mouthing the words, "Bye, bye."

"Asshole," Landon said in a barely audible voice.

Turning back toward Williams, he said, "Well, Eddie, with Sergeant Regan and Mel Graham on the CHP murder, let's give this one our best shot as second string."

They briefly discussed their plans, and while Williams started to process the crime scene, Landon turned his attention to the witness.

The witness was disheveled, dirty, and bearded. His hair and beard were matted from perhaps months without being cleaned. He was obviously homeless. Landon looked at the identification Egan had handed him. It was a soup kitchen identification card issued by a Catholic homeless shelter in Eureka, identifying the man as Fred Norman, about forty. Norman was but another of the many "hippy" types who were drawn to the redwoods and the California North Coast in the 60's. Here, among the natural beauty of the redwood forests and the northern California coastline, they grew their pot, found their 'karma', and stayed.

The more intelligent among them were drawn to Humboldt State University, a liberal arts and forestry college, and soon, many of those, after graduating, couldn't find local jobs in their liberal arts field, and couldn't bear to leave the north coast. Consequently, Humboldt County probably has more short order cooks with Bachelor's Degrees that any other place on earth.

Landon approached the witness and introduced himself, "Good morning sir, I am Detective Landon from the Sheriff's Office. I'll be the lead investigator on this case. I need to get a statement from you."

"Thank God!" Norman said, "I thought I was going to be stuck with that asshole all day."

"Don't worry about him. Just tell me what you saw."

"I have been a little down on my luck, sir, and I was asleep in those bushes over there. The park is a pretty good place for homeless people, because there is usually food left around, and when everyone goes home, no one bothers you at all. I was asleep over there, under that bush, and in the middle of the night, I heard this guy (motioning at the victim) walking up the road. The crackle of twigs on the sidewalk woke me up, I guess, and I rolled up onto my elbow and looked. Damn, the guy's walking straight toward me and I thought maybe he saw me. I got really scared, 'cause he looked like a real hard case, and he was all alone and carrying something under his coat in a paper bag. Just before I was going to get up and run, he turns and walks behind the snack bar. He looked around and just stood there against the wall."

"A few minutes later, I hear a car come up from the south where I couldn't see. It stopped and the other guy gets out and walks around the corner there, and comes to the back of the snack bar, too. Boy was I scared; I didn't take a breath or move a muscle."

"Go on, Mr. Norman."

"Well, this dead guy here says, real tough-like, "OK, dude, it is a done deal. Here is the stuff you wanted, just like you wanted it; but first I've got to see the rest of the money." The other guy doesn't say a word, takes a step toward him and reaches into his pocket and pulls out a gun, and before the first guy can say squat, the other guy shoots him twice as he walked toward him, then once more in the face when the guy falls backwards against the wall. I 'bout jumped out of my skin. I never seen a man murdered in cold blood before. The shooter reaches down and grabs the bag, and walks away slowly, just like he came.

I was so scared I was shaking, and when he got right about there, I cracked a twig, and he turned around and comes back toward me, like he knew I was there. He looks right where I'm laying, in the pitch dark, not breathing, not moving. Then he walked away, not even in a hurry, in the direction where he came from. I hear the car door close and the car drives away southbound. Only then did I breathe again"

"What did the guy look like?"

"I never got a clear look at him. He was wearing black pants and a black parka with the hood up."

"What about his size, race, anything unusual about his voice?"

"No, Sir. Like I said, he never said a word. I'll tell you what; he had to be like, like an assassin. He was cold and calm. Knew what he was going to do, and he did it in cold blood; man, I mean in COLD blood."

"What about his size? What race was he?"

"He was small, slender build, I don't know if he was black, Mexican, or white … Hell, he might have been Chinese."

"Describe the car."

"I never saw the car. He parked it around the corner. I just heard it."

"Did it sound like a small car, a big car, V-8? Come on man, give me something!"

"Just a regular car. Sounded new, probably a big car; didn't sound like a 4 banger."

"Did he touch anything that you saw? Something he left behind that might have his prints on it."

"No, Sir. He just walked up, killed that guy, picked up the bag real casual-like, and walked away, like he done this a hundred times before. Cold, man! Like in the movies."

"Where can we find you if we need to talk to you again, Fred?"

"Oregon! Frisco! Man, I don't care, I ain't gonna stick around here and get myself killed."

"You have to stay around for a few days. We'll get you into a shelter somewhere in town."

"Can you make me go there? I mean, you probably better arrest me and put me in jail, because otherwise I'm not going to stay and get killed by that cold-blooded SOB."

"I don't want to do that, but you have to stick around, so if that's what you want, I'll have to arrest you for something, then you'll have to wait around for a trial. You got any outstanding warrants? Tell you what…you sure you wouldn't rather stay a couple days at a shelter? We can put you there under another name."

"OK, I'll stay at your shelter for two days. I can use a good meal or two for the road. But you gotta come by and check up on me every day. You miss a day, and I'm outa here."

"Fair enough," said Landon. He picked up his radio and called for another Deputy to come by the scene and pick up the witness for transportation.

Then he turned his attention back to the Evidence Tech, who was photographing the scene from every conceivable angle. "Come up with anything?"

"A little. Looks like he was shot with a .38 or better. Shot him twice, and then iced him with a third shot to the face at close range. The shooter was small to medium build and wearing a black heavy parka with the hood up."

"Wow. It's incredible what you guys can come up with just looking at the scene. I get the first part, but how did you know about the shooter's size and the parka?"

"I didn't. I heard the witness tell you," Williams laughed.

"Asshole! Anything else?"

"His prison tattoos indicate he's a former big-time loser. Quentin kind of tats. Oh, and papers in his pockets say he's Anthony Garcia, about 27."

"Tony Garcia?" Landon interrupted. "Let me see." Walking over to the body once again, he looked closer and said, "'El Gato. Tony Garcia. I didn't recognize him. He's a big-time gang banger around here. I thought he was still in the joint for robbery, attempt murder, and witness intimidation; big time stuff. I didn't know he was out and dealing in drugs now. That's a big come down."

"El Gato, eh? Well, even a "cat" has to eat, I guess."

Back at the Office
10:00 a.m.

It was mid-morning when Sheriff's Detective Sergeant Regan arrived at the CHP Office to interview Officers Brennan, Coughlin, and Gibson. Seeing the familiar face of Sergeant Regan walk in, Brennan got up and greeted him, "What do we know so far, Sarge?"

"Not much, Dean. The team is still at the scene looking for any scrap of evidence. They'll be there awhile yet. What we know now is that Sonny was apparently shot twice, immediately, from close range with a handgun. The killer may have even suspected Sonny would be wearing a vest and appeared to aim above it to kill him. It happened between the cars. Sonny never got a shot off. One bullet apparently nicked the artery, and he bled to death. They will do an autopsy today to see what else there is to learn from the rounds themselves. No casings on the ground, so it was either a revolver, or they took the casings with them."

"They?" asked Brennan.

"We don't know. We found only one set of footprints in the uncontaminated area, so I assume there was only one, but we can't discount that there were more. Maybe others in the vehicle. I need to take your uniform and boots with me, but first, let me look at the bottom of your left boot."

As he took off his left boot and handed it to Sergeant Regan, Brennan said, "Why the left boot?"

"We did find a peculiar boot pattern at the scene; that is, a fairly common boot print, but with a particular chunk out of the sole pattern. The pattern was all over, even where the ambulance crew never walked, and if it doesn't match yours and the other Officers who were at the scene, we may have a really good clue."

He looked at Brennan's boot and said, "Good. No match."

Then, pulling out his notebook from his pocket, he began, "OK, Dean, take it from the top and tell me everything you saw from the moment you got there."

Multi-Agency Debriefing
12:47 p.m.

The room was very quiet and the mood was somber when Captain Richards walked into the room, two minutes late, for the first multi-agency debriefing called by Sergeant Regan. The meeting was convened at the Sheriff's Office, because the CHP Office had become a meeting place for off-duty Officers, family members, and friends who were arriving at the office to get the latest information and grieve together.

Seated at the table were several Sheriff's investigators and technicians. Sergeant Regan was going over his notes, a deep frown etched across his brow. His boss, Humboldt County Sheriff Herb Tatum, was seated to his left in deep thought. Across from him, Dan Freeman, Humboldt County District Attorney, was offering his condolences to CHP Sergeant Anderson, who was already seated. Freeman was newly elected as the county's primary criminal prosecutor, taking office almost one year ago, when he upset the law enforcement-favored candidate in what was considered a last-minute upset fueled by his soft stance on possession of small amounts of marijuana.

Although his election as District Attorney made him a key member of the law enforcement community, his lack of police training and certification caused the other seasoned law enforcement leaders to view him as an outsider. Being much more liberal toward marijuana and other 'recreational' drugs made the other men at the table uncomfortable in sharing enforcement plans with him. Consequently, he was rarely included in top law enforcement meetings, but this was too big to exclude him from, and he knew it.

"How is Mrs. Tyler handling this, Kurt," asked Sheriff Tatum.

"She is extremely distraught. She's taking it very hard, just like any wife we've seen go through that situation. But she's a tough cookie, though, and she'll be okay. It will help if we can get the killer."

"OK, fellas," Regan interrupted, "We'll all have time to mourn later. We've still got a lot of work to do today, so let's get through this fast and get back to work. Let's review what we know so far." Motioning to his right, he continued, "This is Mel Graham, the Evidence Tech on the Tyler case. Mel, tell us what we know so far from the evidence at the scene."

"OK, Sarge. We don't know for sure how many shooters there are, but we suspect only one. We got one really good footprint at the scene, size ten or eleven, fairly common boots, but with a unique chunk out of the pattern on the left sole." He put the plaster cast of the boot print on the table and pointed out the place where a unique chunk of the sole had been torn from the sole of the boot.

"The suspect appears to have shot Tyler twice right off the bat, point blank to the chest and neck before the Officer could get off a shot. It looks like he shot him intentionally above the bulletproof vest; that may prove significant. After he left, Tyler staggered back to the right front door and got in one call for help before he collapsed and died. No casings on the ground, and the footprints don't indicate the shooter stopped to pick up any casings; that says we're probably looking at a revolver. It appears to be a mid-caliber, probably a powerful .38 or .357 magnum from the damage. We scoured the scene, grid by grid, but that is about all we found that ties into this shooting."

Regan continued without hesitation, "Oh, and CHP had an unidentified caller alert them to the Officer's location, but he may not be involved. CHP is trying to ID the caller."

"Also, Kurt, tell the group about the guy you were telling me about, the kid who has had it in for Tyler for a couple years."

"He is a young punk named Alden Snider. He's a 'hot rod' car buff; drives a souped-up white 1967 Chevy Malibu, and was seen this morning in front of Tyler's house, as if taunting Mrs. Tyler. He's a white male adult, age 25. Got a few small raps on his record: petty theft at 18, a prior misdemeanor assault from a bar beef when he was 22, and a possession of stolen property from earlier this year. On the driving side, he's got a reckless driving last year, and a few speeding tickets over the years; likes to drive fast. That's where he and Sonny have tangled. He's a neighbor of the Tylers, and likes to harass them."

"We're looking seriously at Mr. Snider, but we can't afford to overlook anything or anyone else," Regan added. "We don't want to get our minds too focused and closed this early. Statistically, these types of 'traffic stop' murders happen from stopping someone that the Officer didn't know was wanted for a crime; maybe a recent robbery or burglary, maybe even one that hasn't been discovered yet. Could also be some parolee or felon just passing through the area. We've got Detectives checking all the hotels, restaurants and gas stations for suspicious persons or vehicles matching the description."

"As for the vehicle," Regan continued, "The CHP log shows the suspect vehicle to be a white late-model Chevy, license plate ARM 601. Plate comes back with no active record for it for at least the last five years."

Captain Richards interjected, "All current license plates in California are 1963 series license plates, yellow on black. This means all previously registered vehicles were issued new plates in 1963, and subsequently manufactured vehicles just filled in after the previously registered vehicles were issued plates. This is very significant, because this license plate is six digits and begins in "A", meaning it was one of the first license plates issued to a vehicle in 1963. It couldn't have been issued to a 1967 Chevrolet or similar. That means the murder vehicle was 'cold plated,'

"Cold plated?" Freeman asked.

"Sorry, Dan," Richards continued. 'Cold plated' is a law enforcement term for replacing the 'hot' or wanted license plates on a stolen or wanted car with license plates from another vehicle which is not wanted, which we call 'cold' plates."

Richards continued as Freeman nodded at the new information, "Here is the rest of the story. DMV 'active' records only go back five years, and this vehicle isn't in the system since at least 1964. That means that after being issued to a car in early 1963, or possibly even late 1962, the vehicle was removed from the road before renewal time in 1964, never to be registered again. I'm guessing it was totaled in an accident, or was an old vehicle removed from service. DMV is hoping a hand search at headquarters might give us some information, but they had a big fire at DMV headquarters last year which destroyed many of their old no-longer-registered files over five years old."

Regan shook his head and said, "Another obstacle we will have to overcome. But we know the late-model Chevy is still out there, so we will keep looking."

"What about the other homicide this morning, Sergeant, any possible connection?" asked DA Freeman.

"Maybe the guy who shot Tyler was fleeing from the Sequoia Park murder, or something,"

"We looked into a possible connection, and we'll keep looking at it, but right now it looks like an unrelated coincidence. If it was the other way around, it would look like a real possibility, but the Sequoia Park 187 occurred 45 minutes after the Officer was shot. That one clearly looks like a drug deal gone bad, according to the witness and Detective Landon, who is working the case."

"So, that's it for now. Not much to go on, so we need to get busy before the trail goes cold. Okay, assignments. Captain Richards, have one of your best guys go out to the original call and see if they can identify the people involved in the original accident call, or anyone who saw something suspicious. If you find anyone, let us know ASAP, and I will have a Detective interview him in detail. Also, keep trying to ID the guy who called in the location of the patrol car and hung up."

"The Medical Examiner is performing an autopsy in about an hour; hopefully he will learn something important. I've got my guys checking the Highway 101 all-nighters for possible suspects passing through. Detective Landon is working the gang-banger 187. He's interviewing the victim's family right now, or he'd be here. He'll keep looking for a possible connection between the two homicides. Detective Ed Gretel and I will contact this Snider guy within the next hour or so. We will secure a search warrant if necessary to get his attention. Let's all meet back here tonight at 1800 hours. It's going to be a long night tonight until we've checked every lead. I want this SOB in jail by tomorrow morning."

The men began to file out of the room, when Captain Richards held back and got Regan's attention, motioning for him to stick around for a moment. When the room was empty, Regan said, "What's on your mind, Kurt?"

"Maybe nothing, Don, but I thought you should know something. I thought a lot about whether this is significant, but I decided that it is better to have all the possibilities on the table. I'm absolutely sure it has nothing to do with this, but we have a little 'situation' at the office that I want to make you aware of."

"Sounds serious, Captain, what do you have?"

"As I said, it is probably nothing, but you need to know every possibility. We've just started working an Adverse Action against one of our Officers, Randy Allen, which could result in termination in a week or so. Here's the catch. The only witness, and the one who brought it to my attention, was Sonny Tyler. I was thinking about it, and without Tyler's testimony, we probably won't be able to proceed with it."

"Wow! That's serious. Do you really think that Allen would do something like that to save his job?"

"No! Absolutely not at all. I'm sure it isn't related, but … it's your investigation, and you need to know the whole story. I keep thinking … Allen was going to lose his job, but now he probably won't. He may just be lucky as a result of Tyler' demise, but he'd know Tyler's schedule and about the vest Tyler wore. I just wanted you to know … "

"What can you tell me about it?"

"Pretty straightforward. Last month on swing shift, Allen helped Tyler at a rollover accident scene. The car was totaled and debris scattered around the scene. When Allen was impounding the car, Tyler saw him pick up a nice pair of racing-style gloves and put them in his pocket. Tyler called him on it, and told him to put them back in the car. Allen said he couldn't prove they belonged to the driver since they were lying on the ground. Tyler didn't back down, and Allen put them back in the car. At the end of the shift, he sees Allen put them in his locker and tells the Sergeant. The Sergeant finds them there and Allen denies everything, says he bought them and Tyler is lying. The office did the AA interview two days ago, and even though no-one else at the office knows about it, there's been some open bad blood between Allen and Tyler."

"Shit. All over a pair of gloves? Would a guy really do that?"

"A pair of gloves on one hand, but a career on the other. I don't know. But since no-one else knows about it, I'd like to keep it between us unless you decide it is a lead worth following up on."

"Sure, Cap, I'll keep it in the back of my mind for now, but it may move up to the front real soon if we don't get any good leads." In the meantime, get a good look at Allen's boots, size and style, and let me know if Allen's actions seem out of the ordinary in the next couple days."

"He's at the office with the others right now and seems pretty shaken up by the murder. I'll take a look at any boots he has at the office, and I'll look at his schedule and see if it lends itself to suspicion. I'll keep you posted of anything I can find out on my own.

The Apartment of Sylvia Santos
1:15 pm

The word was getting out about the murder of Officer Tyler, and other off-duty Officers, family members, and friends were arriving at the office to get the latest information and grieve together. Outside the office, community members were quietly offering flowers, candles, poems, and condolences at a makeshift shrine outside the front door.

Sylvia Santos felt the same immeasurable grief, but she wanted to be alone more than anything else. As soon as the opportunity presented itself, she had slipped out the back door of the office and drove straight home.

Captain Richards returned to the CHP office and quickly briefed those who were gathered in mourning. In doing so, he noticed Sylvia was not around with the other grieving employees at the office. As the Commander of a small office, he knew the complexity of his role in an emergency such as this. Careers were made and lost at times like this. The CHP "brass" did not like <u>not</u> knowing what was going on. Unofficially, his highest priority, according to their expectations, was to keep the Division Chief informed at all times, so the Chief would, in turn, look good to the Commissioner and his staff, by providing instant up-to-date information at a moment's notice.

But Richards also knew that his job was much more important than that on the local level; he had to show strength and guidance for his CHP "family," and he had to assure that the basic needs of those involved were met. Toward that end, he had called in an extra off-duty dispatcher several hours ago, and now the Trauma Counselor he had also called in had finally arrived at the office.

When Captain Richards went into the Dispatch Center to tell Sylvia, she was not there. The relief Dispatcher, Art Lindstrom, was talking on the phone. He motioned for Art to pause a moment.

"Hold on a moment," Lindstrom interrupted the caller on the line. "I need to see what my Captain needs."

"Where's Syl?"

"Not sure," Lindstrom said, looking around the room. "She was here just a few minutes ago. Maybe she went home. It's past her shift time."

Richards walked back to the briefing room in the rear of the office, looking in rooms as he walked. "Has anyone seen Sylvia?" he asked those assembled in the briefing room. When no-one responded in the affirmative, he realized, for the first time, that while they had been absorbed in the loss of the Officer and the initial investigation, they had probably neglected to realize the full impact the loss had on the on-duty dispatcher. At a time when the extended CHP family was gathering to support and grieve together, it worried him that one of the key players had gone off by herself. He hoped it was just a case of one person's desire to grieve privately.

Ten miles across Humboldt Bay, at about the same time, Sylvia slowly pulled her red Volkswagen into the driveway of a small apartment complex in downtown Eureka. She had been relieved of duty after her interview with Sergeant Regan, and she knew a Counselor was being called in. She wasn't ready to talk to a counselor, yet, and wanted time to herself to sort out her emotions.

She stopped the car in the parking lot, turned off the engine, and sat transfixed for several moments, staring out the windshield. Tears welling up in her eyes, she slowly got out of the car, slipped quietly through the gate and headed for the last of three one story apartments that fronted onto F Street.

Approaching the door of apartment 3, she produced the key and fumbled with the front door lock. Her small, trembling hands could scarcely grip the key to open the lock on the door, and as the ring of keys slipped from her hands and fell to the ground, she pounded her right fist on the door, laid her head against the jamb, and began sobbing. After a few seconds, still crying, she bent down and scooped up the key and, this time she was able to force it into the lock, open the door, and go inside.

Throwing her purse on the table, she went directly into her bedroom, opened the top drawer and pulled out a wrinkled scrap of paper. Clutching it to her breast, she sat back onto the bed. "Why? Why? Why him?" she sobbed into the pillow. Relieved of the burden of maintaining control, she drew up into a fetal position and cried herself into exhaustion.

Investigators Interview Alden Snider
1:50 pm

The sound of 'In A Gadda Da Vida' rattled off of the corrugated metal walls of the Old Town Speed Shop, where Alden Snider worked, when Sergeant Regan and Detective Ed Gretel approached the garage.

The speed shop was one of those greasy mechanic shops that are a throwback to the past. Calendars of naked and scantily clad women dating back ten years adorned every wall, and the only counter top was covered with greasy parts and empty parts boxes. These were mechanics that could tear down and rebuild a fast engine in a flash, but couldn't touch the new high-tech smog-equipped cars. But they didn't care, because they were only interested in making customer's muscle cars go even faster.

Before going into the garage, they looked at the vehicles parked outside. They paused and stepped over to a 1967 Chevy Malibu Super Sport parked near the roadway. "He's not trying to hide it," Gretel said as he stepped around to the rear of the vehicle to check out the license plate. "George Henry X-ray 743, he said aloud as he wrote the number down. Looks like the right plate for a '67 Malibu."

Regan motioned toward the garage and they walked over and stepped into the open doorway. They sized up the employees, busy working on cars in three bays, looking for the one who looked like he might have an attitude. The trouble was they all had variations of the same look about them. One of the mechanics, shirtless and sporting a beginner's set of prison tattoos that only covered his upper arms, spotted the men first. He reached up and turned down the radio, prompting one of the others, without looking up from the wiring harness he held in his hands, to say, "Hey, what the ...? I like that song."

Regan and Gretel surveyed the men, and their eyes stopped on one mechanic, young and slender, who hadn't looked up yet, working under the hood of a blue Mustang GT coupe. He had on a T-Shirt that said, "Shut up Bitch!" on the back. Without a word being said, they walked across the greasy floor up to the mechanic and said, "You Alden Snider?"

"Who wants to know?" he demanded, as he turned his head and looked up at the two men. Without taking his hands off the carburetor he was working on, he looked left at Detective Gretel, then focused to his right on Sergeant Regan, the taller of the two men, who was wearing a Sheriff's uniform.

All work in the shop ceased, and the other two men exchanged glances and stepped out into the open to hear the conversation. They spoke briefly, and then moved apart.

"We'd like to know," said Regan. "I'm looking for someone. Are you Alden Snider?"

The mechanic looked back at Gretel, as if trying to size up who was in charge, and said nothing. Suddenly, the younger of the other two mechanics, who had moved over toward the doorway, took off running out the open doorway and down the street. Detective Gretel started to pursue him, when the mechanic with the tattoos pushed a toolbox over, crashing into the cluttered pathway, between car parts, blocking Gretel from the open doorway through which the man ran. "Oops," he said sarcastically, then stepped into his path and bent down to pick up the tools that fell. As Gretel stepped around him, he said, "Oops, again. Sorry, I keep getting in your way, Officer."

Detective Gretel took up the chase after the fleeing man, who had a half block lead by the time he got out the door. Sergeant Regan turned to the remaining two men and said, "OK, guys, let's see some ID. We can make a big deal out of this or not, it's up to you." Both men started fumbling for their identification, protesting that they hadn't done anything.

Meanwhile Detective Gretel started to gain on the mechanic, who was having trouble running in his oversized blue coveralls. A quick left onto Fifth Street, and another right on Bay Street, and the Detective had cut his lead in half. The suspect ran around a blind corner to his left, and Detective Gretel heard the squeal of tires braking and a 'thump'. As he rounded the corner, the young man was picking himself up from bouncing off a pickup truck. Detective Gretel pushed him down again, hard, and stood over him as he rolled to a stop. "Don't … make me … hurt you," he said, panting like an old dog on a hot day. The young man rolled into a sitting position and said breathlessly, "OK, OK, I quit. I was going to pay it off right after payday. Honest."

"What … are you talking about, Snider?" said the Detective.

"The warrant. And I'm not Snider."

"What? Let's see some ID. Why did you run when we asked for Snider?"

"I thought you were checking us all out, and you'd get to me. I was really going to pay off the warrant on payday."

"Where is Snider?"

"He's the guy you were talking to."

"Come on, you dumb son of a bitch!" He pulled the man to his feet and checked the driver's license the man produced. Sure enough, his name was Willie Nixon, not Alden Snider."

When they got back to the garage, Sergeant Regan said facetiously, "Where did you go, Ed? I want you to meet my new friend, Alden Snider," gesturing to the man they originally approached. "But I don't think you are going to like him very much." Changing to a pretend whisper, he continued, "Seems he has an attitude."

"Yeah, I don't like pigs," said Snider.

"Tell us about this morning at the Tyler house," Regan asked.

"I don't know what you are talking about"

"How about when you pulled up in front of their house and honked the horn and peeled out when she looked out the window."

"I never did that! She's lying. She's a lying bitch!"

"Where were you this morning about 6:00 a.m.?"

"Let's see. Oh, yeah. Like most everyone else in the world, I was sleeping at 6:00 a.m."

"Sleeping where?"

"None of your fuckin' business."

"Yes, it is kind of my "fuckin'" business; I'm investigating a murder, and you might be someone I need to talk to."

"Murder? What murder?" he said defiantly.

"CHP Officer Sonny Tyler was killed this morning. I understand you know Officer Tyler, professionally speaking that is; and you might have the desire to see him dead. Now do you remember this morning?"

"Tyler is dead? Good." he said, apparently amused by the news, "But that bitch is the one that should be dead." Then realizing why they are there, he says, "Whoa! Let me guess. You guys are here because you think I did it? You don't know who did it, so here you are trying to pin a cop's murder on me. Well I'll tell you, I'm glad he's dead, but that don't prove nothin'. If you think I did it, arrest me; if not, get the hell out of here and don't come back unless you have a warrant, and I have my attorney present. And tell that bitch to go screw herself!"

"Look Snider, are you sure you don't want to cooperate if you have nothing to hide."

"I told you I was asleep. I told you I wasn't anywhere near the Tyler house this morning. Now arrest me or get out of here."

"I'm sorry you feel that way, I think we'll be seeing a lot of each other, Snider." As they turned to leave, Gretel turned toward Willie Nixon and said, "Get that warrant taken care of by next week or bring track shoes to work!"

"Yes, sir," Willie said, avoiding eye contact while looking down at his shoes.

Back in the car, Gretel asked, "What do you think, Sarge?"

"Hard to say. He is a cocky, arrogant little bastard. With his greasy skin, he could probably pass for Hispanic or Indian. We'll be on him like stink on shit for a while. In the meantime, let's turn up the heat a little bit. I think we have enough to get a search warrant to search his house for his boots, to match up to that print we have from the scene. I noticed he was wearing boots today at the garage, but I couldn't get a look at the bottom. We checked everyone who was at the crime scene, and no one's boot matches the cut mark on the print. That looks like our best link to the killer."

CHP Follow up Investigations
2:50 pm

Captain Richards, after his fourth update to the Division Chief, walked to the back of the office, glancing into the locker room, where Officer Brennan was seated on the bench in front of Sonny Tyler's closed locker. He walked in and sat down next to Brennan, who looked a little embarrassed at being caught in such deep thought.

"What are you still doing here? After what you've been through, we told you to go home two hours ago."

"I can't just walk away, Captain. Give me something to do. I feel helpless. Some asshole just killed my best friend, and he's still out there. You know I'm a good investigator, but it's out of my hands, and I can't do anything and it's killing me. Just give me something to do that won't be stepping on someone else's toes."

"I can't, Dean. You are too close to the case. Good protocol says I keep you out of it, just in case you stumble across the killer."

Brennan winced and pleaded with his eyes. "Anything Captain, some background work, some peripheral interviews, anything. There are always people who need to be contacted."

Richards looked at the ceiling, as if for guidance, took a deep breath, and said, "OK, Dean, maybe it's just what you need. Here's what you can do. The Sheriff's Homicide Team has asked me to have someone go out to the original accident scene and look for witnesses and accident evidence. I was going to assign another Officer, but ... but you have to promise me that if something happens and you find something, you won't do anything stupid. You know what I'm talking about, don't you?"

"Yes sir, I know exactly what you mean. I won't kill the son-of-a-bitch, ... unless it is provoked, of course."

"Provoked? Right. Don't let me down, Dean, it's my career, too."

A half hour later, Brennan pulled up to the intersection of Myrtle Avenue and Freshwater Road, the scene of the morning accident call that was 'Gone On Arrival'. 'GOA' calls usually occur for one of three reasons; the location was wrong, someone thought they heard an accident when there was none, or, most often, an accident has occurred and the drivers end up exchanging names and going their separate ways before the CHP arrives. In the latter instances, there is usually always some evidence at the scene to indicate it occurred: tire tracks off the roadway, broken glass, clods of dirt or other debris that is dislodged from under fenders, or skid marks.

He stopped in the parking lot of a small market on Myrtle near the 'T' intersection that is the beginning of Freshwater Road, and walked up to the edge of the roadway surveying the scene for signs of an accident. He saw nothing. As he turned around to walk eastbound, he was startled that a stranger, wearing a deep burgundy robe and a turban, was standing quietly right next to him in his path.

"Jesus," he jumped back, "You scared me."

"Sorry 'bout that Officer who got killed," said a voice in broken English.

The speaker was a slight built man in his 50's. The man was obviously of mid-eastern decent. If the clothing hadn't given it away, the strong smell of incense that came from his clothes would have. Brennan sensed he had come from the nearby convenience store, and wondered why he hadn't smelled the man's arrival before he was startled by him.

"Thank you," Brennan responded, knowing that was the first of many such condolences he and his fellow officers would receive over the next few weeks. The people in Humboldt County, and particularly around the Eureka vicinity, were a tight community and generally supported law enforcement, except when the cops interrupted the source or transportation of marijuana. Then the younger generation thought they were assholes, while the older citizens applauded the effort.

Officers were always spread pretty thin, and more than once he had seen private citizens get involved at accident scenes, assisting Officers with taking individuals into custody, and providing information that helped to make a case.

"I think maybe I was de last' person to talk to him," said the man. "He ask me if I seen a car wreck here."

Brennan perked up at the possibility of a key witness. "Tell me all about it," he said, as he pulled a small notebook from his pocket.

"I was jus' standing' outside my store smoking," he said, motioning toward the convenience store about 100 feet from the intersection, "when the Officer came down Myrtle. He slow down, real slow, then go straight down the road," indicating south on Myrtle Avenue. "Then, a few minutes later, he comes back again, an' he drives east on Freshwater. Then a few minutes later, he came back again. He looks over here at me, and he comes right up to me where I'm standing next to the store."

"What did he say?"

"He says 'do I see a car wreck here'. I say "No." Then he says 'do I hear anything like a car wreck around here." I tell him "No." He says thanks and drives over there and stops and calls someone on a radio."

"What did he do next?"

"He just sat there, like he was thinking."

"Were there any other cars or people out at that time of the morning?"

"Let me think? Maybe ten minutes before, the newspaper delivery man came by. He stops here every morning and has coffee, black, and a maple donut. We talk a few minutes about the weather, and he drive up Myrtle to deliver his papers. It's pretty quiet at that time of morning, never anyone around. Oh, I remember, after the Officer talked on the radio, another car come by and drove up Freshwater, and the Officer jus' pull out in the road and drove off in the same direction."

"Did it look like he was after the vehicle?"

"No, he just pulled out and drive that way, kinda slow."

"Do you remember what kind of car it was?"

"Yah, it was a white car, in the 60's, I think a Chevy; like my brother-in-law has."

"Really?" Brennan said excitedly, eager to hear of a possible connection with the killer's vehicle. "A Chevy?"

"Yeah. A Chevy. Like my brother-in-law's. Only my brother-in-law's Chevy is blue."

"Was the other car driving bad or speeding or anything?"

"No. He just drive by, and turn onto Freshwater. I wouldn't of notice him but the Officer was there, and I was watching' him."

"How many people in the vehicle?"

"Jus' the driver. He look right at the Officer, and he look like a Mexican, I think."

"What is your name, Sir?" asked Brennan.

"Sam Hassam. Do I have to get involved?"

"We'll see, Sam. I hope not."

Brennan returned to the car and drove up Myrtle in each direction, inspecting the roadway for accident debris. Then he did the same on Freshwater for a half mile to where Greenwood Heights Drives intersects at a 'T' from the north. There was nothing to indicate an accident had happened anywhere near the intersections.

Brennan steered the big Dodge toward Eureka. As he did, he couldn't help but think about the ironies of fate. Someone thought they saw or heard an accident, and called the CHP to report it at that location. That precise sequence of events placed the fate of Officer Tyler on that road, at that very moment, to cross paths with a killer. *How are we supposed to make a difference, when we have no control over fate like that?"* he asked himself.

Acting on the information he got from the store owner, Brennan contacted the circulation desk of the Eureka Times-Standard, and got the name of the man who delivers papers in that area. From the Times-Standard building, he called the man, Clark Elder, who was just leaving his home and agreed to meet with the Officer at a local coffee shop.

Ten minutes later, Brennan was seated at a corner booth, when a tall, slender man in his early sixties slid into the booth across from him. "Officer Brennan?" he asked. His face was gaunt and his cheeks drawn in from a lifetime of smoking or other hard life decisions. His clothing, wrinkled, stained and out of date, suggested that there was no woman in his life.

"Yes. Hello, Clark. I'm Dean Brennan. I'd like to ask you a few questions about what you might have seen while you were throwing your route this morning."

"I heard about the cop … I mean Officer, who got shot this morning. I been thinking about it all morning, and I think I heard it, and I might have seen the shooter. I'm kind of scared. What if he remembers seeing me and comes back to get me?"

"Everyone who is a witness worries about those things," said Brennan. "We still need your help or we'd never solve a case. I can tell you that we will do all we can to protect your identity and keep you safe. It is really very rare that a crook goes looking for someone who isn't a direct witness. This is very important, sir. I need you to tell me what you remember seeing and hearing."

The man took a deep breath and let it out slowly. "I was delivering my paper route going north on Myrtle Avenue, north of Freshwater. I remember the patrol car coming toward me on Myrtle heading toward Freshwater. About 10 minutes later, I had doubled back onto Freshwater, and a white car passed me and turned onto Greenwood Heights, and then the patrol car passed me again, following the white car, and also turned on Greenwood Heights."

"Was the CHP going after the other car?"

"No, the Officer just seemed to be following the white car when they passed me. They were both just driving along going about the speed limit. The Officer was about 100 feet behind the car."

"Maybe 3 minutes later, I heard two loud 'pops' from the direction of Greenwood Heights, 'Pop' ... Pop.'"

Brennan winced at the description of what certainly were the shots that killed his friend.

If Elder noticed, he didn't let on, as he continued the story without pause. "I thought they might be from poachers. I know guys poach deer at night, and I've heard poachers before out in this area. A minute later, the same white car came back by, going much faster this time, and drove past me going the other way."

"What kind of car?"

"I don't know. I'm not up on cars like some people."

Did it look big, like an American car or like a foreign compact car?"

"I'm sure it was an American car."

"How many people were there in the car, Clark?"

"Just the driver."

"What did the driver look like?"

"It was a man. I looked straight at him, and I think he saw me looking at him, because just when he got to me, he put his left hand up to cover part of his face. I didn't get a good look at him, but he was dark skinned, Mexican, Indian, or a light skinned black man."

Brennan thanked him for his time and told him the Sheriff's investigators might want to interview him also, to which he agreed. "Just get him, and I won't have to worry."

When they parted ways, Brennan returned to the convenience store. Sam Hassam's store was the only business in the area, and the only pay phone for a mile or more in any direction. Brennan found Sam standing behind the counter at the register when he walked in. The smell of incense was strong, coming from a room in the back.

"Sam, I have another question for you. You said you didn't see or hear an accident at the intersection. But, did you see anyone use the phone to call in an accident? Usually there is some reason someone thinks an accident happened, to take the time to call it in at that hour."

"No. No-one."

"How about around 6:25 am? Did anyone use the phone after the shooting? Say, just before the Officers responded to Greenwood Heights for the shooting?"

"No sir. I was standing there for quite a while, smoking and waiting for the morning beer delivery truck, and I never saw anyone use the phone."

"Beer truck?" Brennan said softly. "I suppose there were other delivery trucks in the area also. Bread. Milk. Fritos?" *You name it,* he thought, *"the delivery truck might have seen something. I need to get on those delivery guys quick."*

Brennan got a list of possible delivery trucks, one regular early morning customer, and other possible witnesses from Sam. On that morning, the only delivery trucks to serve the area was the beer distributor and a bread truck, and one regular commuter, whose wife didn't know he was still smoking, who stopped for a pack of menthol cigarettes and a roll of breath mints every morning. He began the arduous task of tracking them down. However, two and a half hours later, he headed back to the office with no other new leads to go on.

Second Multi-Agency Debriefing
6:05 pm

The meeting room was quiet as a morgue when Sheriff Tatum walked into the debriefing room at exactly 6:05 p.m. and greeted the men who were assembled there.

District Attorney Dan Freeman was poised to take notes in his leather-bound portfolio, whereas the "real cops" at the table scribbled into small pocket-sized notebooks. The men, except for Sheriff Tatum, were seated in the same chairs as earlier that day, as if they had never left. But the mood was much different now. As this horrific day wore on, and the investigation appeared no closer to finding the killer of Officer Tyler, the mood was clearly even more despondent than at the first briefing earlier that day.

Sheriff Tatum, midway through his fourth term, was a remnant of Sheriffs from earlier times. Gruff exterior, out-of-shape, ill-fitting uniform, always chomping on an unlit cigar. Most long-time residents of the county approved of his old-fashioned head-bashing approach to police work, but it didn't seem to fit in with the new breed of Humboldt County environmentalists, or "hippy-dippy, pot smokin' tree huggers" as he referred to them. To his dismay, they seemed to be gaining a stronghold on the county. As for the men who worked for him, they were comfortable knowing he would be there for them if they were even close to the imaginary line they tried not to cross. He took the cigar from his mouth as he stepped up to his chair at the table.

"Gentlemen, Sergeant Regan has been delayed following up on a possible lead, and he will be a little late in updating us on the status of the case. I'm sure he'll be here in a short time. Thank you for your patience. Maybe he'll have some good news to share."

"Can you tell us anything about the lead he's following up on, Herb?" asked Captain Richards.

"I don't know much. He called in and advised he'd be late doing interviews and follow-ups; I think the prime suspect is turning out to be that young man we discussed this morning; name is Snider."

"Snider?" Captain Richards repeated. "That's the guy Bonnie Tyler told us about. Lives near the Tylers, and has been harassing them for years. Just this morning he was in front of the house as if to mock Bonnie."

At that moment, the door opened and Sergeant Regan walked briskly into the room, threw his notebook on the table in front of the chair, and took the seat at the head of the table next to Sheriff Tatum. "Sorry I'm late, gentlemen. Detective Gretel and I were on a stakeout of Alden Snider, who remains our best suspect; although I'm not 100% sure he is involved. He's either the guy, or he's such an asshole that he isn't even smart enough to cooperate to prove he's innocent."

"We shook him down this afternoon, and he doesn't intimidate easily. Now we've got guys tailing him wherever he goes until we can get a search warrant to search his house, car, and his jock strap if we have to."

"Here is an interesting tidbit; remember this morning I told you he had a reckless driving? Well, guess who the arresting Officer was? Yup, Tyler. And there's more. It was the result of an off-duty Complaint filed by Tyler last year resulting from some antics in front of Tyler's house. Sound familiar? It gets better. That possession of stolen property arrest earlier this year? It was another CHP arrest by Tyler's partner on graveyard earlier this year. Of course, Tyler was there at the arrest. Snider's still going to trial on that one, so we have a lot of motive on his part. Let's not jump to any conclusions, though, and keep looking at all possible scenarios."

"Sounds like the harassment might have gone both ways," mumbled Freeman.

"Actually, Dan, the first was an idiot challenging an off-duty officer in front of his house, who apparently didn't know an officer is never 'off duty'. The second was a routine arrest of a punk who just committed a car burglary. In fact," he paused as he shuffled through the papers in front of him. "Here it is." He flipped the report in front of Freeman, and continued, "Here are the reports."

As Freeman glanced at the reports, Regan continued, "September, 1968, Alden Snider had gotten a speeding ticket from another officer the day before, and stopped in front of Sonny's house, who he knew was a CHP Officer. Sonny was out front doing yard work. Snider yelled, "Fuck you pigs!" and accelerated off, squealing tires and leaving skid marks as he fishtailed down the street displaying his middle finger as he left. Sonny mails him a ticket, and Snider paid a huge fine, but continued to harass the Tylers, particularly Bonnie, in other ways for several months.

"I bet Snider was pissed when he got that ticket in the mail," said Tatum.

Regan continued, "Then, on May 16, 1969, Sonny and another officer were working graveyard shift and stopped the Chevy Malibu driven by Snider for exhibition of speed on Fourth Street in front of Denny's in Eureka. Lying in plain sight on the right floorboard was an expensive car stereo with all its wires freshly cut. Sonny ran the serial numbers on the stereo for wants. Coincidentally, at the same time, Eureka Police were taking a stolen report from a citizen reporting that same stereo stolen from the dash of his car a half mile away. The Eureka Police Officer heard Sonny's inquiry on the scanner, made the connection, and Sonny's partner arrested Snider for possession of stolen property."

"Harassment? Hell, they don't get much easier than that," said Tatum.

Freeman shrugged as if to concede the point, but not the match.

"Let's talk evidence. Not much new at this time. The medical examiner did his thing and recovered the rounds from Tyler's body. He confirmed that Sonny was killed by two rounds from a "high power" .38 or a .357 caliber bullet, so we're looking at a .38 or .357 magnum handgun, probably a Smith and Wesson, because of the lands and grooves."

"Lands and grooves? Is that more cop talk?" asked Freeman.

"Sorry Dan. Lands and grooves are the markings made on a bullet from the barrel of a gun when it is shot. Everyone is unique to that gun, so if we find a gun we can determine whether that bullet was fired from that gun."

"Okay. Thanks," said Freeman.

"Back to the autopsy, Tyler was shot point blank to the throat and upper chest just above the vest from less than two feet away. As for the ammo used, we are looking into a couple leads that I don't want to get too deep into right now. More on that later if it pans out."

"We talked this morning about the unique boot print as evidence. That continues to be our best evidence from the scene. We showed you the boot casting this morning, and we'll have a photo of the print available at tomorrow morning's briefing."

"The CHP has done a great job following up on the original call. They interviewed a nearby store owner who saw Tyler follow a white car, driven by a Mexican male, northbound toward the crime scene. They located a paper delivery man who saw the same car, and then heard two gunshots come from the general area of the shooting. A few moments later, he saw the same white Chevy speeding away from the general vicinity driven by a single male, of medium or dark skin, possibly Mexican, Indian, or a light skinned black man.

"They are also looking at some info that may bring a new suspect into play, but we don't know anything to share yet. Also, they are following up on other delivery trucks that might have been delivering in the area and seen something."

"The Sheriff's Records staff has also stepped up to the plate in a big way. We put a skeleton crew at the public counter, and the rest of the staff has been poring over information from our files. They put together the information from the arrest records I told you about Snider.

They are also going through recent F. I. cards for any potential leads or information."

Freeman raised his hand slightly off the table and interrupted, "Excuse me, Sergeant Regan, but what is an F. I. card?"

Sergeant Regan just looked at Freeman for a few seconds, as if he expected him to laugh and say he was kidding, but he could see that Freeman really didn't know the answer. Around the room, the experienced lawmen rolled their eyes and glanced furtively at each other in disbelief.

"It is a Field Interrogation Card, Dan." As he heard his own words, Sergeant Regan was actually pleased that his disbelief had not shown itself too obviously. "Cops use them to record contacts with people they come across in situations that arouse their suspicions; wrong time, place, who they associate with, what vehicles they are known to be around, what their story is, etc. They come in handy when a crime is discovered later that they seem to fit in with. Cops file them and we can refer to them later for possible leads."

"Is that legal?" Freeman asked. "It seems like it might be a violation of the person's rights."

"No, Dan, it isn't a violation of their rights," Sheriff Tatum interjected. "Cops have been doing it for years. It's been challenged in the courts and determined to be 100% legal. It's simply a record of what occurred. Relax. You can rest assured that no felons were injured or offended in the process." A murmur of snickers rippled through the room, which Freeman ignored.

Sergeant Regan quickly diffused the personality conflict by continuing the briefing, "My guys are checking all the all-nighters along Highway 101, but nothing unusual has come up so far. If the guy was just passing through, Eureka is the only place to get food or gas for 80 miles north or south."

"I thought of another angle," Captain Richards said, "I'll have my Auto Theft Officer contact all the local auto body shops to see if there are any newly damaged cars that might shed some light on the original call of an auto accident that was GOA. Maybe a white Chevy will turn up. I'll have my Officers keep looking for similar vehicles with fresh damage, as if they were involved in the accident."

"Be real careful you don't offend someone if you do an F. I. Card on anyone driving a white Chevy, Kurt," said Tatum.

As Freeman turned in his seat to say something, Sergeant Regan quickly continued, "Everything still points to a single shooter. Motive is open, so our best suspect is Snider. You should have seen him this afternoon; cocky, arrogant and he hates cops, especially Tyler. He even said he was glad Tyler was dead, and he meant it, too. Turning to DA Freeman, he said, "Dan, we're going to need a search warrant for Snider's house, his car, his workplace, and his girlfriend's house. Any problems with that?"

Freeman paused for an uncomfortable few seconds while he put his pen down on the tablet. Now the ball was in 'his court' and they would finally have to give him his due. *"This could be sweet,"* he thought. "Depends, Sergeant Regan. It depends. I'm sure there will be no problem. Tell me, what do you have in the way of justifying a search warrant for all those places?"

"Justifying it? Jesus, we got a dead cop and a dirtbag with a history of harassing the cop and his wife, and she says he was there this morning taunting her after the murder. Isn't that enough?"

Freeman looked around the room at the men who were all staring back at him. He knew this was the moment they had all been waiting for for over a year. The test.

Would he safely toe the line of strict propriety and be overly cautious in favor of the criminal's rights, or would he be like them and write up the warrant with minimal direct supporting evidence.

"Not exactly." said Freeman. This was where he was going to hold the line and show them he, not Herb Tatum, was the new face of Humboldt County law enforcement. "Under your scenario, Snider would have as good a chance of getting a search warrant against Tyler for harassment. Seems like every time Snider gets busted, Tyler is there. You only have one person's word against his that he was there this morning. You are going to have to show me a more convincing tie-in before my staff can write up the justification for a search warrant of his home, his workplace, or his car. You'll need more than motive and an allegation he was in front of Tyler's house this morning. You are going to have to show opportunity, that he was there at the murder scene to be able to do the crime. You've got nothing to tie him to the scene."

The others squirmed silently in disbelief.

He continued. "I know. You're going to tell me he has a car similar to the one seen near the scene. Do you know how many white late-model Chevy's there are in

Humboldt County? You said yourself you might even have another suspect to add to the mix. You've got to show me something more."

Regan's face was scrunched up in a you-gotta-be-kidding-me look as Freeman finished. "Yeah, OK, I'll get my guys on it right away," Regan said. "In the meantime, maybe you could put one of your most experienced staff on the case. Would that be possible? Say someone like Ken Steele?"

"I understand where you are going, Sergeant. Ken Steele is experienced all right, and coincidentally, a good friend of law enforcement. But he may have a tendency to bend the rules of evidence to try to help too much. This case is going to be scrutinized by a lot of people for a long time down the road. I think I'll stay on the case myself, for now." He turned in his chair and glanced directly to Sheriff Tatum. Everyone in the room knew this was about much more than a search warrant. The new kid in town was staring down the old school Sheriff, and Officer Tyler's murder suddenly took second stage. "Gentlemen, I want to solve this murder as much as any of you, but we need more to bust this guy's door down; much less his girlfriend's."

Sheriff Tatum redirected the confrontation, "You are right, of course, Dan. I'll have my men get their information together and we'll see if we can put together enough Probable Cause for you to proceed with a warrant."

"We've got a lot of work to do before morning,' Regan said, "Let's meet again at 10:00 am tomorrow morning. OK? Any questions?"

As the men began to file out of the room, Sheriff Tatum grabbed Sergeant Regan's elbow as he passed, "Let's talk a minute, Don."

Once the room cleared, Tatum looked down the empty hallway to assure they were alone and stepped back into the room. "Screw him and his 'Probable Cause' bullshit. We don't need him. This is a dead cop. You write up the request yourself before you leave, and we'll go over his head and get Judge Hilliard to sign it tonight. We'll knock down his fucking doors tonight or first thing in the morning."

"I'm already ahead of you, Sheriff. Thanks."

Investigators Stake Out Alden Snider.
8:00 pm

Sergeant Regan and Detective Ed Gretel pulled up in their conspicuously 'unmarked' sheriff's car and stopped directly across from Alden Snider's home, the first house on Redwood Trail. Just 200 yards away, well off the road out of sight, sat a marked Sheriff's unit waiting to be called in to assist with the warrant search.

Redwood Trail is a private road off of Walnut Drive, about a half mile south of the Tyler residence. In fact, both residences backed up against, and had access to, the huge Federal Forest located behind their respective parcels. A miles-long, meandering, sometimes overgrown trail followed along the creek, hidden from the road, and traversed behind all the residences that backed up to the forest. The presence of the trail was mostly known only to youngsters who grew up along the street through the years, and who had forged and maintained it during their adventures over several generations.

The Snider house was an older, small house that had to date back to the '40s or earlier. A renovation in about 1960 had modernized the exterior and added a new bedroom to the house. Across a patio, to the right, about 20 feet away, was an equally old detached single car garage, to which a lean-to had been added years ago, which was now full of car parts, motors pulled from cars, etc.

It sat back from the street about 150 feet at the end of a tree lined driveway. At the entrance of the driveway onto Redwood Trail, there were a dozen or more acceleration tire marks going toward Walnut Drive. It was clear that the young Mister Snider liked to squeal his tires -and burn rubber when he left home.

It was dark already, and there were no lights on at the house. Regan glanced at his watch; it was 8:05 p.m. The good news was that Snider hadn't been at the house since the morning, so he couldn't have disturbed any potential evidence since their confrontation earlier in the day. The bad news was that it was getting late to serve the warrant tonight. Regan slapped the newly obtained search warrant against his free hand while they waited. He reached over and picked up the radio. "D-3, S-2," he said

"Go ahead, Sarge." crackled the radio.

"What's your status and location?"

"I picked up the subject driving his white 67 Chevelle Super Sport when he left work, and followed him to an apartment on Harris Street, 1600 block. From the looks of the greeting he got from a young female, he may be here awhile."

"D-3, I'm interested in anything he tries to move from one location to another. Make a note of anything he carries in or out of his car or the residence. If he returns to his house, don't let him carry anything out after he enters his residence. We'll serve the search warrant as soon as you advise he is at his residence. 10-4?"

"10-4, Sarge."

Regan looked at his watch again and said to Gretel, "I really want him to be here when we serve the search warrant. You can learn where to look by watching the suspect's eyes and reaction. Looks like he'll be there a while," he repeated. "If he leaves his girlfriend's house, these Deputies will let us know. Let's go back to the office and figure our next step while we wait to hear from them."

Regan left instructions for other surveillance units to monitor Snider's actions for the entire night. Regan and

Gretel would pick up the trail in the morning. "He's too good a suspect to let him dump some evidence. If it looks like he is staying there all night, maybe we'll just start there in the morning with the search warrant," Regan said. "Let's break for the night and get an early start on him in the morning, say about 5:30 am. Let's see what he does in the mornings. If he doesn't come home in the morning, we'll kick in the door. I want this search warrant served before Freeman hears we went over his head to Judge Hilliard."

"He's going to be really pissed," Gretel said. "I'd like to be there in the morning when he finds out Tatum trumped him. We'd be screwed if it weren't for Judge Hilliard."

"Yeah, he's one of a kind."

Section Three

Day Two; The Search Warrant
5:20 am

What started as a "day from hell" yesterday was looking to be even worse today as Detectives Regan and Gretel waited, lost in thought and total silence. Regan knew yesterday afternoon that this wasn't going to be an easy case, but now, he felt for the first time the enormous weight which had been dumped on his shoulders. He knew that his reputation as a Detective Sergeant probably rode on the outcome of the six-page warrant he was tapping against his thigh. In a few hours, he was going to be a hero, or he and Sheriff Tatum were going to be the laughing stock of Dan Freeman, forever. Worse yet, he might never get another warrant from Judge Hilliard.

The morning was still unbroken and the streets seemed to be deserted when Alden Snider turned his Chevy Malibu into his driveway. As soon as he did, his headlights picked up the silhouette of Sergeant Regan's unmarked cruiser parked facing him next to the house. Sergeant Regan, who had been alerted by the stakeout Deputies that Snider was arriving, was leaning against the right front fender, slapping the warrant nervously against his left hand. Detective Gretel was standing behind the open left front door. Immediately after, the headlights of a marked patrol car turned into the driveway behind Snider, appearing to have come out of nowhere. In the mirror, he could see the familiar shape of a lightbar on the roof of the marked patrol car now effectively blocking his exit. Another unmarked patrol car pulled in behind the patrol vehicle.

'What the...?' he thought. He hurriedly exited his car and confronted Sergeant Regan. "What the fuck are you doing on my property? I thought I told you this morning to leave me alone ..."

"... Unless I had a search warrant and your attorney is with you? Well, Mr. Snider, you'll have to call your own attorney, but I've done my part." He slapped the search warrant against Snider's chest. Snider raised his arm and the warrant fell into his hands as Regan walked past him toward the front door, motioning with his right thumb over his right shoulder to Detective Gretel, who nodded knowingly, and stepped forward and reached out to pat down Snider's pockets and waistband. Snider pulled away from him and said, "What are you doing?" Gretel stepped toward him again with a more serious intent, and said, "I'm checking you for weapons. Trust me, Snider, you don't want to do this the hard way. Don't give me an excuse to kick your ass."

Regan continued as he walked toward the door. "It's a pretty standard murder search warrant, Snider; guns, clothing, boots, anything that might lend itself to evidence of the crime we are investigating. You going to open it, or are we?"

"Fuck you, you pricks," Snider said while being searched by Gretel.

"I'll take that as a 'we will'. Okay boys, get the master key." With that, an undercover Deputy who had been standing by, immediately stepped forward with a four-foot-long steel battering ram and headed for the door.

"Wait, wait." yelled Snider. When Gretel completed the weapons search, he nodded to Regan, and stood to the side as Snyder approached the door with his keys in his hand.

"My attorney will be all over your ass. I'll have your job for this. You got nothing to tie me to that cop's murder. This is harassment."

"You want my job, Snider? Okay, but I'll warn you. You aren't going to like the hours and working conditions. You see, we have to work with dirtbags like you, all hours of the day and night, every day. I'm sure you have a great lawyer, so let's just go ahead and assume you are going to get me fired, so you don't need to keep repeating it. Got it? Now shut up and stand aside while we do our thing. Oh, and take off your boots, I want to look at them."

"My boots?"

"Yeah, your boots. And by the way, since you are an official suspect in the murder of Officer Tyler, I need to advise you of your rights in case I ask you any questions during the search. You have the right to remain silent. Anything you say can, and will, be used against you in a court of law. You have the right to have an attorney present with you before being questioned, and if you can't afford an attorney, one will be appointed to represent you free of charge. Do you understand these rights?"

"Fuck you."

"That's a yes, isn't it?"

"Fuckin' A."

"I'm going to put that down as a conditional 'affirmative'. And do you want to waive your rights and talk to us?"

Screw you and the horse you …"

"… I'm going to mark that down as a 'No.'"

"You're a prick, Regan, just like Tyler was. Is that a requirement to be a cop?"

"No, but sometimes it makes things more fun."

Their dialogue was interrupted by the arrival of a tow truck in the driveway.

"What is that here for?" asked Snider as he looked out the open front door.

"Oh, that," Regan replied. "We're going to take your Chevelle down to the Sheriff's Office where our evidence guys can go over it with a fine-tooth comb. Don't worry, we should only have it for a couple days … unless, of course, if we find evidence in it, in which case you'll probably never see it again."

"You mothers are going to try everything you've got to pin this on me."

"We're going to try everything we've got to catch our killer, and this is the first step. If it's not you, you have a funny way of acting innocent."

In spite of Regan's optimism, two and a half hours later, they had thoroughly searched the house, the barn, and the lean-to, having exhausted every possible search location their experience could recall, and they emerged from the house with two boxes; one containing a black plastic bag with a marijuana plant found in the utility porch, the other with a pair of nunchuks from the bedroom drawer, and two pairs of boots. The only handgun they found was in the bedroom nightstand; a .22 caliber revolver. They left it, since it physically could not have been the murder weapon, and no other laws were broken regarding it.

As for Snider, he had been badgering them throughout the search until they found the nunchuks, at which time they convinced him to shut up and they might not charge him with a felony for possession of nunchuks.

Now, as the end drew near, he was getting cocky again, and he stood in front of Regan and said, "Well, Sergeant Regan, you've trashed my house, where is your evidence? Where is the murder weapon? Where is the gun, the knife, whatever? All that bullshit, cops with guns and everything, and all you can come up with are nunchuks and one little pot plant?"

"You aren't the first murderer to get rid of the weapon. In fact, only the really stupid ones don't. You won't be the first cocky and arrogant asshole who thinks he's too smart to get caught, either. If you are innocent, you'd cooperate with us. But since you aren't, I'm going to assume you are just a little smarter than the average guilty dirtbag, or a little stupider than the average innocent dirtbag. Either way, you are going to see a lot of me in the future, until you screw up and we get enough evidence to take you down."

Looking at his watch, Regan continued, "Well, look at what time it is. It is 8:00 a.m. The garage you work at should be opening up about now. We also have a search warrant for areas under your control at the garage, just in case you hid something there. You want to follow us down there? Oh, that's right, you don't have a car. I'm thinking you probably want a ride to the garage so you can borrow a car."

"Have a blast, you pricks, you still aren't going to pin this on me. You ain't going to find anything there."

"No ride? Okay, see you at the garage."

"Okay, I'll take the ride. But you're still pricks."

"Yeah, but now we're the nice pricks who are giving you a ride to work." As he opened the rear door of his car, he said, "Are you still going to get me fired now that you can see what a nice guy I really am?"

Snider just looked past him as he got into the back seat of Regan's car.

When they arrived at the garage, another Sheriff's marked unit was already on site to assure nothing got moved until the arrival of Regan and the search warrant. The Deputy was standing next to Carl Everham, the owner of the Old Town Speed Shop.

"What's going on, sir," Everham asked when Sergeant Regan walked up to them, followed by Alden Snider. Then looking past Regan to Snider, he said, "What did you do now, Alden?"

Regan handed him a copy of the warrant and said, "This paper will explain. We are going to look around. We only want to focus on areas available to, or under the control of, Mr. Snider when he's at work. We will cause as little disruption as possible."

"Is this legal," he asked.

"I assure you it is, or Judge Hilliard wouldn't have signed it. Now tell me, what parts of the building are under his control or available to him."

"Everything except the tool boxes of the other mechanics. He has access everywhere."

"Okay, we'll start with 'everywhere'. Let's go boys."

Another hour passed, and Regan and the other Deputies had satisfied themselves that there was nothing related to the crime at the garage.

"Okay. Let's see, house, car, workplace … three down and one to go."

"What do you mean by that?" asked Snider, but his tone was now one of resignation more than defiance.

"Didn't I mention it? We have another search warrant for your girlfriend's house, just in case you dropped anything off while you were there last night."

"You bastards. Now you are going to harass my girlfriend. You are going too far, now. I think I better get my attorney on the phone."

"You do that, Snider. In the meantime, we are in kind of a hurry, and while you are wasting your time talking to your attorney and finding a ride, we will be at your girlfriend's. I hope she's there to open the door, so we don't have to use the 'master key'. Or, ... , or you could shut up and come with us and let us in and save the door."

"Someday, I'm going to get even with you for this, Sergeant Regan," said Snider as he got into the rear seat of the car again.

"Really? Like you got even with Sonny Tyler? Careful now, Snider, or you might give me a statement I can use in court."

It didn't take long to search the girlfriend's apartment, and again, no new evidence was discovered.

As they started to leave, Snider again taunted them, "Four hours of this bullcrap, and you got shit to show for it. My attorney will be all over your asses for harassment. Are you going to leave me alone, now, assholes? You going to apologize to me? You assholes should get busy looking for the real killer and get the fuck off my back."

As the Deputies turned and walked away, he said, "Someday, I hope you all get a bullet like Tyler did."

Regan stopped and hesitated, staring straight ahead. Everyone held their collective breaths, waiting to see what Regan would do. Then, he took one slow step forward, then another, as he continued out the door without looking back at Snider. He was frustrated up to his eyebrows, and now, the final taunt by Snider almost pushed him over the edge. But there was something else that also stopped him in his tracks.

As they got into the car, he turned to Ed Gretel, "Did you hear that? He said, "I hope you get a bullet like Tyler did." I went out of my way not to mention that Sonny was shot. Did someone else mention it that I didn't hear, or did he just screw up?"

"I don't know, Don. I'm pretty sure it was on the news last night, and maybe when we found the .22 revolver and got excited for a moment, he might have put it together."

"Nevertheless, we're going to be in his pocket for a while. Come on, let's head downtown. I've still got a briefing at 10:00 am, and it ain't gonna be fun."

Day 2 - Agency Debriefing
10:10 am

It was about 10 minutes after 10:00 am when Detectives Regan and Gretel arrived at the Day 2 debriefing. Once again, the room was filled with the same familiar faces from the night before, sitting in the same chairs. Taking his seat at the head of the conference table, Sergeant Regan began, "Gentlemen, thank you for taking the time to meet again this morning."

"Dan, I might as well start off with this. I took the liberty to write up a search warrant for Snider's car, house, work and girlfriend's apartment, and I had Judge Hilliard review it, and he agreed to sign it last night. Ed and I have been out all morning serving them and we have no news to report at this time, pending the car search, which is going on at this time."

"You what?" Freeman shouted as he stood up at his seat.

"I didn't feel we had the luxury of time to allow him to get rid of any evidence."

"You want me to sit here and give legal guidance to you, and then you disregard it and go to a 'cop lover' judge and go over my head? What the hell am I even here for?" He slammed his leather binder closed and pushed his chair back to leave.

Sheriff Tatum spoke without looking up. "Shut up and sit down, Dan. Save the theatrics for your pot-loving' hippy constituents. You've got a job to do, and so do we. You gave us your best advice, and a Judge agreed with us, instead, and last I heard, judges trump D.A.'s. – now get over it and sit down."

"You are giving *me* advice, now, Sheriff Tatum?"

"No," he said, as he took a long draw on his unlit cigar and looked up until his eyes locked on Freeman's. "I'm just asking you. You've been wanting to make your political points, and you will, in time. But you've got to ask yourself, 'Is this the case you want to gamble your whole career on?' Really? A cop murder case still resonates loud and clear with the citizens, even most dirtbags, and do you want tomorrow's paper to say, 'D. A. REFUSES TO COOPERATE WITH COP KILLER INVESTIGATION!' I don't think that would be smart. But what do I know? I'm just a dumb old Sheriff."

"Have a seat, Dan. Let's get to work on finding our killer." Regan said. As Freeman slid slowly down into the chair, Regan continued, "We got a lot of grief from Snider, who was present at each, and all we have to show for it is a pot plant from his utility room and a pair of nunchuks."

"Don't even think about submitting the case for prosecution for that!" Freeman said as if it vindicated his actions.

"10-4," Regan said. "But since both are still illegal to possess, Dan, you know we had to take them for destruction. If you'd prefer, I'll have the plant shipped to your office and you can 'dispose' of the pot as you see fit. Now, back to work. We still haven't found a match to the boots, and we are looking at all possibilities. Obviously, we didn't find anything that matches at Snider's."

Freeman was taking notes, but looked up over his half-framed reading glasses and scanned the room, one man at a time with his eyebrows raised, but resisted the urge to say, *"I told you so."*

"Any connections between the murders, Don?" Someone asked.

"Absolutely not, but our records people did pull another rabbit out of the hat. Seems in March of 1968, our gang banger murder victim, Tony Garcia, was arrested on warrants by Officer Tyler.

"There we go again," said Freeman. That's quite a coincidence, don't you think? Or has Tyler arrested everyone in town?"

"Not really, Dan. Sonny Tyler was well recognized as a tenacious investigator who liked nothing better than to put dirtbags in jail for drugs or stolen property. He made a lot of arrests; way more than the average Chippie. Tyler liked throwing assholes in jail; Tony Garcia and Alden Snider were assholes. Match made in heaven; it's not surprising to me that they crossed paths. There is still not a shred of evidence or an ounce of reason to believe the cases are connected. Nothing. Detective Landon and I have gone over the reports and witness statements from the gang-banger homicide, and they are clearly unrelated; one is a traffic stop that went bad north of town, the other is a drug deal gone bad south of town about twenty minutes later.

We're checked them out, and now we're wasting valuable time trying to link them by grasping at straws."

"Probably, but at least it is a real motive, not just speculation based on a neighborhood feud," said Freeman. "Maybe Sonny stopped Garcia yesterday, and he recognized Sonny and shot him for revenge. I'll have my staff pull the file on that prior arrest just to be sure it's not more than just a coincidence." suggested Freeman.

"Good idea, Dan. That's what we need. It still doesn't answer why Garcia was murdered a half hour later."

"One step at a time."

Regan continued the debriefing. "Officer Brennan followed up on the phony accident call that led to the time and place of the murder, and no new information has come to light beyond what we shared last night. However, …"

Regan glanced at Captain Richards and took a deep breath. Richards grimaced in anticipation of what was to come next. "There are a couple new wrinkles we have to look at, especially if Snider doesn't look as promising as he did yesterday."

"Captain Richards has an Adverse Action going against one of his Officers. It just started three days ago. Officer Randy Allen is accused of taking a pair of racing-style gloves from the road at the scene of a rollover accident. Instead of throwing them back into the wrecked car, he took them. The only witness, and the complaining party in the allegation is ... Officer Tyler. Without Tyler's testimony, no case, and Officer Allen doesn't get fired from the CHP."

"Now *there* is a motive," said Freeman. "A dirty cop kills the good cop who turned him in. I heard about a case like that back in the Midwest a few months ago. Read about it in one of the law journals. I'm telling you, it happens all the time. You should hear the stories I get about what cops are doing to offenders. There are more bad cops out there than you know about."

"Jesus, Dan. Get a grip," said Sheriff Tatum. You're watching too much TV. You ought to get to know the cops in this county, personally, and you'd change your mind. You are listening too much to your dirtbag friends who have an axe to grind."

"Well," said Regan, "the timing sucks, but we might as well get everything out on the table. We've also just uncovered some information about the ammo used to kill Sonny. The ammo was Remington .38 caliber "Plus P" ammo."

Some of the men in the room gasped and sat back in their chairs in unison.

Sensing this was a bombshell by their reactions, Freeman said, "What? What's Plus P ammo? You guys look like you just saw a ghost."

"True," Regan continued, "'Plus P' ammo was developed by Remington just a couple years ago to offset the advancements in ammunition on the open market. Since most .357 magnum revolvers are not readily available due to the war in Viet Nam, cops in the United States have been forced to carry a .38 caliber revolver. They were outgunned by the bad guys, so Remington developed a .38 caliber bullet with added powder to help law enforcement officers get more power from their .38 caliber handguns."

"So?"

"So … they were only issued to law enforcement agencies around the country for issuance to police officers and deputies."

"Wow!" said Freeman. "That kind of points straight to the dirty cop, Randy Allen, doesn't it? How long were you going to keep that information from me?"

Regan took a deep breath and sat up straight, looking directly at Freeman. "With all due respect, Dan, go screw yourself. Are you going to be part of this team or just take cheap shots from the sideline? Nothing is being hidden from anyone, especially the guy who will be prosecuting the case. You are getting this as fast as I get it. What you don't know is that there are plenty of 'Plus P' rounds available on the black market, and you don't just jump to conclusions and accuse a cop of murder. Your insinuation is offensive to all of us who are trying to solve a cop's murder one step at a time, looking at all possibilities. What I can also tell you, if you'd stop long enough to listen to all the facts before jumping to conclusions, is that we're already looking at Randy Allen. He was on days off and supposedly was in Sacramento visiting family over the weekend. Should be easy to prove. We are already arranging to question Randy Allen today about this case."

"One last question," asked Freeman. "Are you planning to break down Allen's door like you did for Alden Snider?"

"No."

"Double standard. I rest my case."

"We'll do what we've got to do, when the time comes. I've got work to do, let's all get to work," Regan said as he got up, pushed his chair hard against the table, and walked out. The others got up and made their way to the door, grumbling in small groups, and avoiding Freeman.

The Next Few Days.

This would be the last of the daily briefings as there was little change to report regarding the case, as Detectives fanned out their efforts and fell short on all counts.

All efforts to identify the man who called in the location of Officer Tyler's patrol car proved to be futile. Sergeant Regan believed the caller was just a concerned citizen, who was somewhere he wasn't supposed to be, and didn't want to get involved, but wanted to report something suspicious, anonymously.

Everyone got their hopes up briefly when a local body shop owner reported a white 1965 Chevy was brought in with minor front end damage and the owner asked the shop to expedite the repairs, "as soon as possible." It resulted in one very scared individual explaining to Sheriff's Detectives how he had borrowed his girlfriend's car and accidentally wrecked it and was trying to get it fixed before returning it to her. To his relief, the story checked out and no more came of it.

Detectives Regan and Gretel turned their attention to the "Plus P" ammo itself. The most likely connection to the 'Plus P' ammo continued to be Randy Allen, and Sergeant Regan finally got permission to interview Officer Allen, who insisted that an attorney be present when he was questioned.

As expected, Allen was appropriately indignant at being considered a suspect, and, after chastising Sergeant Regan for wasting their time talking to him while the killer gets away, he offered an "iron clad" alibi showing he was in Sacramento on the night of the murder, including signed credit card receipts during a night of partying and an early morning golf outing to celebrate a brother-in-law's birthday.

After offering the above statement, on the advice of his attorney, Randy declined to waive his 'fifth amendment' rights, refused to answer any direct questions, and declined the opportunity to take a lie detector test.

After reviewing handwriting samples, and confirming the sales receipts from Sacramento, Regan had to concede that it appeared Officer Allen was not physically able to commit the crime in Eureka, while in Sacramento, a six-hour drive away. Unless some evidence were to surface showing a possible conspiracy to murder Sonny Tyler, such as a murder for hire, Officer Allen was apparently just a very lucky beneficiary of good fortune resulting from Tyler's demise.

Attempts to identify the specific lot or batch from which the 'Plus P' ammo came from were equally fruitless. Other than to conclude the ammo was distributed to law enforcement in Northern California, it was not possible to narrow their distribution any more.

Undercover officers from all local police agencies made several covert attempts to buy 'Plus P' ammo on the black market in the next few days, looking for a possible source, but there was none available from the usual sources and informants.

Grasping at straws, Regan asked Officer Allen to submit his service revolver and off duty revolvers for comparison test firing. To his surprise, Allen freely offered two .38 or .357 caliber guns for analysis, and the resulting tests proved the guns were not involved in Tyler's murder.

After reviewing the expedited test results, Regan threw down the test report and sat back in his chair in the Detective's Office. It was now three days since the murders. Regan threw his left foot up on the desk in disgust. Across from him, Detective Gretel sensed Regan wanted to talk, so he put down the report he was poring over, and sat back and said, "What's on your mind, Don?"

"This is serious, Ed. We've got a dead cop, and here we are sitting on our collective asses doing nothing. We've run out of leads, we've got no more evidence to pursue. Tomorrow is Sonny's funeral, and I've got twenty thousand residents of this county watching me and expecting me to find justice for Sonny."

"We, boss. We're in this together."

"Yeah, Ed, I know you are loyal. But I'm where the buck stops, and I don't know where to look next. I thought we were all over this case, and I know we are good at this, but here we are with nothing. I'm going to look like an idiot tomorrow. I should be doing something, but I don't know where to look next. We are right back at freakin' square one. I'm beginning to think … he paused at the thought … unless we catch a big break, this case may never be solved."

"Don't get discouraged, boss. It's only been a few days. You know most murders that aren't solved in the first day usually take a while to solve, but we get them, eventually. The answer is here somewhere. We'll just keep going on it until we find it."

"Patience, my ass. This is a dead cop. A dead friend."

"I think we're giving up too soon on Alden Snider. He's our best suspect, and he couldn't act more guilty. Yeah, he got rid of the evidence after the crime, before we searched his house. A good crook would do that, so we just got to keep the screws on until we find something more."

"If we could only find that boot."

Section Four

The Funeral

Sonny always hated his CHP graduation photo. But there it was. Sitting alone on his simple gray metal casket for all the world to see. Actually, it wasn't a bad likeness of him, but it was 'the hat' that he hated. Every recruit hated the CHP's 'Greyhound bus driver' hat. With the metal rim band inside, it screamed 'rookie' until the Officer, once in the field, could rip out the band, dirty it up and give it the popular 'forty mission crush' popularized by WWII war movies.

A private man in life, Sonny would have been embarrassed to see the fuss being made over him in death. People who had hardly noticed him in life were there to mourn his death.

Bonnie Tyler sat in the front row, sobbing continuously into her handkerchief. Her eyes were swollen and red; as if she hadn't stopped crying since being notified of Sonny's death. Katie Fulton was sitting to her left, holding her hand and attempting to console her, much as she had done for the past five days.

Casey sat at her right side and turned around in his seat and looked at the hundreds of Officers from different agencies that showed up for the funeral. As the formation of uniformed CHP Officers marched into the church in unison and took their seats behind him, Casey wondered why he had never met so many of his daddy's friends.

Across the aisle, members of Sonny's family, siblings, nieces and nephews, who had come up from Southern California for the services, sat alone in a quiet vigil. Behind them sat a number of Sonny's friends from the community youth sports teams that he had coached. After that, the rows on that side were filled with men in different uniforms, a blur of blue, black, tan and green as members from a score of Police, Sheriff and Firefighting agencies paid their respects to a fallen comrade most had never met.

In spite of the surrounding legion of support, practically speaking, Bonnie was now alone again. Twenty years ago, she had stormed out of her parent's home back in Oklahoma, at the age of seventeen, vowing to never return. She didn't say too much about that part of her life, but once, when Sonny suggested they take a vacation and go visit her family, she told him that she could never face them again. She went on to say she had been sexually abused by her step-father. Then, several years ago, when Bonnie's mother called her unexpectedly, Sonny got on the extension phone and berated her for allowing such a heinous violation of her daughter. The woman broke down on the phone, swearing it was untrue. Bonnie immediately got off the phone and Sonny eventually hung up on her. They never heard from her again, but the conversation had always haunted Sonny. Sonny never pushed the matter again, in spite of his thoughts, and Bonnie, true to her word, never went back to Oklahoma.

"Look at her up there. Have you ever seen such a phony?" Nancy Owens whispered. She was seated toward the back of the church with Mary Lou Sutton. They sat alone while their husbands, CHP friends of Sonny's, joined Abe Fulton and others as pall bearers, while the soon-to-be-off-the-hook former friend, Randy Allen, sat quietly in a pew among his fellow officers. While the husbands were consumed by the loss of their comrade, these two wives were consumed with other, pettier, things. "Poor Sonny. I really liked him. But I have got to tell you, he deserved a lot better than her."

"I hear you. She's probably already counting her beneficiary money."

"What do you mean?"

"You know, the federal government gives a huge lump sum to survivors of law enforcement officers killed in the line of duty." Mary Lou whispered.

"Really? I didn't know that."

"Terry probably never told you, so as not to tempt you." With that, they giggled loud enough that some people turned in their seats to stare at them.

"Shush, girl!" Nancy said as she looked down. After a few seconds, she looked around the room and said, "Is she here yet?"

"No, I haven't seen her yet, but you know she'll be here."

"I'm not so sure. Everyone's knows they were having an affair. This could get *ug...ly*."

"Maybe, but people would talk more if she didn't show up at all, don't you think? Besides, who told you they were seeing each other?"

"Hello? They always work night shifts together, and surely, you've seen the way she looks at him. For God's sake, girl, what's it take?"

"Shush. There she is!"

The women turned in their seats to see Sylvia Santos enter the church alone and quietly take a seat near the rear on the other side of the aisle. She was looking down and didn't notice the women.

"Look at her. You telling me there is nothing there? She can't even look anyone in the eye, and she couldn't get any further from Bonnie."

"I guess. But don't forget, she was working when he got killed. That's got to be tough for a dispatcher to handle."

"Even tougher if you've been screwing him."

Their conversation was interrupted by Captain Richards, who approached from the rear and sat down in the pew next to them. "Good morning ladies," he whispered.

"Good morning, sir." Nancy said.

"Pretty sad day, huh? It has got to be rougher on some than others. I'm glad to see you two seem to be holding up well." He sat alongside the women for a few moments, who sat quietly with their hands in their laps, long enough to spoil their conversation, then he got up. "I think I'll go help some of the others who aren't doing so well." He got up and walked directly over to Sylvia.

"Good morning, Syl," he said. "Mind if I sit down for a few moments?"

"No, sir. Please, sit down."

"How are you doing? Is the time off helping?"

"Yes, sir. It is. Thank you."

"No thanks needed. And the stress counseling. Is it helping?"

"Uh. ... I haven't gone yet, sir. But I will."

"That's what I heard. Listen, Sylvia. Please. I can't order you to go, or I would. It can only help. You are too valuable an employee to lose. Please go and talk to someone. You are in this too deep to think you can handle it on your own."

"In too deep?" She reacted as if the Captain could read her mind, "What do you mean, sir?"

"This has hit us all hard, but you seem to be most affected. I can only imagine the torment you are putting yourself through. You handled it perfectly. Quit trying to find something to blame yourself for. We all need you to get back to your old self, and I'd just feel better if you'd talk to the counselor, or someone. I will always be there if you need someone you trust to talk to. You need to let it out."

"Okay, I will, sir. I promise."

"Thanks, Syl. Well, I guess I'll see if anyone else can use some moral support."

"Thank you, sir, for all you've done for everybody. When do you get to let it out?"

"There will be a time for that, but not right now. I'm the Commander. I need to try to be strong for everyone right now."

The distant sound of a single mournful bagpipe wafted into the church. "It'll be okay with me if I never hear another bagpiper play 'Amazing Grace'," he said, "I only hear it at funerals. It looks like it is getting ready to start. See you soon."

After the funeral, friends and family went to the Tyler home for a reception. The room was alive with a curious mix of chatter, subdued reflection, laughter, tears, and a few guests just sitting in solitude. Bonnie Tyler sat on her living room sofa, with Katie Fulton by her side, accepting condolences from well-wishers who made their way past her.

The services themselves had been the usual mixture of heartfelt condolences from people whose lives he had touched, and public relations appearances by a few local and statewide dignitaries who didn't even know who Sonny Tyler was a week ago, in life, but were "there" for him and Bonnie now, in death.

When there was a break, Sergeant Regan approached her. "I haven't had much opportunity to speak to you, Mrs. Tyler," he said.

The sight of the man responsible for the investigation started Bonnie crying again. "Please, call me Bonnie, Sergeant Regan."

"Okay, Bonnie. I just wanted you to know we've been working on the case non-stop since it happened, ma'am. I wish I had better news to report, but I promise I'll never give up on the case until it is solved."

"I know you will. Have you found out *anything?*" she said between sobs.

"Nothing yet to pin down the perpetrator, but we are looking at a suspect real closely, and it may be just a matter of time."

"Alden Snider?"

"Well, yes. But he's just one possibility. We are looking at other possibilities, too."

"I just know it's him. If you tell me it was him, but you can't prove it in court, I swear I'll kill him myself."

"I know you feel that way, ma'am, but you can't allow yourself to think that way. Please just be patient, we'll bring the person responsible to justice."

"I know. I know you'll find Sonny's killer. And soon, I hope. And please keep me posted on the status of the investigation; I don't care how long it takes."

At that moment, Casey walked up to her, "Mom, can I go outside?"

"No, not now," she said. "Casey, honey, this is Sergeant Regan. Remember I told you about him."

"Are you the man who's going to catch my daddy's killer?"

Regan took a deep breath and knelt down to Casey's eye level. "Yes Casey, I promise you. I'll get the man who killed your father. I promise."

As Casey turned and walked away, Regan choked back a lump in his throat. Just a day before, he had begun to ponder that which he considered imponderable just a few days ago. Might this case go unsolved? All of these people were looking to him to solve the case, and he couldn't get past Alden Snider's arrogance and taunting. He'd never been stumped in a murder before, and he damn sure didn't want an unsolved cop murder to be his legacy. He figured he'd have the shooter behind bars, or at least identified, by now, but every lead had led to a dead end. And now he had just promised a nine-year-old kid that he'd find his father's killer, and he didn't even know where to turn next.

The Plymouth

The brightness of the morning sun surprised Casey as it washed across the room and gently woke him from a deep sleep. He rubbed his eyes and looked at the alarm clock on the table next to the bed. He was surprised to see that it was already 9:00 a.m.

Every morning since the shooting, he awoke and expected to learn that he had merely dreamed this terrible nightmare, and everything would be as it was. But, like every other morning in the last nine days, he awoke with that now-familiar ache in the pit of his stomach. This morning, he didn't have to ask his mommy; he knew it was all too real. He wondered if he would ever feel "normal" again.

He slipped quietly out of the sheets and peeked around the doorway into the hallway. The house was quiet except for the ticking of the grandfather clock down the hallway. He walked quietly toward the living room. The fire in the fireplace was reduced to no more than glowing embers. Obviously, he was the first one up this morning. Even Ralph, the family's new Samoyed Husky pup, was asleep in the corner of the room.

It was Saturday morning. He was glad there was no school today. Since the shooting, his mom and the other adults had seemed obsessed with keeping him busy, but today, there didn't seem to be anyone around, at least not yet. He figured if he hurried, he might get out of the house before anyone came by.

He dressed quickly and put on his coat. He wanted to be alone and he didn't want to sit around the house, so he decided to go outside and tend to his chores, caring for the odd collection of 'farm' animals the family kept in and behind the shed they called the "barn."

He slipped quietly out the back door and into the clearing behind the house, and headed for the barn. Actually, the building Sonny called 'the barn' was just an old garage/outbuilding separated from the house by about 30 feet. It was big enough to hold a barn's worth of the family's collectibles, as well as feed, tack, and supplies for the family's farm animals.

Directly behind the barn was a chicken pen that Sonny had built to protect the 20 or so laying hens that supplied the family and neighbors with eggs.

He fed the chickens and, after a short one-sided conversation with the rooster who chased him from the pen, he proceeded to the pig pen housing "Howard," his 4-H Club project pig. Because Howard was, well, a pig, his dad had built the pen as far as possible from the house, at the very edge of the forest that bordered the rear of the property. He kicked at the ground and said to the pig, "You probably haven't noticed, Howard, but everything has changed around here. I'm not sure what is going to happen to you, or me, but I'm sure it isn't going to be good." He kicked the ground even harder and turned away before Howard could see him tearing up.

Behind him, at the edge of the forest, there were a score of redwood trees that had not been cleared of underbrush for over 50 years. An old logging road, now just a trail, led down an embankment between the trees into the forest. It was on this trail that Sonny and Casey had experienced many adventures together.

Now at the edge of the forest, he walked a few steps toward a nearby tree stump, sat down and looked around.

As far as he could see as he looked around, everything reminded him of his dad. Since his dad worked mostly odd shifts on the CHP, they had plenty of occasions to explore the forest behind the house during daylight hours after school and on weekends like this.

As he sat and recalled those adventures, one in particular came to mind. About two years ago, he and his dad had been hiking and exploring an overgrown trail in the remote area of the forest not too far behind the house, and found an old, long-abandoned car, a 1950 Plymouth sedan among the trees. He hadn't visited that part of the forest in some time, and he wondered about the old car. Instinctively, he jumped to his feet and ran to the opening where the trail led down the embankment into the forest.

The trail dropped off sharply into a shallow ravine, getting narrower as it went. He jumped over a small recently-fallen tree and crossed the spring and continued along the path another hundred yards to a small clearing. From here, one could hike north or south, parallel to Walnut Drive for a mile or more in either direction. He was far enough into the forest that the quiet babbling of the small creek blocked out all the sounds from the highway and homes nearby. He paused to look at the remnants of a fort that he and his friends built the past summer. He smiled as he welcomed the quiet solitude that he always enjoyed in the forest.

He hurried to his right between two trees and found another well-hidden path under some low hanging branches. He scurried another fifty feet or so along a trail, then back across the creek and up a short climb to another old clearing.

The immediate area where he now stood was at a curve on the old, long forgotten, logging road, now abandoned and overgrown. The road was gone, but it created a nice open clearing. He looked across the clearing to where he remembered seeing the car, and suddenly, he spotted the familiar silhouette of the old car, covered with vines and undergrowth, but otherwise just as he remembered it.

The right side of the car, abandoned years ago up against the shrubs and trees of the forest, was always obscured, even two years ago when they uncovered it. Now, the front and left side of the car were again disguised by almost two year's growth of berry vines, shrubbery and ferns.

Walking to the rear of the car, which was much less overgrown than the front, he could see the partially uncovered trunk lid and could clearly make out the chrome emblem proclaiming the word PLYMOUTH just above where the license plate would have been. He began clearing away the newly grown blackberry vines covering the left side of the car, and soon that side of the car was again completely visible.

He stood back and surveyed the scene. The old light green Plymouth was nothing but an abandoned junker, but it was basically intact as it appeared to have been abandoned a number of years before they found it. The side of the car was littered with old bullet holes, as were the side windows. A single bullet hole penetrated the windshield, directly in front of the driver's seat, but the windshield was otherwise intact.

He remembered asking his dad at the time how it got there, and, as always, his dad was ready with a story. Noting the many bullet holes in the vehicle, his dad had convinced him it was the car in which Bonnie and Clyde had been gunned down. Then again, he said, perhaps it might have been the end of the road for some prison escapees passing through the forest years ago. Perhaps they still haunted the forest, his dad mused.

Casey remembered running up to his mom, at the time, when they emerged from the forest and repeating the tale. While Sonny laughed during the re-telling, Bonnie got angry and said, "Sonny, why do you fill his head with silly stories and that kind of nonsense. It'll only get him laughed at by the older kids."

He recalled his dad replied to her, "For Christ's sake, he'll have to face reality soon enough, let him be a kid and have some fun now."

Later, Casey told the story to his friends and showed them the car. They played around the old car for several months, until their interest waned and it was eventually all but forgotten.

Now, here it was again. He gave the left front door a hard jerk, and it creaked open, revealing the rotting interior of the car. A small rodent scurried into the brush through the rusted out floorboard, which startled him. Just as he and his dad had discovered the year before, there, growing up through the rusted floorboard, and right out through the rear window into the open sky, was a sapling redwood tree.

Other smaller trees and vines had also grown through and around the vehicle, but the driver's area was remarkably intact. He sat on the ragged remnants of the driver's seat, and stared out the window. Suddenly, he felt as though someone or some *thing* was watching from nearby.

He heard a loud crackle of twigs from the dark shadows of the forest behind him and leaped out of the car and shouted, "Who's there?" There was a brief moment of silence, then a series of louder crackling twigs coming his way from the forest off to his left. The hair on the back of his neck bristled and he felt a shiver all the way down his spine as the noise came steadily closer. He bolted for the trail and retraced his steps as fast as he could run, hearing the crashing of twigs and branches behind him, and now panting, heavy panting and grunting, overtaking him. By the time he reached the trail opening, he could hear his pursuer directly behind him and gaining on him and then, just as he was about to scream, in a blur of white, Ralph, the family dog ran past him and didn't stop until he reached the top of the trail.

"Ralph!" Casey uttered in disgust. Exhausted and scared, he fell to the ground crying and laughing at the dog, who appeared more scared than him. As he hugged the dog's neck, a week's worth of emotions came to the surface from deep inside him. He buried his head in the dog's soft fur and sobbed for several minutes.

After several minutes, he heard his mother calling him from the back of the house. "Coming," he shouted back, got to his feet, and hurried up the gentle remaining slope to the house, wiping the moisture from his eyes and cheeks.

"Casey," she shouted at him, "Where in the hell have you been? I've been looking for you for twenty minutes. You know better than to just disappear like that. Where were you?"

"I just wanted to be alone for a while," he said, "so I walked down to the ..."

Before Casey could finish, she noticed scratches and dried blood on his hands and continued, "Look at your hands. They are all cut up and bloody. What have you been doing? This better be good, young man!"

He looked down at his hands, and noticed that they were scratched from clearing the berry bushes from around the Plymouth. "Hey, Mom," he said, "Remember the old

Plymouth dad and I found a couple years ago in the forest? I found it again, and I guess I scratched my hands on the berry vines in the forest. And then Ralph scared me and we ran all the way back up here, and then I heard you, and I came right away."

"You went down to that old car? Casey, honey, that is NOT a good idea. It is all rusty and you could get cut on it or something. Now you probably need a tetanus shot. I'd rather you stay away from that car and stay closer to the house."

"But mom, dad and I..." he began.

"No buts...," she interrupted. "I don't like you going down to that old car anymore. There are plenty of other places to play. Do you hear me?"

"Yes, Ma'am."

"Now, come in and let's get you cleaned up for lunch."

Casey dropped it because she hadn't actually said he couldn't go back to the Plymouth, and he didn't want to press his luck any more on the subject right now.

The next morning Casey was up bright and early and seemed to have recaptured his old self. He waited patiently for breakfast, because he knew he would arouse suspicion if he didn't act normal. Promptly after breakfast, he asked permission to go out and play.

"My, you seem to be feeling better, today," said Bonnie, "I'm glad to see that. Sure, you can go out and have fun. Maybe your friend Ricky is available to play with. But first, don't forget to feed the animals."

"Sure, mom. Good idea. After my chores, I'll go see if Ricky can play, or I'll just play in the back. Don't worry about me. C'mon, Ralph." he said to the dog as they scooted out the door.

He made a quick stop at the barn for some paint and an old paint brush, then scooped up an oil can and some old rags and disappeared into the forest.

An hour or so later, he stepped back from the Plymouth and smiled as he admired his handiwork. "Pretty cool, huh, Ralph," he said. The left front door of the old Plymouth now had a new paint job. The shiny white paint stood in marked contrast to the oxidized green paint on the rest of the car, but the writing on the door made it almost unnoticeable. In neatly handwritten letters Casey had drawn a seven point star encircled by the words, "Highway Patrol."

"Now dad will be right here anytime we want him, Ralph."

He opened the door and sat on a clean rag on the seat and stretched to look out the windows. Instead of the forest he saw the day before, today he saw an open highway in front of him. For the next hour or more, he mimicked sirens and screeching tires as he drove the Plymouth on one hazardous police call after another.

Finally, he stopped and got out of the vehicle. Even though the huge forest was well protected by trees, he could feel a gentle breeze against his cheeks. He shivered. "You know, Ralph, I feel like dad is here with me when I am around the old Plymouth." Then, looking at his watch, he said, "We better get back to the house before mom catches us or we'll be in big trouble."

That night, he felt an inner peace that he hadn't felt in over a week. Over the next two months, Casey often snuck down to the old Plymouth and spent many hours alone with his dad's memory. Alone in the forest with the car, he acted out the scene of his father's murder again and again, but always with a different, more favorable, outcome.

Christmas, the winter rains, and other distractions eventually commandeered Casey's thoughts, and soon the old Plymouth was again relegated to a distant memory, as time and the seasons passed quickly by.

Section Five

Life Goes On As Two Cases Go Cold
October, 1976.

Generally speaking, the 1970's were a fun time for a young kid growing up on the remote California north coast, even though the 'disco craze' and other significant social trends of the era were always about five years late arriving in the rural north.

When you are fifteen years old, time passes quickly, as life's new adventures and interests capture your attention. It was easy for a young teenager not to notice that his life was being reshaped by the passage of time, and with sports, school activities, a driver's permit, and, of course, girls, to occupy his time, the summers and winters began to pass seamlessly by, and Casey thought less and less about the nightmare of 1970.

It was tougher on the adults, because jobs, never plentiful in the region, were becoming even more scarce. Before the 1970's there were four industries which sustained the county: tourism, fishing, the logging industry, and illegal pot growing. The gas lines of the early seventies, changes in the definition of 'international waters', and battles between the forest industry and environmentalists had a devastating effect on the former three, and only the latter had been a consistent income producer for the region. So, for the most part, residents denied its existence and looked the other way while huge cash payments were being made for local purchases and services.

Along the way, District Attorney Dan Freeman successfully rode the wave of marijuana apathy into a second term of office as District Attorney in the interim, whereas Herb Tatum retired and was replaced by another, more progressive, new Sheriff.

But local small town politics were of little concern to Casey as he made his way into high school in 1976. Bonnie, on the other hand, could scarcely conceal her desire to leave the bad memories of Humboldt County. Yet, since Casey excelled at school activities and sports, and they kept him happily occupied, she decided not to leave until he graduated.

But life was anything but easy, living in the same city, even in the same neighborhood, as Alden Snider. As if to add to the insult, Snider, on the other hand, had cashed in on his brashness in the years following the murder. The man most people thought killed Sonny Tyler was now a high profile small business owner. Snider had artfully predicted the success of the high-fidelity car and light truck stereo craze, and opened *Alden Snider Car and Truck Stereo and Accessories* on Highway 101 in South Eureka. The business took off with the young crowd and Snider turned to local radio advertising to turn it into the pre-eminent auto and truck accessories business on the north coast. It was impossible to enjoy your favorite radio station without hearing Alden Snider advertising "Alden Snider's, the place you *GOTTA* be!"

It was generally accepted that Snider was making huge profits elsewhere also. Always willing to push the lines between legal and illegal, he was rumored to be heavily involved in laundering thousands of dollars from the lucrative marijuana growing industry. To the hippy and anti-government crowd, he had become a bit of a cultural hero, and there was even talk of running for the Humboldt County Board of Supervisors.

But the last years had not been <u>all</u> good to Snider. To those who remembered six years ago, and knew Snider's background, the sight of his success was almost too much to handle. Many citizens, who had followed the case so closely since 1970, still reminded him periodically that they thought he'd gotten away with murder.

As for Sergeant Regan's two unsolved murder investigations, the lack of any other tangible leads in the case seemed to confirm the suspicion that Snider had committed the perfect crime. In the ensuing years, Snider had been stopped at least a dozen times by CHP and Sheriff's Deputies for minor traffic violations, which provided police with the opportunity to remind him he was still their prime suspect.

In every instance, the attitude was always the same; brash, arrogant, and mouthy. He seemed to enjoy baiting the cops regarding the unsolved homicide. A few speeding tickets was all they had to show for their efforts.

No-one took the success of Alden Snider as a slap in the face any harder than Sergeant Regan. Regan kept photos of Sonny Tyler and Alden Snider on his desk as a personal reminder of his failure to catch the killer. He had personally kept tabs on Snider in the intervening years, and kept in touch with confidential informants, ex-girlfriends, former business partners, etc. Most hated Snider by the time he interviewed them, but he had never mentioned any complicity in the case to any of them.

Once, Regan even planted an undercover female Officer, from out of county, at a bar Snider frequented. Snider hit on her all night, and had quite a bit to drink, but when she said something about the old case, he didn't even flinch.

And now it was October again, and it was time for Sergeant Regan's annual visit to Bonnie Tyler, to update her on the case. Once again, he'd have to confess that he was no closer to solving the case than he was the morning of the crime. With a deep sigh of resignation, he scooped up the keys off his desk and walked slowly and deliberately toward the door. He wondered how he would open the conversation this year.

It was half past noon, when Sergeant Regan pulled his undercover unit into Bonnie Tyler's driveway. The recent rains of the previous evening had freshened up the bark and branches of the huge Redwood tree in front of the house, and it gave off a most pleasant scent as he took a deep breath before walking up to the front door. Without hesitation, he rang the doorbell.

Inside, Bonnie Tyler was doing aerobics in the living room, stepping up and back onto a makeshift step. As she did so, Jim Croce crooned, *"If I could save time in a bottle ...,"* from the oak entertainment center in the corner.

Hearing the doorbell, she grabbed a nearby hand towel and, wiping the perspiration from her brow, stepped to the door. Straining to her tiptoes, she could see the familiar profile through the peephole. *"Sergeant Regan,"* she said to herself. *"I wonder what he has to say this year."* She opened the door and greeted him. "Hello, Don. How are you? What brings you by? Good news?"

"I'm fine, Ms. Tyler. May I come in for a few minutes?"

"Sure, Don, come in and have a seat," she said as she motioned toward the shiny chrome kitchen dinette, and walked to the counter. She poured two cups of coffee and, handing one to him, sat down across from him. "You take it black, don't you?"

"Yes ma'am, that's fine."

"What's on your mind?"

"Ms. Tyler, do you know what tomorrow is?"

"Of course I do, Don, it's the six-year anniversary. And you can still call me Bonnie."

"Okay, Bonnie. I hadn't talked to you recently, and I wanted to talk to you about the case. Nothing has ever bothered me as much in my life as this case. I want you to know that it will always be my top priority. The file has never left my desk and I look at it weekly, but we've just ran out of leads."

"Don, we both know who killed Sonny. And we both know that he apparently got away with murder, and we both know that Casey and I will never see justice. It tears me up, but we've had to come to grips with it so we can move forward with our lives."

"And every year," Regan responded, "I keep hoping something will turn up to prove our case and I'll get to bring you good news. But again this year, nothing has come up. But we'll get him, or whoever did it, some day. He'll screw up someday."

"You can't imagine how hard it is to see him and hear his ads on the radio every day. For years, I was consumed with hatred and thoughts about revenge. But then, one day, I went to church and it hit me. Sonny wouldn't want it to ruin our lives; he gave me a wonderful son, and he worked hard to put us in a comfortable position so Casey can go to college and make something of himself. That is what Sonny always wanted, for his son to have a chance he didn't have. I have come to believe that God had it work out this way for a reason. I can see how you've carried this heavy burden through the years, Don, and maybe you should put your faith in God, like we did, and he will show you the way to peace in your mind.

I'm glad you have found a way to overcome your grief, Bonnie, but I don't see myself there yet. I'll keep digging until I see justice for some lowlife cop killer."

"So, tell me, Don, where does the case sit right now? Any new leads?"

"To be honest," he continued, "we have not had any new leads for a while. Snider is still our primary suspect, but we just can't find any evidence to link him to the crime, and he hasn't screwed up yet. I have gone over everything I have on Alden Snider until I can see it in the dark. Nothing. I'm starting to think maybe he isn't involved, and he just likes the attention he gets as a suspect. In six years we haven't found one piece of evidence, or one actual lead that points to him. Even the word on the street is 'no word'. Our best informants are coming up blank, and they are very reliable and usually accurate with their info. No-one on the street is saying anything about this case. Maybe it was some parolee-type who was just passing through and is long gone. Our informants haven't heard a whisper in six years. Snider is an idiot. He's not smart enough to not tell someone."

"Apparently he's smart enough to get away with murder."

"You know, he and his long-time girlfriend broke up two years ago," Regan continued. "The one who's house we searched. He dumped her for her girlfriend, then he dumped the girlfriend. They both hate him now. They'd give him up in a second if they could, but he never said anything incriminating, not even on the night Sonny was killed, or when we searched her place. There's been two other girlfriends, same situation, but he never said an incriminating word to any of them."

"Keep trying, Don. Maybe someday we'll get lucky."

Steve Davis

"October 15th was the worst day of my life, and the low point of my career. I've been investigating murders off and on for nine years now, and I've only had two that I didn't solve. And both of them happened within an hour of each other on October 15, 1970."

He paused and looked into the coffee cup, as if for answers, or at least sympathy, but getting none of either, he continued, "I'm looking at Snider, Randy Allen, and every random stranger who was seen in Eureka that week. I've gone over every witness statement a hundred times. The witnesses saw a dark-skinned minority suspect. Snider doesn't fit that description unless you consider his greasy skin during that time frame. We've gone over every cash register and credit card receipt on the North Coast for that night, looking for a stranger passing through that fits the M.O. We've milked our informants until they don't want to see us coming anymore. We considered he interrupted a burglar, robber, or drug dealer in the commission of a crime, but, guess what? No known burglaries or robberies went down that night, but, we've shaken down every known thief, robber, and burglar in the county anyhow. Nothing. That leaves drugs. Our informants are desperate people who would rat out their own mother for a fix, but they haven't dropped a dime on this case in six years."

Then we've got the 'Plus P' ammo. That tends to point to Randy Allen."

"I understand he has a foolproof alibi out of the area for that night. Besides, I never thought Randy was capable of such a heinous thing."

"Exactly, but I even have to think that maybe someone hired someone to kill Sonny, then alibis go out the window. If you look at motive, Randy pops up to the top again. But again, there has been not one word on the streets that would lead to it being a hit. I'm telling you, Bonnie, informants like nothing better than to inform, and dopers will say anything to get a hit when they are desperate, but nothing. Nothing ..." the word tailed off as he repeated it.

"I still don't believe it was Randy," she said. "We both know it was Snider, and eventually you'll get what you need to solve it. In the meantime, Casey and I have moved ahead with our lives, and though we'll never forget Sonny, I think this is what he'd want for all of us; including you, Don. You don't look too much at peace with yourself."

Steve Davis

"Peace of mind is what I bring to other people if I do my job. I don't think cops are supposed to have peace of mind."

"Think about yourself once in a while, Don, instead of others. Please keep me in the loop."

"I will. And good luck, Bonnie. You deserve it."

Attempted Suicide.

Then, in late 1977, when the case seemed to have fallen completely from the public consciousness, yet another bombshell shook Eureka as headlined in the Eureka Times-Standard:

CHP DISPATCHER IN SUICIDE ATTEMPT

On the seven-year anniversary of the murder of CHP Officer Sonny Tyler, police and fire personnel responded to a suicide attempt by the CHP Dispatcher who was on duty at the time of the murder.

Upon arrival at the apartment on F Street in Eureka, medical personnel found Sylvia Santos, 34 years, unconscious from an overdose of prescription drugs, the bottle for which was found on the table next to the bed. Ms. Santos was rushed to St. Joseph's Hospital where she was treated. Due to the quick action by ambulance and medical personnel, she is expected to survive the attempt.

> Ms. Santos was the CHP Dispatcher on duty in the
> early morning hours of October 15, 1970, when
> Officer Tyler was shot and killed while on routine
> patrol on Greenwood Heights Drive, one half mile
> north of Freshwater Road, north of Eureka. No-one
> has ever been charged in the unsolved homicide,
> according to a Humboldt County Sheriff's Office
> spokesperson.

The attempted suicide sent ripples of gossip throughout the law enforcement community. Was it guilt at not being able to prevent the murder that drove her to such a desperate measure, or was it a much deeper motivation. The rumors of her having an affair with Sonny resurfaced and caused many to suspect for the first time that they may have been true.

For her part, Sylvia never revealed the reason for her actions to anyone other than the Psychologist who treated her for depression during the recovery period. After several months of extensive psychological counseling, she appeared to recover and she was ready to return to normalcy. However, the CHP wanted more treatment to assure them she was capable of returning to the stress of the job without compromising Officer safety. After another five months of further post-traumatic and stress counseling she was re-instated to her position as Dispatcher. She received a heartfelt showing of support on her return to the job.

Bonnie, on the other hand, was upset that Sylvia had gotten such attention for the attempt and was somewhat unhappy that she hadn't been successful. The newly re-circulated rumors of a possible affair between Sonny and Sylvia were like reopening an old wound. She was embarrassed by the attention, and the whole episode merely added to her resolve to leave Humboldt County at the first opportunity.

Section Six

June, 1981;

Eleven Years After the Murder;

"Casey Aaron Tyler, Honor Society, School of Business"

The announcer's voice echoed through the stadium and reverberated off of the dense forest of redwood trees to the east and came back again, "Casey Aaron Tyler, Honor Society, School of Business." The words sounded just as sweet to Bonnie the second time around.

Casey walked across the improvised stage and shook the hand of the President of the College of the Redwoods. "Congratulations, Casey," he said generically, as he handed him his Associate of Arts diploma. Casey was amused at the man's feigned familiarity with him, thinking he might just as well have said, "Congratulations, anonymous student." In two years at the school, he had only seen the man in person one other time on campus, and that was when he and the college's football coach were escorting a prized recruit around the campus. He guessed it had all worked out for everyone, though; CR got the recruit, the football program flourished, and people around Northern California knew the name of the College of the Redwoods, which might help him when he got to Sacramento State University next year.

Casey looked to his left and smiled and waved toward his mother, as she snapped another picture. He could see her mouth the words "Good one" as she lowered the camera.

The last eleven years had held differing emotions for Bonnie and Casey. As the decade passed, Casey's life had begun to unfold in front of them, from a nine-year-old with a broken heart, to this day, when his future was bright and there was no regret about the swift passage of eleven years.

To a middle-aged woman, however, eleven years was not so easy to ignore. Financially, Bonnie was better off than most. The house had been paid off, thanks to Sonny's insistence on a death benefit on the home loan.

Further, Sonny's CHP death benefits allowed Bonnie to work selectively if she chose to.

The toughest obstacle for Bonnie was mentally dealing with the unrelenting march of time. She was still an attractive woman, considering she was approaching her 48th birthday. Nevertheless, always aware of the 'ticking clock', she was not happy that, other than a year long relationship that ended with a broken engagement three years ago, no-one had expressed any long term interest in her. But now, finally, perhaps she would actually see Humboldt County in her rear view mirror.

Today, however, she reveled in the culmination of their efforts. Now, *today*, with an Associate of Arts Degree in Business in his pocket, Casey would be moving to Sacramento State University to pursue his degree in Business, and they would leave Humboldt County forever.

In Sacramento, there would be a whole new field of mature, professional, men to choose from. Her life might finally get back on track, she hoped.

As they celebrated, they didn't know it, but their lives and plans were about to be derailed by the man who was approaching Casey from behind.

"Congratulations, Casey," the man said.

Casey turned and recognized the face of Sergeant Regan. "You probably don't remember me. I'm Sergeant Don Regan, Sheriff's Department. I was a friend of your father."

"Yes sir, I remember you a hundred percent, sir." Casey stood tall as he addressed the man. Sergeant Regan was visibly older now, beginning to gray at the temples, but he still had the countenance and bearing that made a young man stand a little straighter when he was in his presence. "I've seen you around the campus, sir. I know you teach some classes out here."

"Yes, that's right. I have also seen you around, but I wasn't sure you'd remember me. My neighbor's son is also graduating tonight and I saw you and wanted to say 'Hi', and tell you that I know how proud your father would be of you."

"Thank you, sir, I'm sure he would be also," Casey said. "Listen, sir. Mom and I know how hard you tried for years to find the killer of my father, and we appreciate that more than you know. I'm sorry it didn't work out. I know how hard you wanted to find him."

"I haven't given up yet, Casey. I keep the file on my desk and I've looked at it every week for what, 10, 11 years now. I believe the killer may still be around and I keep hoping for the big break in the case that will bring it home. You know, there's a lot of new technology out there that may give us new resources down the road. I've got a few more years to catch him, I'm not going anywhere for a while."

As they spoke, Bonnie walked up to them, overhearing the exchange. Regan greeted her arrival. "Good evening, Ms. Tyler. I was just congratulating Casey for his success at C. R."

"Thank you, Sergeant Regan."

Turning back to Casey, Regan said, "Say Casey, you are an outgoing, athletic young man. I've followed your sports career in the newspaper through the years. I've also seen you a few times around the campus. I was kind of surprised you never had an interest in the Administration of Justice Program here at CR; it's got a great reputation. Have you ever thought about a career in law enforcement?"

"Hold it right there, Don," Bonnie interrupted. "Casey has already got a career path started. He's heading off to Sac State next year, and looking forward to a real career with a future that doesn't involve getting shot at, and he doesn't need you to derail him. Have you forgotten what law enforcement already cost our family? Please, don't do that to me, Sergeant."

"Yes, ma'am, I'm sorry I mentioned it."

Casey squirmed at his mother's directness. "Mom, he's only asking me a question." Turning to Sergeant Regan, he continued, "Yes sir, I have thought about it. Often. Every day I had to walk past the A. J. building, and I always think about it, but I believe I need to think elsewhere right now."

"Of course, Casey. Stay with it and get a better job. There are plenty out there. Sorry, ma'am, to cause any upset, but I've got to say that law enforcement is a great career for most. You were just very unlucky, and I don't blame you for feeling as you do. I won't mention it again. Say, if you'll excuse me, I see someone I need to go congratulate. Best wishes to both of you. Goodbye."

After he walked away, Casey said, "Wow, mom, you were kind of hard on him."

"Perhaps. But he has no business coming over here, tonight, of all times, and trying to mess with your mind like that. Look at that piece of paper in your hand, Casey. It says 'Business'. It says, 'successful, respected, professional', not 'cop'. We've talked about this, Casey, and your dad would be proud of you for moving up from his profession and setting yourself up for a successful career in business. He always talked about how being in charge of your own business was the best possible profession. He *couldn't* do it, but with that piece of paper and the money we've put away from your dad's insurance, you *can*!

"Okay, mom. You are right. But I know … I saw … how much dad really loved being a cop. Look at Sergeant Regan. He's successful, and I can't think of anyone more respected or professional."

"Oh, my god! You really *are* thinking about it, aren't you? Casey," she implored, "Don't do this to us. For years we've talked about this moment, don't you remember?"

"I know we've talked about it, mom, but right now, I'm not so sure. Look, I haven't made up my mind about anything, one way of the other, so let's talk about it later at a better place and time."

"Okay, but I want you to remember this. I've lost my husband to the CHP; I don't want to lose my son, too…"

"Okay. Hey, mom, there's Andrea Donahue, the girl I mentioned the other day." Pulling at her sleeve, he said, "Come with me, I want to introduce her to you."

"Okay, honey."

Across the stadium grass, near the dais, Bonnie could see the object of Casey's attention. Andrea Donahue was stunningly gorgeous. Her short blonde hair perfectly outlined her face, and her shapely figure could not be hidden by the graduation gown she wore. Although they had never met, Bonnie knew her from pictures in the paper.

She was the daughter of a local prominent physician, Doctor Richard Donahue, and his socialite wife Elaine. Andrea was much too pretty, too rich, and too sophisticated, and Bonnie immediately felt intimidated.

As they walked across the lawn toward her, Andrea pretended not to see them approaching, but she brightened up and pulled her shoulders back a little straighter in anticipation of the meeting.

Steve Davis

Casey and Bonnie walked up to the trio and paused. Andrea turned to greet them and said, "Oh, Hello, Casey. Mom and daddy, this is Casey Tyler, my friend from school. I mentioned him to you a couple days ago."

"Glad to meet you, sir, ... and ma'am," Casey replied, "and this is my mother, Bonnie."

"I'm very pleased to meet you, Mrs. Tyler," Andrea replied, offering her hand.

"And I am so pleased to meet you, Andrea," said Bonnie, "Casey has talked a lot about you recently, and I can certainly understand why. You have a beautiful and charming daughter, Dr. and Mrs. Donahue."

Casey smiled at the thought that his mother seemed to really like Andrea. Until now, she had not seemed to like the girls he had dated in the past.

"Why, thank you, ... Uh ... Have we met?" Mrs. Donahue asked as she extended her hand, surprised that Bonnie seemed to know them. Her eyes quickly took the measure of Bonnie from head to toe, as they had trained themselves to do over the years. She could instantly evaluate whether a new face would help her standing in the local women's clubs. As her eyes came back to Bonnie's face, it was clear that Bonnie had not measured up as someone Mrs. Donahue needed in her life. "Your face looks familiar. Please forgive me if we have met, but I can't remember where."

"No, we haven't met before, but I recognized Dr. Donahue from his picture." Bonnie suddenly felt very inadequate; the way she did as a child when others looked at her clothes and knew she wasn't in their class. She thought she had outgrown that awkwardness by clawing her way to respectability, but she clearly had not, because here were those feelings again. She could only hope that Andrea would be another passing fancy for Casey, and she wouldn't have to tolerate the Donahues' condescending attitude toward her.

"That's a beautiful dress, Mrs. Tyler," Andrea said. Leaning over toward her, she continued softly, "You've raised a sweet young man in Casey. I like him a lot, and I hope we get to see more of each other in the future."

Before she could respond, Elaine Donahue continued to press for answers. "And what of Casey's father. Is Mr. Tyler here?" she asked as she looked across the lawn from whence they had come as if he would be joining them at any time.

"No, Casey's father is deceased." Bonnie said politely, ending the awkward silence.

Andrea whispered to her mother, "*Mother, I told you ...*"

"Oh, that's right. That must have been simply dreadful. The poor man. I'm sure you must be quite relieved that Casey doesn't have to go into such a dangerous profession, Mrs. Tyler."

Bonnie winced. She was extremely offended at Elaine Donahue's implication that cops are people 'forced into the profession due to the inability to get a good job', and choked back the urge to defend Sonny and the very career she had disdained only moments before.

Instead, she drew a breath, and said, "Yes, it was 'simply dreadful'. But actually, like his dad, Casey is a bright young man and will have plenty of opportunities to choose which profession he wants to enter." Turning toward Andrea, she said, "Thank you for the compliment about the dress, Andrea, and I hope we do end up seeing each other much more."

The latter comment was intended to give Elaine Donahue something to fret about rather than a sincere desire to see Andrea again. Besides, it was clear that she and Casey didn't meet Elaine Donahue's expectations for Andrea, and the Donahues would do all they could to derail any interest between Casey and Andrea.

Bonnie smiled to herself; she wouldn't have to do a thing, the Donahues would end it for her and she would just wait for it to happen.

Section Seven

September, 1983
Casey Joins the CHP

Officially, according to the calendar, a scant two years and ninety-one days, plus a few hours, had passed since the last time Casey sat poised on another stage, another place, and another time, but to him, it seemed as if it was another person's life he was reflecting on.

Casey sat on the stage at the CHP Academy and looked out into the crowd. When he graduated from College of the Redwoods twenty-seven months ago, he was still searching for direction, but now, today, he felt like this was the right step toward whatever destiny had in mind for him.

His right hand was subconsciously running up and down the blue and gold stripe on his uniform trousers like his tongue might explore a recently-filled cavity. After twenty-three weeks of wearing the plain gray cadet uniform, the feel and cut of the tailored CHP dress uniform felt a little awkward, but it was a nice awkwardness, since he had put in a thousand hours just to be able to feel that awkward stripe tonight.

His decision to drop out of Sacramento State half way through his senior year and join the CHP had been the source of a hundred arguments between him and his mom. Bonnie Tyler was unaccustomed to not getting her way, and this was a big one that got away.

Nevertheless, he was proud and pleased with his decision, and tonight was the moment he had worked so hard toward for the last 23 weeks, and which he had anticipated for over a year, since the day he had secretly taken the test for the CHP.

The hardest part, of course had been breaking the news to his mother. As he anticipated, it hadn't gone over very well. Furious at Casey's decision, for the past five months, Bonnie had regularly told Casey that she wouldn't attend the ceremony, and he had resigned himself to the thought that she really would miss it. But there she was, seemingly beaming with pride, sitting in the fourth row, alongside Abe and Katie Fulton, Sergeant Regan, and Andrea Donahue.

The latter was a complication that Bonnie had not counted on; Casey not only continued to see Andrea through college, but they were getting quite serious about their relationship, and she found herself having to tolerate Elaine Donahue's haughtiness much too frequently.

The truth was, even Casey had to question the wisdom of the decision to drop out of Sacramento State University just one semester shy of his Bachelor's Degree in Business Administration. Pressed for a reason, he could only say it was what he wanted in his heart, as if in response to a calling. He couldn't tell if Bonnie, or the Donahues, were more irate about the decision, but the important thing for Casey was that Andrea understood him and was supportive of him following his heart. There would always be time to go back to a business career later if he changed his mind, and he hoped the passage of time would rebuild the relationships between himself and Bonnie, and Andrea's parents.

So, for five and a half months, neither family spoke much to him as he inched toward his goal. Andrea, on the other hand, was continuing at Sacramento State University toward her Master's Degree in teaching. The good news to Bonnie was that they had put marriage plans on hold until Andrea's graduation. If it would have given her consolation, which it certainly didn't, Bonnie could take comfort in the fact that, like herself, Elaine Donahue's influence on the young couple also diminished exponentially as her protests intensified. Elaine's mortification that her beloved Andrea was now engaged to a lowly police officer could not be hidden, and neither woman had been able to affect the breakup of the relationship they so despised.

While accepting the inevitable, Bonnie had actually convinced herself that this just might work out for the best. As a new CHP Officer, Casey would be assigned to Southern California for a few years. There was every possibility that, with Casey's absence and Elaine Donahue's constant prodding, Andrea might have second thoughts, or, perhaps they would grow apart, as many young couples do when one becomes a cop. Maybe he would even find that once the glory of following in his father's footsteps had worn off, the CHP wasn't his cup of tea, and he'd go back to College in Sacramento, Andrea would be out of the picture, and, best of all, they'd be out

Steve Davis

of Humboldt County and the ever-present, haunting shadow of Alden Snider.

But, that was in the future. Today was the first part of that journey. As Casey watched her, Bonnie smiled proudly. He could see a wrapped package in her lap with a big bow and card.

He looked back at the podium, as the Academy Commander called out the names of his 97 classmates in alphabetical order. One by one, the CHP Cadet Training Class III of 1983 stepped forward and had their badges pinned on them by the CHP Commissioner or another significant CHP person in their lives. Soon, it was his turn.

The Academy Commander paused, "Officer Casey Aaron Tyler, Riverside Area. Casey was Company Commander of Company B. Pinning his badge on Casey will be Sergeant Abe Fulton, Humboldt Area. Sergeant Fulton was the best friend of CHP Officer Sonny Tyler, Casey's dad, who tragically lost his life in the line of duty in 1970. I'd also like to acknowledge and welcome Bonnie Tyler, Casey's mother and the widow of Officer Sonny Tyler." As he gestured in the direction of Bonnie, many in the audience stood and broke into respectful applause, and Sergeant Fulton stepped forward to pin the badge on

Casey's shirt. Casey knew the applause was not for him, but to honor his dad. *"The CHP is, indeed, a tight family,"* he thought.

"Welcome to the Patrol, Officer Tyler," Sergeant Fulton said as he shook his hand and stepped back.

After only a handful more badges were pinned, the Commander stepped back to the podium and said, "Ladies and Gentlemen, tonight, the CHP Academy and Cadet Training Class III of 1983 is proud to present to you the 98 newest Officers of the California Highway Patrol."

The ceremony ended, the crowd pressed forward to congratulate the new Officers. Bonnie stepped up and gave Casey a hug with her left arm, while she clutched the gift to her right side. "Casey, honey, it may not have been my first choice for you, but I am so proud of you, and your dad would be bursting with pride. I know he would want you to have this to commemorate this occasion." She handed him the wrapped package.

"Open it, Casey," Andrea implored.

Casey recognized the shape of the package. Tears were already rolling down his cheeks as he tore open the bright blue and gold wrapping and revealed the handsome,

Steve Davis

etched wooden case. He wiped his eyes as he opened the box and gazed at the engraved Smith and Wesson CHP Commemorative Model 19, .357 Magnum revolver, enfolded in bright blue felt and mounted in the walnut display case. The collector's edition revolver was his father's pride and joy, and had been proudly displayed on the fireplace mantle at home for as long as Casey could remember. "Mom, this is perfect. I promise I will take care of it like dad did, and like you did after he died. Thank you … thank you!"

"Of course you will. I know it will always be safe with you."

"So, Casey, do you even know where Riverside is?" asked Sergeant Regan.

"Barely, sir. But I reckon I'll get to know it real well over the next few years.

Section Eight

Casey's Return to Eureka.
March, 1987

The first vestiges of light were just beginning to brighten the eastern sky when Casey pulled his Camaro into the Officer's parking area of the Humboldt CHP Office and stopped. He got out and looked at his watch. 5:15 a.m. *"A half hour early for my first shift in Eureka! Christ, you'd think I was a damn rookie reporting in for the first time,"* he thought, as he looked around to see if anyone was around to see him arrive so early.

He'd been in this office a hundred times, sometimes with his dad, as a child, sometimes with his mom, to clear up some paperwork, but this time was different. This time it was HIS office, just like it had been his dad's office some 20 years ago.

As he approached the back door, he reached for the handle and froze. A cold chill passed through his body as he pondered the last time his dad walked through the same door, not knowing that he would be killed just over an hour later. Casey suddenly felt his own vulnerability more than ever before. Perhaps he, too, would meet his ultimate fate on the streets of Humboldt County. Had he made all those decisions, which brought him back to this place, just to be a footnote in the CHP history books? *"There are no guarantees,"* he thought. He hoped that if it happened, his mother could handle it twice.

He opened the door and walked into the locker room, where Sergeant Fulton was waiting, straddling one of the benches that divided the rows of lockers on each side of the small room. Casey had been in the locker room over seventeen years earlier, and he instinctively glanced over at the locker which had been his dad's when Sonny occasionally stopped by to pick up a subpoena or notes for court when he was a child. He always loved it when he got to go to court with Sonny years ago. He even got to sit in the front row and listen to his dad promise to tell "the truth, the whole truth, and nothing but the truth, so help me God." His dad always won the case, and Casey would tell his friends and teachers all about it over the next few days. He was saddened as he realized he hadn't thought about it since 1970. But then, he was startled back to reality, when he saw the black ribbon, which had obviously been draped over the locker door as a safety reminder since 1970.

"Welcome home, Casey," Sergeant Fulton said. "I thought you might be early this morning, so I've been waiting. I wonder if you are as nervous as I am?"

"Yes, Sir."

"I noticed you looking at the locker. You probably could have it if you wanted. No-one has used it since Sonny was killed."

"I'd have to think about that, Sir"

"Casey, I'm sure you are going to go through some pretty bizarre emotions as you begin to work in this office. I feel pretty emotional, myself, and I'm sure you must be a lot worse. I just want you to know that I am here for you, if you need someone to talk to about it."

"Thank you, Sir."

"That's another thing. Protocol says you should call me Sir or Sergeant when it is in an official capacity; but if it's not official, like now, I'd like you to call me Abe, like the rest of the guys. Okay, Casey?"

"Yes, Sir, … Abe." he said, as they both laughed at his awkwardness.

Let's go in the break room and get a cup of coffee, then we'll go up to dispatch and we'll meet the dispatcher on duty. Then we'll get the paperwork out of the way before Captain Webster gets here. He'll want to talk to you before we hit the road."

The break room wall was adorned with a cutout of a huge plywood pig, someone's idea of self-deprecating humor from the seventies. On it, over two dozen pegs were attached, each adorned with each employee's coffee mug of various shapes and sizes. Most were emblazoned with advertisements from various tow services which had served the area for thirty years, but some were more personalized. He noticed one that said 'World's Greatest Dad' near another which proclaimed its owner to be the 'World's Greatest Grandpa'. *"Imagine the odds of that,"* he thought with a chuckle, *'The world's greatest dad and grandpa working in the same little office.*

Sergeant Fulton pulled his own mug from the pig's forward section, emblazoned with a "49ers" logo and offered Casey a 'loaner', with a long ago closed local restaurant's logo on it. "The only pegs available for the new guys are near the pig's ass," he said. "Like everything else on the CHP, you work your way up."

They had just gotten their coffee and began small talk when Sylvia Santos entered the room with an empty coffee cup, which said, 'Not yet! Wait until I've had my first cup of COFFEE'.

"Oh, excuse me," she said. "Am I interrupting something?"

Sergeant Fulton stood up and said, "No. Good morning, Syl. We are going to come up to dispatch in a minute. But since you are here, …" Turning to Casey, he said, "Do you remember Sylvia Santos?"

"Yes, I do. Hello, Ms. Santos," he said as he jumped to his feet.

"Hello, Casey. It's nice to see you again. Welcome back to Humboldt County."

Yes, indeed, he remembered Sylvia. He remembered that in 1970, even though he saw her infrequently, she was gorgeous to a certain nine-year-old boy. He also knew that his mom was never shy about her dislike for Sylvia, which caused him to notice her even more. Then, after her suicide attempt, he was old enough to understand her grief for the first time, and remembered the whispers that she and his dad might have been a little too friendly before his dad died. Later, as a teenager, when he saw her around town once in a while, he noticed that she was also very shapely, and he clearly understood why she might have caught his dad's eye. Yes, she was older, a little more haggard, but, to his surprise, still very pretty and still shapely.

"Thanks. I'm glad to see you are still around," he said. He winced at how stupid that sounded, especially considering her suicide attempt. He hoped she didn't make the connection.

The local newspaper and town gossips had covered her attempted suicide in 1977, and it was occasionally discussed among Bonnie and her friends, sometimes in his presence. He was actually surprised that she seemed normal. From all he'd heard back then, she was a conniving, unstable, mental case that people had better stay away from at all costs.

"I have to admit I've been worried since I found out you were coming here," she said. "I've got to warn you.

You won't get away with anything on my shift, because I'm going to be even more diligent than normal."

"Thanks," was all he could think to say.

She turned her back on the men, and, as Casey watched, she poured herself a cup of coffee, added two spoons of creamer out of the jar, one heaping spoon of sugar, and turned around to leave. "I've got to finish my shift. I will see you gentlemen up front in a few minutes. Nice to see you again, Casey. I'll see more of you when you work graveyard shift. I'll look forward to getting to know you better."

As he stared at her, he realized there was indeed something uniquely alluring about Sylvia, and he thought that if those rumors from long ago were true, he certainly forgave his dad for his interest in her.

"Whoa, Casey," Sergeant Fulton said, as Casey watched her walk out of the room, "She's about twice your age, but I understand the look in your eye. Besides, no-one has been able to crack that nut, and many have tried."

Casey blushed. "No, Sarge, you've got me wrong. I was just surprised she remembered me, and she seems like such a nice person, after all I've been led to believe about her."

"She's been chewed up and spit out by the rumor mongers through the years, but she is a solid person and a great dispatcher. I don't know how much you know about the morning your dad died, but she was a superstar, and when you are on the road, you'll never be in better hands than those. Since she came back from her suicide attempt in '77, she works nothing but graveyard shift. Oh, once in a while the Commander will make her work days or swings for training, then it's back to graves. Her commitment to the guys on that shift is legendary."

"But ... she's still Santos. She never married?"

"Trust me, every 'single' guy, and a few married ones, who have ever worked that shift has tried to hit on her. Deputies and Officers from other agencies come up with excuses to come to the office on graves just to see her, and no-one has ever gotten to first base. She has dated a few guys over the years, but never cops. Then she drops them because they don't measure up to her idea of what a man should be."

"So, what's her perfect man?"

"Well ... nothing disrespectful, but you'll hear it occasionally yourself; most people think he would look a lot like your dad."

"Wow," he breathed, almost inaudibly.

"Just be careful with your emotions, Casey."

"Oh, no, sir. I'm all about trying to get back together with Andrea Donahue, Dr. Donahue's daughter. We kind of drifted apart after college. I'm seeing her tomorrow night to see if she'd be willing to try to start over."

"Good luck with that. And how is Bonnie doing lately? You know, I always thought she hated it up here in Humboldt County, and I'm surprised she didn't move out of here."

"Well, you're right. She has always wanted out of Humboldt County, but she just never could seem to make it happen. First, she stayed here for me and school, and then it was that Fortuna Police Officer. Then after I graduated from CR, she met another guy, and that kept her in Eureka again for a couple more years. Then, when I joined the CHP, I made it clear that I was going to come back here, so she gave up. I'm pretty much all she's got. She still bugs

Steve Davis

me to get out, but this is the only home I've ever known, and I love it, and I'll stay here as long as I can. Bottom line is … she's not really happy right now."

"She's got to be happy to have you around again."

"Yeah, but she might be expecting more attention than I can give her."

"That's tough. … Look at the time. Let's go up to dispatch, then we'll jump on that paperwork."

Section Nine

The Traffic Stop
October, 1987

Casey pulled the big Chevy patrol car off of
Highway 101 at the exit to Elk River Road, turned left and
drove to the end where the service road dead-ends at the
bay. A quick U-turn and he stopped in a well-worn turnout.
This was one of Casey's favorite 'cherry patches', a place
where he could always count on a good 'customer'
showing up for business.

He leaned back in the seat and stretched his hands
over his head. As he did so, he pondered how his life had
come full circle in what seemed like such a short time from
when he lived there as a teenager.

He smiled to himself. After being separated for
several years, he and Andrea had rekindled their romance,
and they decided the time was right to get engaged. He

proposed two months ago, she accepted, and the wedding was planned for early spring. Overall, his relationship with his mom was pretty much back to normal. Even Dr. Donahue seemed to accept Casey, for his personal qualities, if not his job, although Elaine Donahue was going to take a little longer.

As he sat there and contemplated these things, a black Mercedes, approaching from the north at a high rate of speed, would shake that complacency and threaten all those relationships over the months ahead.

Casey actually heard the car before he could even see it; the now-familiar sound of a vehicle pushing the air in front of it takes on a unique pitch when the speed is over eighty miles per hour. He fired up the Chevy and waited for the approach of his first 'customer' of the day. He knew that from his location, he could see it clearly as it passed, but the driver could not easily see him. *"Easy pickings if I don't blow it,"* he said to himself as he dropped the gearshift into 'drive' and urged the patrol car after the black coupe which was fast disappearing down the highway.

About a mile down the road, he began to overtake the unsuspecting speeder. He quickly obtained an "odometer clock" on the vehicle. *"Over eighty,"* he thought, as he closed the gap, then paused long enough to get a 'bumper clock" on the car. "Eighty three," he said aloud to no-one, as he turned on the red light and pulled behind the sleek black Mercedes coupe. *"Nice car,"* he thought.

As he exited the patrol car, and began to approach the rear of the Mercedes, he could see the driver, who appeared from behind to be in his mid-thirties, nicely dressed with slicked back hair, seated stiffly alone in the car. His hands were out of sight, hidden in his lap, and his gaze was locked on the Officer, as he intently watched Casey's approach in the side rear view mirror. In his short career, Casey had already learned that such action was frequently a tip-off that something wasn't normal. It was a trait often used by street-wise criminals, and all too often proved to be a harbinger of a weapon or a potential attack on the officer. It was just one of the intangible signals that caused an experienced Officer to use extra diligence.

"Hey, partner," Casey said as he paused at the rear of the Mercedes, "how about putting your hands on the steering wheel where I can see them?'

There was a short pause while the driver pretended not to hear him. Just as Casey was about to repeat the request, the driver complied and put both hands on the steering wheel.

Casey proceeded to the driver's door, observed the man's empty hands, and said, "Thank you. May I see your driver's license? I stopped you for speeding."

"Are you sure, Officer? I didn't notice how fast I was going, and it seems like you didn't have time to clock me. Did you?" The man, about a dozen years older than Casey, was nattily attired in dress slacks and shirt and he wore a black leather jacket that cost more than Casey would ever be able to afford. Obviously a successful businessman, doctor, or attorney, Casey thought to himself.

"Did I what?" Casey asked.

"Did you clock me?" The man paused, while he looked for the Officer's name tag," Officer …?"

"Officer Tyler," Casey said. "Yes, I clocked you at 83 miles per hour, sir. May I see your driver's license?" he asked, in just a little firmer tone.

The man produced his wallet and plucked the license from it. "Officer Tyler, you say?" said the man as he handed over his driver's license.

"Yes sir," Casey glanced at the license, "Mister … …" He could feel his throat tighten and he almost choked on a missed breath of air, and he tried to swallow with what was now a very dry mouth. "… Mister Snider." His voice tailed off as he pondered whom he had stumbled across.

He had prepared for the possibility that, in returning to Eureka, someday, he would stare into the face of the very man everyone suspected had gotten away with the murder of his father. He certainly never planned that it might happen so soon after his return to town. He took a deep breath.

"That wouldn't be Casey Tyler, would it?" Snider asked dryly. "You know, I think I used to live near a little kid named Casey Tyler. That wouldn't be you, would it? … Casey?"

Casey swallowed hard as he tried to compose himself, 'OK, I guess I knew it could happen, but I hadn't time to formulate a plan for when it did happen, and now here he is, right there in front of me.'

Casey had also never thought Alden Snider would be driving a shiny black Mercedes, dressed to the nines, and acting as cocky as he was. And now, Snider's

Steve Davis

arrogance was making it even worse than he could have
imagined.

Casey could feel himself reaching for his gun to
even the score, right here, right now. He was relieved to
look down at his hand and see it was not moving, except in
his mind. "I'll be back in a moment with your ticket, Mr.
Snider."

"Aw, c'mon, Casey." Snider implored as Casey
walked away from the window, "How about a break for an
old neighbor? For old time's sake," his voice got louder as
it followed Casey's back as he hurried back to the security
and comfort of his patrol car.

"*That son-of-a-bitch*," he muttered to himself as he
thought about what he should do. He knew if he wrote the
ticket, he might be accused of returning to Eureka and lying
in wait for Snider. But he didn't care. This was one ticket
he wasn't going to let go, and the only thing that would
make it better would be if Snider refused to sign the
citation, or had a warrant somewhere, that would allow
Casey to arrest him and tow away his pretty Mercedes.

Somewhere in America there is probably a small
backwoods town where Casey didn't check Alden Snider
for warrants. "*Anything to arrest him and throw his ass in*

jail," Casey begged to himself as he waited. But in the end, he could come up with nothing, and returned cautiously to the Mercedes with the ticket book in his hand.

"Mister Snider, I need your signature on this line, promising to appear in court on this date and time," Casey started to explain, but he was interrupted by Snider, who took the ticket and scratched his signature on the correct line. "I know the procedure. I'll see you in court, Casey Tyler."

As Casey handed him his copy of the citation, Snider looked up at him and said, "Well, I sure feel a lot safer around here now, knowing that Officer Tyler, Junior, and is on the beat." He wadded it into a ball and threw it on the floorboard of the car. As he put the car in gear, he looked up, straight into Casey's eyes, and said, "You know, Casey, you really should be careful out here. Don't let the same thing happen to you that happened to your daddy!" Then he drove away and left Casey standing there watching the car getting smaller as it vanished around the bend in the roadway.

"That son-of-a-bitch just threatened me." Casey thought as he walked back and threw his ticket book hard through the open window. It bounced hard off of the seat,

Steve Davis

hit the dash and fell to the floorboard of the patrol car. *"And, he almost admitted that he killed my father."*

For the rest of his shift that day, Casey drove around aimlessly on his beat and pondered Snider's parting words. *"Was he really threatening me, or just saying something spiteful that he knew would get to me; to get even for the ticket?"* One thing was for certain, Casey vowed. He promised, then and there, to find out if Alden Snider was a murderer, or just an asshole with a bad attitude. Casey knew he would not rest easily until he knew if Alden Snider was truly involved in his father's death.

The Plymouth Reunion

It was Saturday morning, his day off work, and Casey woke up mad, just as he had every day since the confrontation with Alden Snider. Casey found himself more enraged every time he thought of it, and that was about every hour of every day. He went to the kitchen and pulled hard on the refrigerator door.

"Jeez. I need to go to the store. Nothing but crap in here. I could go for a nice breakfast this morning, but this crap isn't going to cut it."

He reached for the phone and dialed his mom's number and, moments later, he had successfully gotten himself invited to breakfast.

Bonnie hung up and smiled. She didn't really mind, since she hadn't seen much of Casey since he got back to Humboldt County, and she appreciated the times when he was around. She had finally resolved herself that she would likely never get out of the County. And with Casey engaged to Andrea now, she was likely to be seeing even less of him.

After breakfast, Bonnie said, "You know what would be great, Casey. Since you are back in Humboldt County, I'm kind of motivated to do some home cooking and canning again. You used to love my cooking and I always liked gardening. I was thinking …how about we clear a place around the old chicken pen to plant a garden, like we used to have?"

"Mom, you never liked gardening, you just liked me, or dad, doing the gardening."

"Well, you got the benefits of the garden, right?"

"Yeah, I guess. I haven't been out there for a while. How bad is it?"

"I think the blackberry bushes might be a couple feet high. Don't worry, I'll help and it will go fast. We don't even have to do it all today, but we could start today and see how it goes."

"Okay, Mom. I've got nothing else to do, and it might help take my mind off work."

"What? Is something wrong at work, Honey?"

"No, Mom. I just keep thinking about that asshole Snider. You should have seen him."

"I know what you mean. I've had to hear his stupid ads for years while you were gone. I hate him, but … we've got to move on."

"How can you say that so casually? He killed your husband in cold blood, and got away with it. How can you overlook that?"

"The bible, Casey. It says you have to let go of your hatred. You can't let it eat away at you. You've got to move on."

"The Bible? When did you get back into religion again?" It seemed to him that every five years or so, Bonnie got back into the Bible, perhaps a subconscious throwback to her Southern Baptist roots in Oklahoma that she had abandoned years ago. "Anyways, I don't think it says that, mom. And if it does, screw it. I'll never forget it, and if I ever get the chance to put him away, I'm going to do it."

"Casey, you won't do anything stupid, will you. You got a job, a future, a fiancée; everything is going your way right now. Let's not talk about doing anything to screw up our lives."

"I'm not planning anything, but if I got the chance…"

"Let's work on a garden, Casey."

It was almost noon when Casey, Bonnie and the now-arthritic old family dog, Ralph, made their way out to the area of the old chicken pen and surveyed the area. Having survived well beyond his expected lifespan, the old dog spent most of every day just lying around the house, but he always perked up when Casey came around. He followed them to the chicken pen and took up a position nearby and lay down, ever vigilant.

The remnants of the old chicken wire still surrounded the hundred-year-old redwood tree, but the wild berry bushes had re-claimed the land and all it possessed. Intertwined with the dreaded poison oak he remembered so well, it was immediately clear to Casey that the overgrowth was going to be a formidable foe.

Bonnie looked at the area and said, "Oh, Casey, it's going to be great, just like old times. We'll plant the garden right up near the old barn, so it'll be easy to fence in."

"We'll need the tools from the shed."

As they approached the shed, Bonnie paused. "Oh, …" she said.

Casey knew what was coming next. He began to count backwards to himself, *'five, four, three, two, …'*

"Oh, I just remembered. I promised Mrs. Moore I'd take her to do her grocery shopping this morning. She doesn't get around much since Mr. Moore passed away. But don't worry; I'll just be a little while. You can go ahead and start, and I'll help just as soon as I get back from town. Okay?"

"Right on time. Some things never change," Casey thought. "Sure, mom. I'll see what I can get done while you are gone."

He and Ralph stared at her back as she walked away toward the house. A sense of resentment swelled up inside him, and for a moment, he was 9 years old, watching her walk away from the same job. She would get Sonny and him to start a work project and then come up with an excuse to stop, leaving them to do the work. And now, here she was pulling the same stunt on him again, as an adult.

He turned to Ralph and said, "I wonder if she really thinks I am that stupid." He let out a sigh of resolution.

Ralph wagged his tail. He preferred to work alone anyhow, and besides, he hoped it might bring back some pleasant memories and take his mind off the man who taunted him the week before.

'I'm going to need some serious tools'. He walked to the door of the old barn and pulled on it, but it didn't budge. He gave it a hard jerk and it squeaked as it broke clear and swung open, dragging across the ground. Even the squeaking and dragging noises couldn't muffle the distinctive, immediately recognizable sound of Black Widow Spider webs being pulled apart, causing him to step back quickly. Ralph sensed Casey's fear and barked into the dark room and took a step back in line with Casey, who shuddered as a chill went down his spine. Inside, he could see the tools and other clutter on the bench, just beyond the spider webs, pretty much just as he had left them as a teenager. He was about to close the door and go to the hardware store for new tools, rather than face the spiders that made the ominous webs he was peering through, when something caught his eye. There, within reach, on the bench, was his dad's old machete, and next to it the sharpening block that he used to keep it sharp. He carefully reached in and removed the machete and sharpening block

and left without closing the door. *'Cleaning that mess up is for another time'*.

After laboriously sharpening the machete blade, Casey walked over to the edge of the chicken pen, inside of which he could see the weather-beaten homemade coop he and his dad had built over seventeen years ago. Nothing appeared to have moved since the little farm was abandoned shortly after his 4H days in the early 70's. It seemed almost sacrilegious to tear down the old pen that he and his dad had built, and it made him feel guilty for abandoning it so long ago.

He cleared only about ten feet of berry vines, accompanied by a thousand memories of those days, when he stopped to rest and put the machete across his lap. As he sharpened it, he contemplated the last time he'd seen it used, and smiled as he again remembered the old Plymouth in the forest. He stood up and said, "Let's take a break, Ralph."

They walked the short distance across the clearing to where the trail used to enter the forest. Feeling the need to reconnect with his dad, he began hacking at the overgrowth until he could see the beginning of the long dormant trail down the old logging road and into the forest.

He was actually surprised that the trail wasn't more overgrown as he worked his way down the path and into the forest.

An hour later, he stood at the edge of the clearing deep in the forest, and could clearly see the outline of the old car once again, even though it was more covered with overgrowth than the first two times he had found it. The front and the far right side of the car were totally engulfed in new tree growth, just as before, but the left outline was clearer than expected. He smiled at the thought of discovering the old Plymouth for the third time.

Without hesitation, he walked up to the vine-covered relic. He leaned down and pushed some vines away with the tip of the machete, until he could barely make out the star he had painted on the door years earlier. "Well, I made it, didn't I?" he said aloud, though he didn't know if he was talking to himself, the car, Ralph, or his dad.

As he hacked away at the overgrowth concealing the old car, he remembered how, as a grieving nine-year-old, he had communicated with his dad in this same location. When he finally laid the machete on the hood of the Plymouth and stepped back from clearing the last of the brush, the left side and rear of the old friend were again clearly visible.

"You know dad, I stopped the asshole who shot you this week, and I swear I won't quit until he gets put away." The moment was interrupted as he could hear Bonnie calling his name from the edge of the forest above. "Well, I'll be seeing you from time to time. I'll be back."

Minutes later, as he and Ralph emerged from the forest, Bonnie was there to meet them. "What in the world were you doing down there?"

He was scratching the back of his hands and arms, and before he could answer, she glanced down at the rash and cuts from contact with berry vines and poison oak. "Oh my God. Look at your hands. Don't touch anything. You've got poison oak all over you. You'd better have a good story, young man."

"Mom, I'm not nine any more. I'm twenty six."

"Well, you couldn't tell from looking at the mess you made of your hands. How did you do that? Bare handed?"

"Oh! The machete. I forgot dad's machete down at the car."

"What car?" Bonnie asked.

"The old Plymouth. You remember. Dad and I found it just a few months before he was killed. I've always feel close to him there for some reason."

"That old car? You went all the way down to that old car? Seems like we went through this years ago, Casey. Forget the berry vine cuts and the poison oak, now you're going to need a tetanus shot for some old rust infection." Turning toward the house, she said, "Come on up to the house, I'll clean it up and we'll see how bad you are."

"Mom. Twenty six. Remember?"

Bonnie shook her head and walked toward the house as Casey and Ralph followed.

The Cold Case is Re-opened

Buoyed by the reconnection he felt with his dad at the old Plymouth, and still enraged by Snider's attitude, Casey spent the next few days anguished over the recent traffic stop and what he considered a tacit threat by Snider. He decided to go into the Sheriff's Office, on his day off, the following Monday morning, the seventeenth anniversary of the murder, and meet with Sergeant Regan. He hoped to ask him to consider re-opening the cold case investigation.

When he broached the idea to Bonnie, she wasn't as enthusiastic as he was. "Not a good idea, Casey. It's taken seventeen years, and a ton of counseling to get beyond it. I finally did, and I feel the wounds are healed, and I hate to see you open the old wounds again. Besides, Sergeant Regan has done everything possible to solve the case. You think you can solve it if he hasn't in seventeen years. And what about your safety? You might be in danger if word gets out that you are re-opening the case."

Steve Davis

"Relax, mom, now you are sounding like Andrea. I'm not doing anything except asking Sergeant Regan to re-look at it again. He's the Detective. I'm just a traffic cop. I say it doesn't hurt to look at it again."

"You'll do what you want to anyhow, you're just like Sonny. But I don't like it and I agree with Andrea if she is against it."

On Monday morning, he went into the Sheriff's Office and asked at the public counter if Sergeant Regan was available.

"And whom should I say is asking?" the clerk asked.

"CHP Officer Casey Tyler."

"Oh," she said, in a manner that told Casey she recognized the name. "I'll check with him."

A few minutes later, Casey was escorted into the Detectives Office, where he was greeted by Sergeant Regan, who was seated at his desk with an open file folder and a half eaten Snickers bar. Once a rising star on the Sheriff's Office, Regan was now just a grizzled veteran Detective Sergeant. Two promotions through the years to Lieutenant had proven the theory that a great Detective doesn't necessarily equate to a good, or even mediocre, administrator. Policing paper clips just wasn't his thing, and each time, he had requested a demotion to his old job.

He had since resigned himself to be a career Detective Sergeant, at which he excelled, except in two nagging cases that happened within an hour of each other on one bad day in October, 1970. His hair was graying, although still cut close and his countenance was still intact, even if a few too many restaurant dinners and Snickers bars were showing on his gut. His face told of a career which included many sleepless nights, hard days, and nightmares of the carnage he had seen while dealing with the lowest of life forms. Cigarettes, Jack Daniels, grief, and more than a few soured relationships had taken their toll on the man who was once supposed to be the future of the Sheriff's Office.

"Casey Tyler. Man, look at you. It is great to see you, again. I heard you were back in Humboldt. I'm thrilled to see you again on familiar turf. What can I do for you, Casey?"

"This is a little awkward, Sergeant Regan, but last week I stopped Alden Snider for speeding and he came on real strong. What a prick. I felt like he threatened me by suggesting the same thing might happen to me that happened to my dad. I'd like to talk to you about the case against Snider, and ask you to consider re-opening the case."

"Well … I can't re-open the case, Casey… ," he said. As he spoke, he closed the file folder and turned to his right in the squeaking grey metal chair. He reached for the shelf behind him, continuing, "because I've never closed it." He pulled a binder from the shelf and said, "This is a summary file I keep close by. I look at it regularly, trying to find a loophole I missed. As for Snider, he still hasn't screwed up and given us even one clue. But tell me what happened."

Casey pulled a matching chair from the nearest desk, and sat down facing Sergeant Regan. He proceeded to relate the details of the traffic stop to Regan, who scribbled on a pad and listened intently.

When Casey finished, he paused, and sat back in the chair. He could see that Sergeant Regan had that same look of anger and frustration that he'd seen years earlier.

"He actually said that."

"Exactly."

Regan looked down as he thumbed through the binder aimlessly, pondering what to say. "I'd like to give it a complete, fresh look someday, but the timing is bad right now. All my Detectives and I are overwhelmed with some big ongoing cases and several recent gang-related shootings. But I know you. I know you aren't going to accept that. I'll tell you what. Since you are a cop now, if we can get approval from our Commanders, we can make an exception and have you look at the case and evidence files, yourself. Then if you see something we've missed, you let me know and we'll look at it.

Later that day, Casey walked into Captain Webster's office. A half-hour later he exited the Office with a signed piece of paper authorizing him to review the Sonny Tyler homicide case files with Sergeant Regan and the Sheriff's Office.

"You got it?" Sergeant Fulton asked incredulously as he met Casey outside the Captain's office.

"Yup."

"Amazing. I thought sure he'd give you the old CHP line about our traffic safety mission, and not being a real cop."

"Oh, I got that, and more. But, in the end, he said he'd want to do the same thing if he were in my shoes. He just asked me not to get him in trouble with Division, and to talk to him before I did anything big. He'd like to see this case solved, too, and he's willing to bend rules a little to get it some attention."

Casey went directly to Sergeant Regan's office and presented the authorization to him. "That was quick," Regan said, as he looked up from the Tyler case binder, which he now had spread in front of him. "I checked, and we're good to go on my end too. I've been thinking; this could be a great idea to let fresh eyes look at the case again. But are you sure you are up to it? There's a lot of pictures, autopsy files, bloody evidence, clothes, etc."

"I've given that some thought, and I'm going to try to look at it as if it was someone else. Can we get started?"

"Sure. I know I don't have to tell you this, but remember, this is the most important case either of us will ever have, so don't overlook the chain of evidence, and log in and out everything you touch. Functionally, you work for me when you are working on this case. Everything goes through me, you must check in with me regularly, and I have to know before you do anything big on the case, okay?"

"Okay," said Casey.

Casey followed Regan downstairs to the Evidence Clerk's Office in the basement. As they walked out of the stairwell, Sergeant Regan was paged to the front counter. He introduced Casey to the Evidence Clerk, Sally Perkins. "Sally, this is CHP Officer Casey Tyler. Casey's going to look at one of our old cold case files. Please give him any assistance he needs." He then excused himself to respond to the page, saying, "Talk to me tomorrow after you've looked at it, Casey."

"Sure, Sergeant."

Casey turned back to Sally. He had seen prettier women before, but he wasn't sure where. There was something about her that put her in a class of style he had only rarely encountered. Sally was just a couple years older than Casey, certainly not old enough to have been at the Sheriff's Office when the original case was filed away. She looked at the Officer in front of her, smiled sweetly, and asked, "What case are y'all looking for, Officer Tyler?"

"Not fair," he thought. *"Gorgeous girl, loaded with class, and throw in a southern accent to melt a mortal's heart."* It wasn't fair that one woman had all that in the same package. He guessed she was from Georgia for some reason, but he was suddenly too shy to ask.

"A homicide that occurred on October 15, 1970."

"Oh, that is an old one," she said as she scribbled the date on a piece of scratch paper and excused herself. As she walked away from him, the click of her high heels on the floor assured that her movements could not go unnoticed.

In about five minutes, she returned with a large heavy, cardboard box. "Here it is, October 15, 1970, Case Number F-70-218. I need y'all to sign here for it."

Casey signed for the file and, as he walked for the door, his heart pounding, he felt as if something big was going to change his life forever.

When he got back to his apartment he placed the file box on the table. He got a sharp knife out of the cabinet, and carefully cut the evidence tape and opened the lid. He signed the OUT box on the line, noting that it had not been checked out in almost a dozen years. It was only then when he noticed the case file card, affixed to the outside of the box, which said;

Case File Number F-70-218

Date: October 15, 1970

Victim: Anthony Garcia.

"Anthony Garcia! Oh, shit. I forgot there was another homicide that day. This isn't a good start. First thing I do, and I've already screwed up and logged into the wrong case file." He closed the file quickly, as if it never happened, and pushed the box away in disgust. Then he slouched back into a chair and leaned on the table with his head in his hands. *"Shit! Damn it! If I'm going to be taken seriously, I've got to be more professional."* He vowed to be more cognizant and careful in the future.

After dinner, he approached the file box and took the lid off. *"Since I've already signed it out and broken the seal, I may as well look through it, and maybe I'll learn something about Sheriff's homicide procedures that will help when I get the right files."* Before long, he was poring over the evidence like a kid looking at a **Playboy**, looking at every crime scene photo and reading witness transcripts from the 'gang banger' shooting that happened on the same date as his father's murder. He went to the shelf and got a blank ledger from his college days and began to take notes on the case.

"Obviously a drug deal with a double cross." He made a note in the ledger. He looked at the crime scene photos. *"The evidence guys sure did a good job of recording the crime scene. Close ups of the wounds, the face of Tony Garcia, and even his clothing and boots. I thought I was thorough, but these guys are pros."* He continued to make notes as he examined each photo thoroughly.

There was some dozen or more photos of the body, taken from all angles, and another two or three dozen of the surrounding scene. *"Good spot for a drug deal, remote but close into town, no residences nearby, and the sound of the gunshots would be muffled by the building and trees. Someone chose the location deliberately."*

Somewhere around midnight, he finished the file, signed all the proper chain-of-custody logs, and replaced the lid on the box and resealed it with evidence tape.

He looked down at his watch and realized that it was well past 1:00 a.m. "Crap!" he said aloud. *"I was supposed to call Andrea tonight after dinner. It's too late now. She's going to be pissed tomorrow."* Shrugging his shoulders, he shut off the lights and went to bed.

The next morning, Casey called Andrea and groveled sufficiently so that she forgave him for the previous night's oversight. He promised to meet her on her lunch break from St. Bernard's High School, where she had just begun working as an English teacher.

He drove to the Sheriff's office to contact Sergeant Regan. When he heard about the mistake, Sergeant Regan laughed and said, "It could happen to anyone. Besides, I'm not sure you ever knew there was a second murder that day." He checked over the box to assure that the chain-of-evidence was properly signed in and out, and said, "Good job. And, if you learned anything from the Garcia homicide file that would help us, let me know."

Casey went down to return the file, and was greeted by Sally Perkins, who got up to meet him. She was dressed even nicer today than yesterday, and her long blonde hair, in a bun yesterday, curled below her shoulders as she met him at the counter.

He explained the mix-up, and she immediately apologized for not getting more specifics the day before. "That is probably the only day ever in Humboldt County that there were two unconnected homicides in the same day. I just saw the date and simply didn't give it another thought." He smiled as her southern accent resonated through his head.

A few moments later, her high heels announced her impending return to the counter with another cardboard box and said, "Sonny Tyler? Was he any relation to you?"

"Yes, he was my father."

"Oh my god, I'm so sorry. Was he that CHP Officer who was killed in the seventies?"

"Yes."

"And his killer has never been caught?"

"No, he hasn't."

"I'm so sorry, Casey. If there is anything I can do to help you with this case, I'll be happy to do so." Reaching down to a card holder on the counter, she scooped up a card and handed it to Casey. "Here is my card. Call me if I can help. Okay?"

"Sure."

"Do y'all want all the boxes now, or one at a time."

"Huh?"

"This is marked Box #1 of 4. There are at least four boxes back there for this case."

"I'll try one or two at a time, please."

Sally went back into the evidence room and came back with a rolling cart with "Box #2 of 4" written on it. Once he returned home, he spent the rest of that day, and the next, late into the night, poring over the case, box by box, making copious notes in his journal as he went.

Casey on the Case

When he finished reviewing all the files, Casey asked Sergeant Regan for permission to contact retired Detectives who had worked on the case, and to re-interview any witnesses he could find, promising to clear all contacts and findings with Sergeant Regan. By the end of the week, Casey had worked out a detailed "special investigation" agreement with Captain Webster and the Sheriff's Office. He was given permission to work on the case off duty, and when time allowed around his normal duties on days and swing shifts, but he would have to work the unpopular graveyard and 1900 shifts when it came his turn.

Within a week, he had contacted all the retired ex-detectives who had worked on the case through the years. To a man, they were haunted by their failure to solve the case. They were pleased that the case would be looked at again. They gladly went over every detail they could recall, from Casey's notes, and offered their own individual hypotheses about the case.

As for the witnesses from 1970, the convenience store owner, Sam Hassam, and Clark Elder, the newspaper delivery man, had passed away several years ago. After the last interview, with no new information, he pushed back in the chair, and took a deep breath. He was already getting discouraged that there was no new revelations forthcoming.

Sergeant Regan didn't help his mood. Sensing Casey's frustration, he said, "Suck it up, Casey. You've been at it a whole week. We've been there seventeen years ahead of you. There is no magic bean that's going to help you. Did you really think you'd have it solved by now? Use your head and come up with something imaginative."

"Yeah," Casey grunted. A few minutes later, he got up and left the room without a word. He left the building through the back exit and headed for home. He was more than a little perturbed that Regan hadn't offered any encouragement, and, in fact, had scolded him like a parent. *'That was kind of cold and brutal,'* he thought as he drove home. He spent all that night sulking and grousing over Regan's lack of sensitivity.

The next day, however, Casey came into the room and walked up to Sergeant Regan, who was sitting at his desk. For the first time, Casey found himself looking down at Regan. He said, "Okay, Sarge. How's this? Willie Nixon and his fellow mechanics. Have you re-interviewed them in seventeen years?"

Sergeant Regan sat up and a smile passed quickly across his lips. It vanished as he rubbed his right hand across his mouth as he pondered the question. "No, I don't think so, Casey. That's what I was looking for from you. Great idea. Do you want me to go with you?"

"If I'm going to be successful here, I'd better learn how to do some things myself. If I forget something, you can follow up with me."

"That's what I wanted to hear. Welcome to the team. Let me know what you find out."

It took most of the afternoon to find out that Willie Nixon was still working as a mechanic, 'somewhere in Rio Dell' a small town about twenty miles south of Eureka. He'd changed employers often, like a man on the run, which he usually was, but always for small warrants. He just had a 'thing' about paying tickets on time, and so he had spent seventeen years looking over his shoulder and changing employers frequently. The one constant in his life was alcohol, however, and like most losers, he preferred to drink at the same bars, no matter where he worked. With Willie, that bar was The Log Jam, in Rio Dell.

That night, Casey pulled up in front of the Log Jam. He got out of the car, reached under the left front wheel well and rubbed off some caked road grease. He rubbed his hands with it, and smeared a little on his left cheek, swiping the excess off with a rag which he threw back on the floorboard. He was dressed in grubby work clothes and looked every bit like an after-work regular. He stopped inside and looked around. He recognized Willie sitting alone at the bar from his latest booking photo. He took a deep breath and walked up and took a seat next to Willie, ordered a Budweiser, and feigned surprise as he looked to his left at Willie.

"Willie!" he greeted him as an old friend. "That's you, isn't it Willie?" Before he could answer, Casey continued, "It's me, Jimmy, from the muffler shop, remember?"

Willie turned in his bar stool and took the measure of the stranger. As he looked at the grease smear on Casey's cheek, he said, "I never forget no face. I don't know you."

His feet slowly moved from the bar step and started inching toward the floor. As the right foot touched the ground, the left was soon to follow, as he was poised to assume his normal solution to his problems --- hit the ground running

"Well, I don't blame you for not recognizing me. I had long hair and a beard then. It's been what --- eight? Ten years? Let me buy you a drink."

Willie paused when he heard the magic words – 'buy you a drink' - and looked at Casey again, this time from head to toe. He relaxed his defenses at the thought of a free beer. Casey breathed a sigh of relief as Willie put his feet back on the bar step. "Oh, yeah, Jimmy. I remember you. How ya doin' man? I'm drinking Coors on tap."

Two hours and five beers later, Casey had used up every fact and trivia he'd ever learned about car engines, but Willie was plastered and was really warming up to his newly found long lost friend. Casey, who had nursed two beers to Willie's five, was ready to get some information.

"Hey, Willie, you ever hear from your old buddy Alden Snider? You used to talk about him all the time. You ever see him now that he's a big shot?"

"Snider? What you talking about Snider for? You wasn't around when we worked together?"

"No shit, man. I'm way too young. Hell, I was probably only about nine when he killed that cop. I just heard his ad on the radio today and now I run into you tonight, and it just reminded me. You used to talk about him all the time, how he was a big shot and you knew him when he was just a punk kid."

"Yes, he was a punk kid, alright, but he didn't take no shit back then. I saw him get his ass kicked regularly because of his mouth."

"You told me once you were working with him the day he killed that cop, weren't you?"

"No, huh uh, I never said that. I never said he killed no cop. No way."

"Tell me again, what'd you say?"

"I might have said I was working with him the day they came to accuse him of it. I almost went to jail myself, but he never killed that cop."

"Really," Casey leaned over as if he was getting close to hearing a secret about to be revealed. He looked over his shoulders and whispered, "How do you know?

You sound like you know who did." He could feel his neck artery pulsing and his heart pounding in his chest as he waited what seemed to be an eternity for the answer. Did Willie himself commit the crime for Snider? He swallowed and waited for Willie's answer.

"Hell, no. I don't know nothing about it. But if he'd killed that cop, he'd have said so. He was pissed that they thought he did it. Then, they searched his house, his car, everything, and he got real scared they were going to pin it on him. Naw, he's a prick; in fact, the big-shot sucker still owes me twenty bucks, but he ain't no killer. I seen him in bar fights and he talks tough, but he's a chicken." He laughed, "Snider a killer, no fuckin' way."

"What about the other mechanic that worked with you? I forgot his name. Where's he now?"

"He's frickin' dead. Killed in a car crash back in '73 or so."

"Hey, man," he continued, "why you keep asking questions about that shit anyhow?"

"I don't mean anything. Hey, you worked on any of those new IROC Camaros? I hear they are balls to the walls hot."

"Oh, yeah. Especially if you put a rocker cam in them, they will fly.

A short time later, Casey looked at his watch and said, "Holy shit, Willie, it's getting late. I gotta go."

"Okay. Hey, Johnny, don't be such a stranger. Come around anytime, I'm usually here."

"Yeah, I just might do that. See you, Willie." He turned and walked out the door and into the night.

'Well, Jimmy, or Johnny, or whoever, not too bad for a rookie detective.' Casey thought to himself as he turned his Camaro toward Eureka and headed home.

The Return of Jeffrey Olson

"So, the Twins have added another run here in the eighth inning on an RBI double by Dan Gladden, and now lead the Cardinals 4-2 after eight and a half. That will be an important insurance run for Jeff Reardon as the 1987 World Series comes down to the Cardinals' last at bat in the ninth."

Sergeant Regan reached over and turned the volume up. "Come on Redbirds, don't let the AL win this thing!" he said.

"Sergeant Regan. Line 1." The intercom blared. Sergeant Regan reached over and turned the volume back down, while he picked up the phone with his free hand. "Detectives. Regan."

"Hello, Sergeant Regan," the voice said. "This is …."

"Good day, Jeffrey." Regan responded to the easily recognizable voice of Jeff Olson, whose words always spoke with much greater authority than its high pitch seemed to empower.

"Jeff, Sergeant Regan. I prefer to go by Jeff. How do you always know it's me?"

"Just a lucky guess, Jeff. You aren't a baseball fan are you, Jeff?"

"No, I never cared much for sports. How'd you know, Sergeant?"

"Just another lucky guess. What's on your mind, Jeff?"

Sergeant Regan had been dealing off and on with Jeff Olson, the former cub reporter known as Jeffrey, on significant cases that had occurred over the seventeen years since they first crossed paths at the Sonny Tyler murder scene in 1970. Now the seasoned chief reporter for the Eureka Times-Standard, he and Regan had long ago settled into a relationship in which Regan used Jeff to get the word out when he needed it, and Jeff used Regan occasionally, for inside access on cases of interest to the community.

"Sergeant Regan, I have heard a rumor that the old Sonny Tyler murder case is being reopened by his son. I'd like to do a story on it. Is that possible?"

"It might be a little premature, Jeff. We're still working out the details of his involvement. And, besides, it has never been closed, so we can't reopen it."

"I understand what you are saying, Sarge, and I assure you we'll make it clear that you have continued to exhaust all leads through the years. I'll make sure it paints the Sheriff's Office in a good light and just looks for new leads. How about it?" In the last seventeen years, Olson had never forgotten his first contact with Regan, when he puked at Sonny Tyler's murder scene. He never demanded anything from him; he always asked. "Do you think that is possible?

"I think it is too soon, Jeff. How about you get back to me in a week or two? Maybe we'll have something by then to share."

Jeff recognized he was being brushed off. He decided to use a different tactic. "Listen, Sarge. This is too big to not cover it right away. Sergeant Regan, I remember the day of the murder you told me to never forget that a good man was murdered that day, and I haven't. I want to see this case solved. I think we can help each other, and I'd like to remind the community of the great debt Sonny paid to protect us. What do you think?"

Regan paused to reflect on the points made by Olson. "Okay, Jeff. I can see you are going to do a story anyhow, so we might as well have some input to make sure it is right. Come down tomorrow about ten."

"Thanks, Sergeant Regan. I'll be there."

Sergeant Regan and Casey met with Olson the next day, hoping any publicity about the old case might generate new leads. Three days later, the October 29, 1987, issue of the Times Standard hit the streets with the story as its lead article:

CHP OFFICER INVESTIGATES
FATHER'S MURDER

In a rare cooperative investigation agreement, the Humboldt County Sheriff's Office announced today that California Highway Patrol Officer Casey Tyler, son of the late CHP Officer Sonny Tyler, who was murdered while on patrol near Eureka in 1970, has been invited to participate in the ongoing investigation of the seventeen-year-old unsolved murder case.

According to Humboldt Sheriff's Sergeant Don Regan, who has been the lead investigator on the case which has stumped detectives for all those years, Officer Tyler recently approached him about reviewing the case in its entirety, and re-contacting old witnesses who are still around, in hopes that a fresh review might produce leads which might shed new light on the case. Officer Tyler has been granted permission by Humboldt CHP Commander Jerry Webster to assist the Sheriff's Office in the case.

"We all want to see this case solved," Webster said, "and Sergeant Regan's Detective Team has exhausted every conceivable lead in attempting to catch the person responsible. If Casey can shed new light on the case it might cause some unknown or previously reluctant witness to step forward with new information which might help the Sheriff solve this horrific murder case."

The news article generated immense renewed interest in the case, and Casey and Sergeant Regan found themselves discussing the case on local radio and television news and special interest shows over the next few days. Unfortunately, the expected new leads never materialized, and of the few 'tips' received, none proved to bring any new information into the investigation. It appeared that if any new leads were forthcoming, they would have to be self-generated.

Section Ten

Andrea is Threatened

December rolled around, and Casey continued to attempt to locate and re-contact old witnesses. Then, about a week later, Casey received a letter in the mail at the CHP office, marked:

> **Special Attention:**
> **Officer Casey Tyler,**
> **Personal and Confidential.**

Anticipating a possible break in the case, he tore open the envelope and opened the half-page, cryptic, typed note inside, which said:

> "Seen you in town today. Pretty Girl. What did you call her? Andrea? Back off and go back to chasing taillights before something bad happens to the pretty girl. THIS IS SERIOUS!"

Casey stood and stared at the note. He had never considered that his involvement in the investigation would place his loved ones in jeopardy. Maybe he was getting in over his head, and should go back to "chasing taillights," and leave the serious crimes, like murders, for the Sheriff's Department. He wondered how Sergeant Regan handled this type of pressure. But then, Regan was divorced for many years, having discovered he was not prepared to make the kind of commitment needed for a successful marriage. Perhaps he wasn't the best person to ask. In any event, he knew that this isn't how law enforcement works. If this type of threat worked, there would be no cops. He concluded he would simply have to be more diligent with his family life.

As he looked at the note, he got excited as he realized that the note provided several clues; for one thing, obviously the murderer was still in the area, dismissing Sergeant Regan's theory that the murderer might have just been passing through. The cryptic note provided a number of other relevant clues that perhaps would assist investigators.

Whoever it was, they really didn't want him investigating the case. Apparently, for seventeen years, it hadn't bothered the murderer that the Sheriff's Office was investigating the crime, but now, the killer didn't like Casey reigniting interest in the case.

He had heard CHP Officers called "taillight chasers" before, but mostly only as a joke between branches of law enforcement. So, there it was again, that nagging 'possible cop' connection. Again, he silently vowed to look at that angle, and Randy Allen in particular, seriously again. But Randy was not going to be an easy target. Since he refused to waive his rights when he was first questioned back in 1970, they can't interview him without an attorney. They're going to have to have some evidentiary link to execute a search warrant, even if they knew what they were looking for. No, to get Randy, they were going to have to have some real, tangible evidence to tie him to the murder.

In any event, the killer must believe Casey might actually solve the case, and that meant he might be on the right track on something.

He carefully secured the letter and envelope in a manila evidence envelope and turned it over to the Sheriff's Office Evidence Tech for prints. He decided not to tell anyone other than Sergeant Regan about the letter, until it could be analyzed in full. In the meantime, he continued with the investigation, albeit more discreetly than before.

That plan seemed to work, until six days later, when Bonnie and Andrea went Christmas shopping and had lunch at the Eureka Mall. Afterward, when they returned to the car, while Andrea was putting some shopping bags in the rear seat, Bonnie said, "Oh, there is a note on the windshield."

She walked up and retrieved it, unfolding the paper note. "Oh my God!" she screamed and dropped the folded note. Andrea dropped the Macy's bag on the seat and ran up to the front of the car. "What's wrong, Bonnie. Are you alright? What happened?"

Bonnie was looking around, frightened, to see if they were being watched. She bent down and picked up the note, and handed it to Andrea.

"Oh, my God." Andrea echoed Bonnie's words.

> Your time has run out.
> Your cop won't leave it alone,
> so now someone else has to die.
> Which one of you will be first?

The women rushed back into the mall and went directly to a pay phone and called Casey at home. Bonnie told him about the note, and he responded quickly to the mall. When he got there, he found Andrea still sobbing and Bonnie very upset. He looked at the note Bonnie handed to him, and after a moment, he said, "There's something else I have to tell you."

As he related to them about the mystery letter, he could see that each of the women was getting more and more angry, until Bonnie finally exploded, "I can't believe you, Casey! Someone threatens Andrea with death and you didn't think it was important enough to tell her. And now they are threatening both of us, and just now you decide it might be worth mentioning. That's it. You don't have the skill, training, or judgment to be investigating murders, and dealing with murderers. I'm going to talk to Don. You've got to stop this before Andrea or I get killed."

"I understand you are mad. But how would any cop ever get through an investigation if he ran and hid every time he gets threatened?"

"HE gets threatened!" Bonnie shouted. "What do you mean HE? I don't see your name on this note. I don't know what you are doing, Casey, but I do know this. You became the cop! Not me! Not Andrea! You volunteered for this case! Not me. And certainly not Andrea. You didn't ask us if we wanted to take the risk of getting killed, you just volunteered us for it so you could …." She stumbled for the right words, then abandoned the sentence. "Nothing is ever going to change, Casey, it's time you think about someone else for a change."

Casey looked at Andrea. She had stood there, attentively, but silently, while Casey was getting reamed by his mother. If he thought Andrea was going to offer him some support, he was greatly mistaken. "Andrea?" he pleaded.

"Sorry, Casey. I have to agree with her on this. You had a business degree, but you pulled the plug on that to be a cop. I love you, and I've tried to support you, but I never was consulted, and now someone is going to kill me. Maybe times were different when Sonny was a cop. Now, it's more personal."

"He was murdered in cold blood," Casey reacted defensively. "You can't get much more personal than that!"

"You know what I mean."

Bonnie interrupted, "Let's go Andrea. The killer may be stalking us right now and we'd better keep moving. Thanks for the security, Casey."

Andrea turned and headed for the passenger door. In doing so, over her left shoulder, she said, "Don't forget, Casey, we're supposed to have dinner tonight with my parents. You'd better work on a better story between now and then, because the old one isn't going to please my dad and mom."

The women got into the car and drove off quickly, throwing a cloud of dust toward Casey, as if to emphasize the point. Casey stood in the parking lot and waved away the dust. "Fuck me," he said, to no-one in earshot.

Casey drove immediately to the Sheriff's Office, where he cornered Sergeant Regan in his office and closed the door.

"Looks serious, Casey," Regan said. "What's up?"

Casey told Sergeant Regan about the second note and the berating he took from Bonnie and Andrea. "And, to make matters worse, tonight I have to have dinner with Dr. and Mrs. Donahue, and I'm going to hear it all over again in spades. What did you do when a dirtbag threatened your family?"

"Well, Casey, first of all, that might be why I don't have a family. I don't know 'quit'. I'm a cop. That's all I know how to be. Whenever I got threatened, it just aroused my competitive instincts. If I could, I'd kick their ass. I'd work harder to put them away for a long time. When I did have a family, I made it clear that I'd give it all up, and kill them if they touched my family. I guess I got lucky because no-one called my bluff."

"But, then again," he continued, "I never got threatened by an unknown person. The way I see it, you've got two choices; back off, give up, and keep giving up every time someone threatens you or your loved ones, or work harder to get them before they can follow through with their threat. If you want to drop your involvement with the investigation, it is okay with me. I understand. You've given me some new leads to follow. But if you want to fight back, I'm with you all the way. You've hit a nerve with the murderer, and he's given up some info about himself. But you've got to know, the risks are real, and someone you love could get hurt or killed."

Dinner at the Donahue's

That night, Casey arrived at the front door of the Donahue's, and was met outside by Andrea, who was sitting on the bottom step of the front porch, waiting for him. "Casey, my dad is furious. You don't have to go in there. I can tell them you want to discuss it another day."

"Another day isn't going to change anything."

"I'm scared," Andrea said. "I love you, Casey, but I don't know what to do."

"I wish I had the answers," he said softly.

Andrea was clearly looking for encouragement from Casey, and his answer visibly disappointed her. "If you don't know, why are we in this position?"

Before Casey could answer, the conversation was interrupted by the opening of the front door. Dr. Donahue stepped into the opening and said, "Suppose we bring this inside, where we can all talk about it."

"Yes, Sir," said Casey. He raised his eyebrows and took a breath, then motioned for Andrea to enter and followed her inside.

Casey knew it wasn't going to go well, especially when Dr. Donahue lead them past the front room, from which all previous welcomes had originated, and walked straight to the dining room table where the chairs were already pulled out from the table in a pre-arranged manner.

"Sit down, please, Casey," Dr. Donahue said, motioning to the open chair at the head of the table.

Casey sat down as directed. Dr. Donahue sat down to his left, facing Casey with his left elbow on the table top. Eleanor Donahue walked around the table and sat quietly to Casey's right, across from the doctor. Andrea took the only available seat, at the opposite end of the table. The seating arrangements were deliberate and prophetic, Casey believed. Andrea was at the far end of the table, with both Dr. and Mrs. Donahue between them in a clearly dominant and aggressive position. From the look on everyone's faces, Casey knew his life was about to change, and Andrea was slipping away.

"Casey, Andrea told me about the note … no, make that the two notes … threatening her life. Tell me, young man, is this what you have in mind for my daughter, your fiancée, a life of fear and threats of death?"

"No, sir, I intend to protect her from harm …"

Dr. Donahue interrupted him. "And tell me, Casey … Officer Casey … how do you intend to do that? Are you going to go and kill the man responsible for these threats? Oh, that's right, you can't. You don't know who it is. But yet, he knows everything about you. And my daughter. And your mother. It seems the person threatening to kill my daughter is the only one who knows who he is and what he is going to do. But wait, I interrupted you. Tell me, Casey, what is your plan to solve this problem?"

"I plan to keep putting pressure on him until he screws up and we can catch him."

"Oh, good. For a minute there, I thought you didn't have a plan. I'm relieved to hear you have a plan and everything is under control. But then, what does your plan say we are supposed to do when he slips through your dragnet and kills my daughter in the meantime? You know, don't you, Casey, that she is the only daughter we have, right?"

"Yes, sir, but I don't intend …"

"Excuse me for interrupting you again, Casey, but did you intend he would stalk Andrea while she was Christmas shopping? That one apparently slipped through the plan. And is this the same plan as the one that included your decision to not tell any of us about the first threatening note?"

As Casey squirmed, he continued, "Casey, there is nothing you can say that is going to make me feel comfortable about you using my daughter as bait in your attempt to trap an unknown killer."

"Wait a minute, sir. That isn't fair. I love Andrea and I will do anything to protect her. I resent your implication that I would use her as 'bait' for any purpose."

"Can you GUARANTEE her safety, Casey?"

"No-one can guarantee anything, sir, but, …"

"You are wrong, Casey. I can guarantee you this. Neither Mrs. Donahue, nor I, are going to stand by while you jeopardize the life of my daughter, while chasing shadows. Either you give up this nonsense and get back to reality, or I will forbid my daughter from seeing you again. Is that clear? I want to hear from you within two days that you have dropped out of this case entirely, or else! Are we clear on that, Casey?"

Casey looked at the end of the table for support from Andrea, who was crying softly and wringing her hands, while looking off to her left.

"Yes, Sir. I'm real clear on what you have said."

Before another word could be said, Mrs. Donahue smiled and stood up from the table, "Good, I'm glad that is settled. Now, let's have dinner. I made some wonderful fresh salmon for dinner." She scurried off to the kitchen.

Dr. Donahue just looked at Casey as if he was hoping Casey would say something that would allow him to continue. Casey, in turn, just stared at Andrea, who sat frozen in silence and deep in thought. After an agonizingly long time, Dr. Donahue got up and walked toward the living room. As Casey and Andrea finally made eye contact, she said, "I'd better set the table." And got up and also went to the kitchen, leaving Casey alone at the table.

Casey drew a large breath and blew out through pursed lips. He got up and walked into the living room. "Excuse me, sir. Under the circumstances, I'd like to be excused from staying for dinner. I need to think this through."

"Actually, Casey, I'm greatly disappointed that you even feel the need to think about it. Yes, I think it might be better if you left and gave it a great deal of thought."

As Casey turned around, Andrea and Mrs. Donahue were standing in the doorway listening. Andrea nodded. Casey said goodbye and walked out the front door, followed by Dr. Donahue. "Remember, Casey," Dr. Donahue said as he stepped onto the porch and closed the door behind them, "I'll be in touch with you in two days to get your answer on that question."

Casey walked away quietly without responding. He knew he was not going to give up the case, and he knew Andrea would follow her father's direction.

Steve Davis

The Intruder

Casey and Andrea had previously arranged to go out together with friends the next night, and he wondered if she would cancel it. To his surprise, when he called her the following afternoon, she seemed somewhat upbeat, as if she was certain the resolution to the problem was near. It was inconceivable to Andrea that Casey would choose his job over her, and she anticipated that tonight he would give her the answer that she and her parents expected to be forthcoming, that he was going to give up the detective case and return to CHP patrol duties, or better yet, get out of police work altogether.

Shortly after 5:35 p.m. she stepped into the shower to get ready for the evening. As she was rinsing her hair, she paused suddenly. There was a sound; not a real sound, but a subtle, quiet sound, like cloth being moved. She turned off the water and stood perfectly still, half frozen in fear, just waiting to hear the sound again.

Seconds went by, and all was quiet. She reached up and gingerly pulled the curtain back just a few inches and peeked out. Nothing. *"Thank God,"* she thought. She replaced the curtain, laughed at her insecurity, turned the water back on, and finished her shower.

When she turned off the water, she opened the curtain a few inches and reached for the hair towel she had left on the hook just outside the shower stall. She stared in disbelief at the empty hook. The towel was gone! She shivered at the thought that she might be in danger. She quickly glanced at the floor to see if it had fallen, when her heart stopped and she let out a low squeal. There on the damp floor was a dirty, smudged, footprint.

Frozen in fear, she listened for any sound coming from inside the house. Hearing none, she grabbed her robe from the counter and listened again. Silence. She bolted toward the front door, grabbed the cordless phone from its pedestal as she passed, and dialed 911. She ran outside through the front door, which was already open. Wearing only the robe, she hid alongside a redwood tree between her house and her neighbor, poised to sprint again, and waited. When the 911 emergency operator came on the line, she pleaded for help and told them of the intruder.

It was exactly 5:45 p.m. when Casey left home on his way to Andrea's. On the way, he was passed by a Sheriff's unit with red lights and siren activated, heading in the same direction. He grimaced and his heart began to pound into his now-dry throat.

Upon arrival at Andrea's apartment, Casey found Andrea with a blanket around her next to the Sheriff's unit, and two additional Deputies in the house checking for suspects. "He was here, Casey. I think he was here to kill me. I'm so scared. Where were you? You are supposed to protect me!"

"I was on my way over here ...," Casey began, but she cut him off.

"I think daddy is right. You can't stop him and he's not going to stop until I'm dead, your mom is dead, and maybe you, too."

"But ...," Casey began again, but she just waved him off and said to the Deputy, "When can I go back inside the house to get dressed? I need to go to my parents' house tonight."

Casey tried to comfort her, but it was clear that she no longer considered him capable of protecting her. When the Deputies cleared the house, Casey escorted Andrea into the house so she could put clothing on. Other than the missing towel and the single dirty boot print in the bathroom, there was nothing out of order.

As he waited in the hallway outside the bedroom, Casey could hear Andrea on the bedroom phone talking to Dr. Donahue. "OK, I won't. Please hurry, Daddy," she said as she hung up.

She exited the bedroom and passed Casey without a word, and went to the Deputy, who was writing on a tablet, and answered a few more questions. Casey attempted to stand nearby and hear her description of the events, but Andrea looked at him with a go-to-hell look that sent chills down his neck. He backed off down the hall about ten feet.

When Dr. Donahue arrived, he walked right past the Deputy and Andrea, and approached Casey aggressively, so much so that Casey stepped backward a step, avoiding contact from the Doctor's outstretched left index finger.

"What in the world are you thinking?" he said as he poked at Casey's chest. "Have you lost your mind? How many people you love will have to die? And for what? An old murder case that no-one cared about for fifteen years, and now you're willing to kill your fiancée and your mother for some obsession you have with it."

"It's not just some old case," Casey said defensively. He could see the writing on the wall; he was going to lose his fiancée, but he couldn't stand to hear his father's murder trivialized by Dr. Donahue. "He was my dad, and it *IS* important. And I've got to be getting close."

"Bullshit, Casey. I won't have it. My wife and I have invested our whole lives so that our daughter can have an extensive education and a career she loves, and we aren't going to stand by while you play cops and robbers and get her killed? If you choose to chase shadows and risk your life, that's fine, but you aren't going to risk my daughter's life for this foolishness."

"Can I speak now? I wanted to explain …"

"No. Damn it, you stubborn asshole. It is too late for explanations. I don't care to hear any explanations for your behavior. We gave you a chance, but you've obviously decided that you aren't going to give up this 'policeman' nonsense and get a real job, so you can provide for my daughter and guarantee her welfare, not jeopardize it! Get out of here, Casey. I forbid you to see my daughter anymore. And we will put an article in the paper that the engagement is off."

"What does Andrea want?"

"She didn't know what to do until tonight. Now, she trusts me. After running naked for her life, now she agrees that you are acting irresponsibly and risking her life for no reason. We tried to reason with you, and now this! I have taken it out of her hands and that's why I'm here to tell you that you have to leave and don't contact her again."

"I need to talk to Andrea."

"No. She's leaving with me and moving back in with us. She's scared to death and wants to leave town for a while. She trusts us to make her choices for her on this."

Casey looked over at Andrea, who was listening to the conversation, and questioned her with his eyes for a sign of hope. She didn't say a word, but motioned with her head that he should leave.

As he walked toward her to leave, he started to speak, and she just put up her hand and turned away. The Deputy overheard the whole conversation and just looked down. Casey turned to him and said, "Sergeant Regan will want the boot print saved as evidence, it may be involved in a homicide." The Deputy just said, "10-4, Casey."

"See what I mean, Andrea," Dr. Donahue said mockingly from behind him, "His fiancée is attacked and all he thinks about is some stupid evidence for his big case."

Casey walked out of the house, as Dr. Donahue continued to berate him as he walked away.

Casey tried for the next two days to contact Andrea, only to have her calls intercepted by her parents, who rudely hung up on him. When he finally caught her leaving work on the third day, she said it was too late; she was scared and afraid to die. "This is too real, too dangerous. I didn't think it would be like this to marry a cop. We need to let it go." She walked away, got in her car, and drove away without even a glance back at him.

Just as Dr. Donahue promised, the next day's issue of the Times-Standard carried a quarter page advertisement announcing that Andrea Donahue had called off her engagement to Casey Tyler, effective yesterday.

Section Eleven

The Hit Man
January, 1988

"What do you mean, dinner ain't ready?"

Eduardo Corona looked around the room as if he expected to see an excuse written on a wall somewhere. The small kitchen was filthy and cluttered. He kicked the chair away from the table so he could sit down disgustedly. "What the hell do you do all day, Maria, that you can't have dinner ready when I get here?"

Maria got up from the couch in the small living room next to the kitchen and walked toward him. "What do you think I been doing," she asked defiantly. As if on cue, one of the three small children let out a loud shriek. "I got home late from lunch with the mayor's wife," she said in her most sarcastic tone. Then she ducked backward to avoid a wild slap he half-heartedly attempted. After six years together she pretty much knew just how far she could

Steve Davis

push her sarcasm and how to stay just ahead of his temper and out of his reach, although she still bore the remnants of the fat lip she got several days ago when she pushed his "hot button" too far and paid the price again.

She pushed past him and retrieved a can of refried beans from the near-empty cupboard and a package of tortillas from the refrigerator. "I couldn't make up my mind whether to have a big juicy steak or baked lasagna." she continued, "So … I think I'll just make burritos tonight."

"Shut up, Bitch, or I'll…" His words were interrupted by the phone ringing in the living room. As he walked out of the kitchen toward it, he said, "Bitch, canned refried beans on a tortilla isn't a burrito, it's dog food. All you've ever been is a good fuck, and lately you're not even good at that."

Before she could answer, he turned his attention to the phone. "Yeah?" he greeted the caller.

"Eduardo … Eduardo Corona?" the voice on the phone asked.

"Yeah, this is him. Who's this?"

"Just shut up and listen." the voice demanded. "You want to make a quick grand?"

"A grand? Sure." Eduardo played along, even though he wasn't sure what was going on. "What do I gotta do, kill somebody?"

"Of course," the voice responded, "You think I'm just giving money away? You interested or not?"

Eduardo paused as he wondered if the caller was serious. "Who is this?"

"I told you. Shut up and listen. That's part of the deal. You interested in a grand … cash … or not?

"Maybe yeah, maybe no. I gotta hear more."

"It's simple. I got a little job for you to do for me. You do the job, you get a grand. Are you interested, or do I go to someone else?"

"Who the fuck is this?" By now Eduardo was starting to worry the call wasn't a hoax. But still, who couldn't use a thousand bucks. "I gotta know who I'm whacking someone for."

"Maybe I got the wrong Eduardo Corona. Maybe the real Eduardo might need an easy thousand more than you do. Maybe you should ask your wife if you need a grand or not."

Steve Davis

"Hey! You leave my old lady out of this. I'm the boss around here. How do I know you ain't trying to set me up? How do I know this isn't a cop?"

"You don't. But do you think a cop is going to call you out of the blue and hire you to off someone?"

"How do you know me and how'd you get my name."

"I said shut up with the questions! You interested or not? Maybe I picked the wrong gang banger. Maybe you got plenty of money and don't need a grand. So, like, why don't you tell me now asshole, are you interested or not?"

Eduardo paused just long enough to realize if he passed up a quick thousand bucks, some of his old homies would jump at the chance to get that kind of cash. "Maybe. Tell me more and I'll let you know."

"That's more like it. Go to the McDonalds and go to the back booth along the windows. There will be a burger and fries on the table. Sit down and eat it and wait for me."

"Hey asshole, I don't take orders from no-one. Don't mess with me, you hear me?" He barked. Then, realizing he was talking to a dial tone, he threw the phone down on the couch in disgust and yelled at the absent caller, "Fucking asshole! Eat your own fucking burger. Who the fuck you think you're talking to. No-one fucking talks to me like that and tells me what to do."

"Who was that, Miho?" Maria asked. What did he want?"

"No-one," he said, "and he didn't want nothin'."

"I know it wasn't no-one." She mocked him by bouncing her head back and forth. "Who was it?" she repeated.

"Shut up, bitch. It ain't none of your business"

"What do you mean, it ain't none of my business? You got three kids and a wife to take care of. Of course it's my business." She took the rolled tortilla and beans from the microwave and slid it across the table, and said, "Here's your dinner, mister macho 'none of your business' man."

"Stick it up your ass," he gestured as he turned away, grabbing his jacket off the back of the chair. "I'm going out for some real food. Don't wait up."

Maria was still yelling as he slammed the door. Her voice trailed off in the distance as he walked down the stairs of the apartment complex and made his way to the carport and his motorcycle. He straddled his beloved

Steve Davis

Harley. The only thing he truly loved in the world was his ride. Others wouldn't give it a second look, but it was his, it didn't talk back, and it never reminded him that he was a loser.

He told himself the caller had nothing to do with the fact that he decided to go to McDonalds to get something to eat. He eased his Harley into the parking lot, and looked around to see if anyone was watching for him. The Harley was quite loud, so he was used to seeing people look disgustedly when he pulled into the stall nearest the door. But, as he looked around, no-one was looking at him. From the motorcycle seat, he could see that the booth at the end by the window was unoccupied.

As he entered the restaurant, he swore to himself he wouldn't even look at it, but he couldn't resist looking back at the end booth in the corner next to the windows when he walked in the door. There on the table was a McDonalds bag, alongside of which was a Big Mac, laying open on the paper and a bag of fries neatly placed alongside with a small drink. No-one was around the booth and it appeared to be waiting for him, as promised. He looked around the restaurant, and no-one seemed to take any interest in him. He went back outside and walked around the corner. He looked around at all the cars, but no-one seemed out of the ordinary.

He convinced himself the meal must be someone else's, and went back inside, casting a side glance at the unoccupied booth. Seeing no-one around, he slid into a nearby open booth and just sat there, trying to look 'cool' while he watched the booth in the corner.

After a few minutes, no-one approached the corner booth, so he eased out of his seat and walked over by the booth as if he was going to the bathroom. As he passed, he glanced down at the cash register tag, which was lying face up near the edge of the table. On it was written the name Eduardo. He stopped short and gave up the attempt to disguise his actions. He quickly looked around yet again, to see if anyone was watching him with interest, but, again, no-one seemed to care about his actions.

Now he was mad; mad at himself for being so predictable, mad at the unknown person on the phone who knew his name, his wife, and knew he would show up at McDonalds, and now mad that, by his actions, the caller knew that he would consider killing someone for a thousand bucks.

Steve Davis

He slid into the booth where he could see the door. He sat there for a few moments waiting to be contacted. He hated the thought of being manipulated like this, but here he was, like a wild animal drawn into a trap. And like the animal caught in the trap, when no-one approached him, he reached across and grabbed the now only lukewarm burger and fries and quickly ate them.

When he finished the meal, he looked into the open McDonalds bag and was surprised to find a huge wad of money wrapped in a note. He looked around again, and slipped the money out of the note and slid it into his jacket pocket. Then he read the typed note:

> **Here is one half payment on the job. If you want the job, keep it and go to the pay phone at Harris and "K" Street and wait for a call. If you don't want the job, leave the money in the bag and go. Don't even think about taking the money and not doing the job. My boys will hunt you down and kill your daughters first, then Maria, then you. Trust me. You don't want to screw with us. Make up your mind now.**

Eduardo didn't like it. Not the killing part; the thought of killing someone didn't scare him or even bother him much; he'd been working up to that for twenty or more years. As a member of the Norte Gangstas as a teenager, he was involved in plenty of violent crimes, although no-one had actually died *yet* at his hands. He'd even done time for knifing a rival gang member as a teenager, and later for parole violations.

No, what bothered Eduardo was that he hated the thought of someone leading him around like a puppet; especially when he didn't know who they were or why they chose him. It smelled like a trap of some kind. Maybe it was a trap by the cops, they were always harassing him; or maybe it was a rival gang member trying to get even for some past wrong he'd done.

He stuck his hand in his pocket and pulled out the wad of cash. He counted it under the table; five hundred dollars in assorted used bills, nothing over a twenty. *"Whew,"* he thought.

He toyed with the idea of just taking off with the money, but he didn't know who it was that was paying for a hit, and that worried him. The voice knew a lot about him personally, his family, and where to find him. Anybody who could pay a grand for a hit could pay to have his family killed if he double-crossed him. *"I better not screw with him; I'd better just take it - or leave it."* His hand tightened around the wad of money in his hand. The thought of leaving five hundred dollars behind on the table was too much to pass up, so he stuffed it back into his pocket and headed for Harris Street.

There was no-one around when he approached the vacant pay phone at Harris and "K" Streets. As he approached the phone, it rang. It unnerved him to know that he was being monitored so closely, and he looked around for a clue about the caller. Seeing none, he grabbed it on the fourth ring and said, "Yeah, I'm here. Look asshole, just tell me who you want killed and I'll decide if I want the job."

"Good news," the caller said, "I changed my mind. You don't have to kill anyone, just make them think you tried to kill them. You'll shoot at him and miss on purpose. In fact, if you kill him, you don't get paid the rest of the money. Understand?"

Eduardo let out a silent sigh of relief to know he didn't have to kill someone. Maybe the caller wasn't a real gangster-type, and maybe it was just a routine hit after all, and a grand for scaring someone was going to be easy money. His posture became instantly more macho. "Yeah. Just make sure my old boys don't hear that I shot at and missed the guy. I wouldn't want it to get around that I missed. Quit hustling me, man, and tell me who the dude is?"

"In due time, my friend. What kind of gun do you have?"

"I got a piece that'll do the job, don't worry about it."

"That didn't answer the question. It's got to be a .38 or a .357 Magnum."

"I got a .38. Why?"

"I'll supply the ammunition. Go look on the ground near the trash container next to the phone booth; in the McDonalds bag."

Eduardo retrieved the bag and came back on the phone. As he opened it, he said, "What's with you and fuckin' McDonalds?"

"I will call myself Mr. Jones. I'll be in touch with you soon."

"When?" he asked, then he realized he was, once again, talking to a dial tone. Once again, the caller had "dissed" him, and it was starting to piss him off. "Mother fucker, maybe I'll kill *you* for free when I find out who you are!" he said to no-one as he slammed down the receiver in anger.

He looked inside the bag and found a napkin wrapped around six rounds of Remington .38 caliber 'Plus P' half-jacket hollow point ammunition. "*Wow, this is good stuff,*" he thought to himself, as he thrust them into his pocket.

Several days passed before he heard again from the mysterious caller. Again, the call was short and very precise. It was around 4:00 p.m. on the following Wednesday when the phone rang.

"Don't touch the phone!" Eduardo yelled at Maria as he walked toward the phone, "How many times I gotta tell you? I'm expecting a 'business' call."

"Yeah, that's you, Mister Businessman. I know it's some little chickee; she calls and you take off. I'm gonna find out who she is, asshole."

"Yeah," said Eduardo into the phone, "Who's this?"

"It's Mister Jones, Eduardo. Are you ready to earn the rest of your money?"

"I'm not sure," he said, "I still don't know who the victim is."

"You took the money, Eduardo, don't mess with me, and don't ask questions; just do the job."

"And if I don't?"

"Let me put it to you this way, Eduardo. The guy you're going to scare has had a bad run of luck lately. He owes us a few hundred bucks. That's why we're only going to scare him. Now you, you are a different story. You took my money, so you owe me five hundred bucks, and are talking about double-crossing me. That's really bad Eduardo. You see, I can't afford to let the word get out to the rest of my 'clients' that I let some gang banger punk rip me off for five hundred bucks. For five hundred bucks, you think I couldn't get one of your little "homies" to put a bullet in your head? You aren't *that* popular back in your old neighborhood, you know."

"OK, OK. What do I do?"

"Since you don't like McDonalds, go to Burger King. Take the Harley, your .38, and the ammo. Look on the ground next to the dumpster by the Highway 101 exit, and you'll find a McDonalds bag. Follow exactly the directions on the note in the bag and the money will be paid. Remember; he's a valuable client, and I just want him scared, not killed, so don't screw it up."

"Hey, chump, I don't dig through no dumpsters." For the third time, Eduardo heard a dial tone in response. "Mother fucker, I'm gonna kill *you* next!" he said as he threw the phone on the couch.

"Victim. Dumpsters. Kill you next? What's going on Miho?" Maria said in her sweetest, most concerned tone.

"Never fuckin' mind," he said. You never care about anything except how much money I bring home. You never worried before about how I earned it."

"But Miho, we don't need it bad enough to get in trouble. You've been in too much trouble before. Don't kill nobody, Miho."

"Listen to you now, you phony bitch. All lovey-dovey. You're just afraid you'll lose your meal ticket. Don't worry, I can take care of myself. I gotta go out for a while."

"Please, Miho, don't go. I'll screw you right now if you'll stay."

He shook his head and walked out the door without another word. He wondered how the caller knew so much about him. *"Is there anything about me the caller didn't know?*

A few minutes later, he pulled into the Burger King parking lot and went to the dumpster as directed. There he found a McDonald's bag tucked behind it, which he retrieved and opened. The note was printed in crayon in block letters on the inside of the bag. It read:

> Tonight 6:30 p.m. He'll Leave Ironworker's Gym - '80 Camaro - 2CBQ305. North on H Street. This part is IMPORTANT. Memorize the license and tear up this bag before you do it.

He turned his head and looked around to see if he was being observed. As he had come to expect, no-one seemed to show any interest in his presence or actions. He walked around behind a nearby rhododendron bush and pulled the revolver out of his pocket and opened it. He pulled the ammunition 'Mr. Jones' had provided out of his pants pocket and started to replace the cheap target-practice wadcutters that were already in the gun, but he stopped. *"No sense wasting this good stuff if I'm just scaring him,"* he thought. He thrust the 'Plus P' ammo back in his pants pocket.

He looked at his watch. Four thirty. *"Two hours before the job,"* he thought, *"I think I'll go back home and take Maria up on her offer."*

Section Twelve

Attempt on Casey's Life

"C'mon Casey, just two more reps."

Casey grunted and squeezed one more repetition out of his aching arms, but couldn't get the last one to the arms-extended position. "Can't!" he grunted, and CHP Sergeant Bill Hitchcock, his spotter and exercise partner, grabbed the bar and helped it onto the rack above his head.

"Almost. ... Almost a new high," Casey gasped as he regained his breath. "Maybe next time."

"For sure," Hitchcock said. Then, looking at his watch, he said, "I've got to get going; I'm working the 7:00 pm shift tonight, and I've got to get ready for briefing. Tomorrow?"

"Busy tomorrow, but I'll see you same time Monday," Casey said.

"Okay, lady." Hitchcock chided as he headed for the showers.

Casey was pleased to have met Sergeant Hitchcock when he transferred to Eureka almost a year ago. Hitchcock, an avid weightlifter and fitness 'nut', was ten years older than Casey. Over the past year, he had tried to get Casey started on an exercise routine, but Casey hadn't been interested until recently. Since his breakup with Andrea, he had more free time than he could stand, so he began what he referred to as 'three-days-a-week torture', while Hitchcock breezed through it every day.

In the locker room, Hitchcock asked, "Say, Casey, how is the investigation coming along? Any new leads?"

"Nothing really, Bill, no-one is talking. But we hit a nerve somewhere. It must have scared the killer out of hiding. Now we know he's still around. Unfortunately, it cost me my fiancé, and mom is pretty cold to me right now, but the killer has left a few clues around, making us feel pretty confident about the investigation. We're following up some possible ideas, but most of them seem to dry up as soon as we get them.

"What about Snider? Does this mean you have ruled him out?"

"No. He fits, but he doesn't also. He doesn't seem smart enough to cover his deeds for seventeen years, yet I can't figure out why he acts so guilty if he's innocent. Maybe he paid someone for the hit on dad. I keep thinking I'm close to some real evidence, but nothing concrete is coming up. I'll just keep working at it. Say, you see Captain Webster all the time, how long do you think he's going to let me stay on this case?

"He's happy about how you are keeping up your beat activity. And the rest of the guys are still okay with it, but it can't go on forever. At the last Staff Meeting, he said he thought maybe another month unless something breaks open on it." Then he said, "Have you thought about what you are going to do if you find him?

"Good question. I've asked the same thing myself. I hope I'll keep it professional. Maybe, if I'm lucky, I'll get to kill him, but I've got to get there first."

"Lucky for Snider, I think I'd have whacked him years ago. It's got to be tough, being it was your dad and all. How do you do it?"

Casey just shrugged and looked away. With his frequent contact with the criminal element, he could probably have easily found someone who'd kill anybody if the price was right. Yes, he'd thought about it, but he knew he couldn't do it that way. It would have to be done the right way, just to prove to himself once and for all that the 'system' works, but sometimes … . His thoughts trailed off as they parted company. By the time Casey walked out of the gym, it was exactly 6:30 p.m.

The sun had set over the pacific, and as darkness overtook the city, the lingering clouds effectively covered the rising moon, adding to the darkness of the evening. Casey quickly surveyed the parking lot, as he had come to do all the time now. Seeing no-one, he got in his car, turned on the headlights, and turned his Camaro westbound on 4th Street. After a few blocks, he turned south on 'H' Street and, after crossing 5th Street, he accelerated normally to the 45 mph speed limit.

When he glanced in the mirror, he noticed a single headlight overtaking him from the rear at a high speed. When the vehicle got within 100 yards behind him, he could make out the shape of a full-sized motorcycle. The rider changed lanes behind him, slowed to match his speed, and hung back about ten car lengths.

Casey thought it was curious, but couldn't really bring himself to believe that he was really being followed.

Nevertheless, his "cop" instinct caused him to keep an occasional eye on the motorcycle as he drove. After a while, the motorcycle seemed to just be driving normally behind him, and he disregarded it. Another few blocks and he could hear the motorcycle behind him, and realized it was much closer now. Casey changed into the right lane and signaled for a right turn. The motorcycle also changed into the right lane behind him.

His curiosity was now piqued. He turned right on Harris Street and drove two blocks and stopped at the small market at the corner. As he drove into the driveway, the motorcycle drove by, and Casey shrugged and paid no further attention to it as he went inside and bought a six pack of beer. He came out of the market a few minutes later and retraced his route back to "H" street and turned south again, accelerating to the speed limit. He glanced in the mirror and was surprised to see a motorcycle was again behind him. It appeared to be the same bike as before. He slowed to around 38mph, and the motorcycle also slowed to that speed. The loud mufflers told him it was, indeed, the same bike.

"He is following me," Casey thought to himself. A chill ran down his spine and the hairs tingled on his neck as

he pondered who would be following him. "*Why? Maybe it's some yahoo I wrote a ticket to, or maybe ... .*" The thought trailed off as he wondered if, just i̲f̲, he had gotten too close to the killer, and now he himself might be the prey. Could this person behind him be the very person who killed his father?

He told himself not to over-react to the motorcyclist. Once before, in Riverside, he had been followed home after work. It turned out to be a fellow he had written a ticket to earlier in the day and the guy thought he'd intimidate Casey by following him home. That night, Casey turned the tables on the guy; by slowing and timing it just right to go through a yellow light, he baited the guy into running the red light, then stopped. The guy drove past, and Casey identified him and sent him a ticket in the mail. He never saw or heard from the guy again. This was probably the same thing, or even one of his buddies pulling a practical joke on him.

Still, he decided not to take any chances as he waited for the biker to make his move. He reached into his gym bag and pulled out his 9mm automatic, used his left hand to rack a round into the chamber and released the safety. By now they had left the residential area and they

were in a rural area approaching the community of Cutten.
At the next intersection, Casey abruptly slowed and turned
right onto a side street, drove about fifty yards and stopped.
He turned in the seat and pulled the gun across his chest
into a 'ready' position. To his surprise, the motorcycle
continued straight on 'H' Street.

He chuckled at his paranoia. *"You're getting a little
paranoid, Casey boy. Now you're imagining killers
following you."* He placed the gun on the passenger seat
and slowly turned his car around. He was still scolding
himself when he pulled up to the stop sign at 'H' Street,
preparing to turn right and continue on his way. He looked
to his left and saw that traffic was clear. As he glanced
back to his right, he was staring in disbelief at the
motorcycle rider, sitting astride the motorcycle, now parked
alongside the bushes at the corner, not more than 12 feet
away. Even in the poor dusk lighting, he could make out a
black handgun silhouetted against the rider's dark red
jacket. The gun was pointed directly at his head!

"Shit!" he yelled as he choked on his own saliva.
Instinctively, he dove across the shifter console and ducked
down with his upper body onto the passenger's bucket seat.
Just as he moved, he heard four rapid gunshots and heard

and felt the right window shatter and spray him with shards of glass. Grabbing the gun he had placed fortuitously on the seat beside him with his left hand, he raised his arm above the window and blindly fired two rounds in the general direction of the shooter. The ejected shell casings slapped him in the face and neck.

Eduardo Corona, the shooter, was visibly startled that he was being fired upon. All of his previous shooting encounters had been drive-by shootings as a gang member. They all involved shooting at unarmed and unsuspecting victims, and no-one ever shot back at him. This was supposed to be the same. But this time the shooter was returning live fire at him. He didn't feel nearly as macho as he had only moments before. Panicked, he abandoned the "scare tactic" and fired two more wild shots at Casey, who had ducked again. When the revolver clicked on empty chambers, both he and Casey knew he was out of ammunition. He threw the gun to the ground and, kicking the motorcycle into gear, turned and peeled out, speeding away southbound, as Casey raised up and fired two more shots in his direction as he fled.

The first of those shots missed Eduardo completely, as had the first two, but the next shot struck him in the left arm below the shoulder. The impact and the pain from the wound caused him to almost lose control of the motorcycle, but Eduardo was a skilled rider, and was able to save it and accelerate southbound on 'H' Street at high speed.

Casey sat up in the seat. He slammed the shifter into low gear and gave chase. He had five more rounds in the clip of his weapon. The high-powered Camaro began to catch up to the wounded motorcycle rider as he slowed for the 'T' intersection of 'H' Street and Walnut drive. Due to his wound, Eduardo had great difficulty making the 90-degree transition turn to westbound Walnut Drive, nearly crashing in the process. Eduardo knew he couldn't drive very far like that and accelerated to over 90 mph, hoping to evade the pursuing Camaro, who had smoothly traversed the turn and was gaining on him on Walnut Drive.

By driving at unconscionable speeds, Eduardo began to pull away from his pursuer, and by the time they approached the sweeping curve at the intersection with Elk River Road, two miles to the west, he had managed to put a quarter-mile between himself and Casey. Casey was familiar with the intersection and he suspected the motorcycle would have trouble negotiating the curving transition lane, so he began to slow down. Sure enough, as he approached the intersection, a cloud of dust completely obscured the roadway. Casey knew that meant that the motorcycle had crashed hard off of the roadway. He pulled to a stop, took cover behind the car, and waited for the dust to settle. Looking to the south, from where the dust cloud seemed to terminate, he could make out the shape of the mangled motorcycle in the ditch to the south of Elk River Road. As he listened, the quiet chill of silence, permeated only by expansion noises of rapidly cooling broken engine parts, were all that could be heard. Far in the distance, Casey could hear sirens from two converging directions.

He grabbed his flashlight from his car and, gun in hand, cautiously approached the general area of the motorcycle. Flashing the light around, he recognized the red color of the rider's jacket lying about 150 feet south of the motorcycle in the open field. He climbed the barbed wire pasture fence and approached the apparently lifeless form, lying face down with his head and neck at a grotesque angle.

He reached down and felt Eduardo's carotid artery for a pulse. Detecting none, he was satisfied that the rider was deceased of an apparent broken neck. He did not move the body, but got down on his hands and knees and leaned down close to the rider to try to get a look at his face. The man's features were unknown to him. He got up and walked back to the road, and leaned against his Camaro and waited.

Before long, a Sheriff's unit arrived at the scene; a Deputy Sheriff Casey had seen once or twice named Jim Belton. Casey introduced himself to Belton, in case the deputy didn't recognize him.

"Sure, I know who you are, Casey," Belton responded. "We are all pulling for you to put your dad's case together after all these years. Are you okay?"

"Yeah, I'm fine. But I'm pretty shook up to know that the killer has escalated from threats and intimidation to actually trying to kill me."

Belton gestured toward the motorcycle in the ditch, he asked, "Is he dead?"

"Yes, I checked. His neck is broken."

"You think he's the murderer?"

"I don't know that for sure, but I've got to believe it's related. I've never seen this guy before. There was no other reason; he just tracked me down and tried to kill me."

"You must be onto something big, or he wouldn't be so worried."

Casey nodded in agreement. As they spoke, ambulance personnel, who had arrived just after Belton, approached and confirmed that the rider was dead.

Another deputy arrived and called Belton aside. After a short conversation, the other deputy left the scene. Belton turned and said, "There was a good witness who reported it." Belton said, "He called in from a home nearby. He was watering his lawn and saw it go down. Other Deputies are responding to the location and securing that scene, too."

Deputy Belton got a quick summary of the incident, and said, "I'd better get over there before they ruin any evidence that may be near the body. Oh, by the way, Sergeant Regan has been notified.

The next Officer to arrive was a fellow CHP Officer, who, after assuring himself Casey was okay, began to document the accident scene along the highway.

Within minutes, responding Officers arrived at the original shooting scene and found Eduardo's gun and the broken glass. They isolated the second crime scene and waited for Detectives.

Casey sat against his Camaro. While he waited, he replayed the incident in his mind. "Why would this punk want to kill me? Who is he? Have I ever stopped him or crossed his path? Is this young punk the killer after all these years, or was he just hired to shut me up? If he was just hired to kill me; to stop the investigation, I wonder if we can make a connection between him and Alden Snider. I've still got to believe Snider's involved." Casey knew at that moment he was more committed than ever to the investigation. "Don't worry, Dad, I have a hunch we're closer than I thought."

"We're going to get him," he said aloud to himself as he cast a glance skyward.

His internal inquisition was interrupted by a familiar voice approaching from behind him. "Looks like you may be getting closer than you thought with your investigation, Casey." The voice was that of Sergeant Hitchcock, who had just gone on duty and responded from the Office in Arcata. "I heard the radio call go out reporting the assault, reckless driving with shots fired, and when I heard the description of the vehicles involved, I knew it had to be you. Someone really wants you dead."

At that time, Deputy Belton approached the men. "We just got the R.O. info on the motorcycle. You ever heard of a local badass named Eduardo Corona? He's got a long rap sheet dating back to the 60's and 70's, when he was a teenager."

"I don't recall the name or the bike from any stops I've made." Casey responded.

"Well, he knew you." Look at this. Belton produced a baggie and held it out. The crudely written crayon message spelling out Casey's itinerary was clearly visible on a torn portion of a McDonald's bag. "Corona had this in his pocket. Doesn't follow directions very well. He was supposed to throw it away. Apparently, he was hired to kill you and he kept the note to remember the details."

"I knew it!" Casey said emphatically. "He was on me soon as I turned off of 4th Street onto H St," Casey continued. "I spotted him, and he was looking for me all the way. He wasn't trying to be inconspicuous, or if he was, he wasn't very good at it."

"It's got to be connected to the investigation." Hitchcock said.

"Another thing. He was serious about it, look at these," Deputy Belton said, showing the men six rounds of half-jacket hollow-point ammunition in another plastic baggie. "We found them in his pocket. Must have bought them on the black market."

"Why?" Casey asked, "What's so special about those rounds."

"These are Remington .38 caliber 'Plus P' rounds. They increase the knockdown power of a .38 load to about the equivalent of a .357 magnum."

"I remember reading about them in the case reports. The ammo manufacturers made them in the 70's for police use only. Dad was killed with the same kind of bullets."

"DOJ is trying to trace the weapon Eduardo had. I'll let you know if they come up with something. We'll check both the rounds and the note for finger prints," Belton said as he walked toward his car."

"Well, we know he was after you, specifically, and that someone put him up to it?" Hitchcock said after the deputy walked away, "Consider this, Casey. If you were the target all the way, someone who knows your schedule pretty well had to tip him off about your gym schedule, so he'd know where to find you."

"That could be anyone at the gym or at the office, Bill," Casey contemplated. "Everybody knows everybody, and we're pretty regular on our workouts. But the bullets? It keeps coming back to those special police-issue bullets. Somehow, it keeps looking like there is a cop involved."

Who was the Hitman?

That night, Casey could hardly control the wide range of emotions that ran through his mind. Coming that close to death brought a terror that he'd never experienced in his life, yet surviving such a nightmare created a euphoria unlike anything he'd ever felt. He didn't know whether to laugh or cry; to run away, or to 'high-five' everybody.

As he tried to sleep, in between the highs and lows, he kept reliving the adventure, trying to find, in hindsight, some clue he missed when it unfolded in 'real time'.

The next morning Casey and Sergeant Regan were in the Detectives' break room at the Sheriff's Office, going over the incident and studying the evidence to consider the endless possibilities.

"The 'Plus P' ammo only had Eduardo's prints, but it is from a very old batch of ammo," Regan said. "We'll try to narrow it down, more. And the McDonalds bag was also …""

The conversation was interrupted mid-sentence by the sound of high heels coming down the hallway. Both men stopped and looked toward the door in anticipation. High heels at the Sheriff's Office meant only one thing; Sally Perkins, the Records Supervisor, was approaching, and her approach was always a highly anticipated event. So much so, that it could make a man briefly forget that someone tried to kill him just a day ago. Sally also enjoyed the attention she received from the men. Several years ago, though, she stopped an advance from one of the detectives, making it very clear she was not interested in a relationship with a cop. Since then, the men at work knew she was just for looking at, so they made the most of the opportunities when she made her infrequent trips upstairs from the Records Section, like this morning.

Casey and Sergeant Regan watched in silence as she walked through the door. She was looking particularly good today, Casey thought. She acted surprised that they were quietly watching her arrival, but her thin smile told them she knew they would be looking. "Well. Good morning, y'all. You're awfully quiet this morning. I understood you wanted this as soon as it came in, so I thought I'd bring it up myself. Hello, Casey. We are all so relieved you are okay."

"Good morning, Sally. Thank you. You look nice today."

"Thank you, Casey," she said with a broad smile, as she walked to Sergeant Regan and handed him a packet of papers. "Here is the DOJ Gun Record and the NCIC Rap Sheet you were looking for, Don."

"Good," he said as he took the papers. Sally turned and walked toward the doorway while Casey and Sergeant Regan watched her walk out the door and disappear down the hallway. After she left the room, Regan looked over at Casey, raising one eyebrow in approval as Casey nodded in agreement. The Sergeant then looked down at the papers in his hand while Casey hovered over his left shoulder.

"What were we talking about?" Casey asked facetiously.

"Someone tried to kill you, remember?"

"Oh, yeah. I knew it was something important."

After a few moments of scanning the documents, Regan said, "No record on the gun – a Saturday Night Special. But your guy has been pretty busy for a 39-year-old. Lots of misdemeanor arrests, but only two convictions. Two felony arrests, one for Assault with a Deadly Weapon, and one for Strong Armed Robbery. Reduced each time to a misdemeanor with deductions for time served." Just then his eyes focused on an entry that leapt off the page at him. "Whoa, this is unreal. April, 1967, when he was 18 years old; the arresting officer on the Possession of Stolen Property conviction was, can you believe it, your dad?"

"What?" Casey stood upright. "Where?" As he bent over and followed Regan's finger to the entry half way down the page, he couldn't believe it. "El Gato...Eduardo Corona...and Snider...all previously arrested by dad. This is getting too unreal."

"It is bizarre. Were they in this together? All this time we were looking for an individual, and maybe we should have looked for a conspiracy."

"I can't imagine they could be connected. That would mean that Corona waited twenty years to try to kill me for dad's arrest. We're talking about twenty years apart. But I think we need to go to the court or the CHP office and get the full reports and see if there is anything to this."

Within the hour, Casey and Sergeant Regan had obtained copies of the Garcia and Corona arrest reports from the CHP Office archives, and walked back to the briefing room, spread them out on the desk, and began to study them in detail, making a ledger entry about each case.

April 21, 1967

Sonny Tyler stopped a car for no front license plate on Old Arcata Road south of Indianola Road. As the car was stopping, the driver was observed pushing something under the seat. The driver, Eduardo Corona, was very nervous and didn't have a driver's license. There was another male passenger in the vehicle, who was also acting "hinky." Tyler asked the Officer on the nearby beat, Brice Tomlinson, to roll by and cover him on the stop while he searched the vehicle. After both occupants were removed from the car, Officer Tyler found a purple cloth Crown Royal bag under the seat. Both men claimed it wasn't theirs and they didn't know anything about it. He opened it and found jewelry inside. Further checking revealed the jewelry to be stolen in a recent burglary in McKinleyville. Both suspects were arrested for possession of stolen property.

"Pretty straightforward. Doesn't seem like anything unusual," Casey said, as he set the report aside and picked up the second file on Tony Garcia.

March 12, 1968, 2045 hours,

Sonny Tyler stopped a 1961 Ford Falcon on Samoa Road, north of the Samoa Cookhouse entrance, for weaving across the centerline. According to the report, the driver was Tony Garcia, who didn't have a driver's license. The stop was pretty routine, until Tyler ran a warrant check on Garcia and ended up arresting him on a Failure to Appear Warrant out of Arcata Justice Court. Garcia tried to run, but his baggy pants slowed him down and Tyler was able to easily catch him and arrest him after a brief scuffle. Garcia was booked without further incident. The warrant and resisting arrest were dropped when he was sent back to prison for violating his parole. He was sentenced to another eighteen months in Lompoc.

"Nothing unusual about that one either. Nothing that would suggest a motive for anything like murder, or even a connection between them." Casey said.

"I'm not sure, Casey. Both were within about 6 years of the same age in 1970, and both were gang bangers from the North Coast. There weren't that many gang bangers around back them. It stands to reason they knew each other, a connection seems quite possible." Regan said. "Then again, Eduardo was from McKinleyville, and El Gato from Eureka. They were probably from different gangs. Probably shot at each other back then."

"What if they met in prison and vowed to get even with the man who put them there?" Casey made a note in the ledger and underlined it.

Regan scooped up the copy of the rap sheet on Eduardo Corona. "No, that doesn't add up, either. They never appeared to do time together, but it is a possibility we need to look at. I'll have Sally get a full NCIC Rap Sheet on Snider and El Gato tomorrow, and we'll compare them all."

Casey picked up the Eduardo Corona arrest report and looked closely at it again. He glanced at the bottom of the last page of the report at the 'Signature' line. The report was signed by Sonny Tyler, but on the far end of the line were the small initials 'RA'.

He picked up the Garcia report again, and flipped to the last page and looked at the signature line; again, there was his dad's signature, and at the end of the line were the initials 'RA' again. *Must be the initials of the Sergeant who reviewed it,* he thought. But then he looked on the following line, and in the box labeled 'Reviewed By', he saw the respective signatures of the Sergeants who worked there at the time.

"I write these things up all the time, and they haven't changed much in seventeen years. But, I don't know what these initials are there for," he said as he showed them to Sergeant Regan. "I wonder what 'RA' stands for?"

"Really?" asked Regan facetiously, "How about Randy Allen? I wonder what he's up to these days?"

"Randy Allen? Of course. R. A.! But why would his initials be on dad's arrest reports back in the '60's? I understand he resigned about ten years ago, under a black cloud, before they could fire him. I don't know any details, but I heard he still lives in Eureka, serves legal papers on people for a living, and tries to keep a low profile."

"Maybe we need to look at Randy seriously again and see how low that profile really is?"

Graveyard Shift – A Break in the Action.

The following month brought a welcome break in the action for Casey. It was his turn to work the graveyard shift; 10:00 p.m. until 6:30 a.m. Under the ongoing agreement with Captain Webster, his participation in the murder investigation would have to be put on the back burner for a month, and daytime sleeping cut into his off-duty time at the Sheriff's Office. He was actually enjoying the break to get his thoughts in order.

He was still saddened by the breakup with Andrea, the only girl he had seriously dated in his life. It was going to take some time to get over her, and the investigation had been his refuge in the interim. He had made a conscious decision to avoid any dating relationships for a while, since the killer had already demonstrated his willingness to discourage Casey by attacking those close to him.

Also, with Andrea gone, Bonnie felt even more threatened that her life was in danger and was getting quite resentful, making her feelings clearly known at every

Steve Davis

opportunity. He knew she was right to be fearful, but he knew he couldn't quit now, and besides, unlike Andrea, his mom had a gun in the house and knew how to shoot it. He decided to avoid her for a while, for her own sake, and hoped graveyards, time and positive results would make it up to her.

Yes, even graveyard shift was a blessing; a needed break from the stresses on his personal life, and he was relieved that all he would have to do this month was focus on and arrest drunk drivers, and other normal duties.

Midway through the month, Casey and his partner, Officer Greg Cooper, were in the middle of a successful month. So far, eleven drunk drivers had been arrested between them, and accidents were down. Toward the end of the month, he arrived at work one night to find that Officer Cooper was going to be late for the shift. This meant he would have to wait at the office until Cooper showed up in about one hour. He talked for a while with the officers going off duty, then after the last of the swing shift officers left the office, he walked up to the dispatch center and sat down to visit with the graveyard dispatcher, Sylvia Santos.

After a few minutes of small talk, the conversation turned to the status of Casey's recent involvement in the homicide investigation. After a short discussion, there was a queer silence in the conversation, and then she said, "Your dad was a fine man, Casey. A fine man." Her words tailed off as if she wished she hadn't said anything.

"Thank you, ma'am."

"It's true. And, I'd ask you to quit calling me ma'am, but Sonny raised you to be a gentleman, and it wouldn't do any good."

"Sorry, ma'am."

There was another awkward silence for quite a few seconds. Casey was lost in deep thought about this woman across the table from him. Then, out of the blue, even he was surprised to hear the words coming from his mouth, "Sylvia, can I ask you a personal question?"

"Yes. And no."

"Yes and no?"

"Yes, you can ask me a personal question; and no, your dad and I never had an affair."

Steve Davis

Casey blushed and looked down. "Thanks," he said. Casey stared left and right at the desk, avoiding eye contact, embarrassed that he was so transparent. *"How could you have asked such a personal, stupid question,"* he thought.

"Not that I didn't try. I did. Do you really want to hear the story?"

Another pause. Casey knew it was now or never. He took a deep breath and said, "Yes."

"I was young and single and I was pretty taken with your dad. He was more of a gentleman that the rest of these guys. While the other guys were sometimes crude, he always treated me with respect and I soaked it up. I think I was in love with him, or at least the image I had of him. I used to dream about him, and I got to thinking we deserved each other. Nothing personal against your mom, I just never liked … never felt comfortable around her. Sorry for my bluntness."

"It's OK."

"He never gave me an opening. Then, one night on graves, his partner went home sick about 0330, and he had to hang around the office on call until day shift came on. If no calls came in, it meant we were going to be alone for over two hours, and I came on strong.

We were flirting and I gave him my best 'come on' for a twenty-eight-year-old. I thought it was working; I know he was thinking about it, and flirting back, and then I stepped over to him, and kissed him. It was a great kiss, but then he pulled back and said, 'I've got to go', and he left the room.

I could hear him in the squad room while he waited for day shift to get here. I was embarrassed and crushed, and didn't know how to take it. It was pretty awkward for a few days." After a short moment of reflection, she said softly, "And then ..."

She pushed herself away from the table and got up, turned on her heels and without another word walked over to the nearby dispatcher's locker cubicle and returned with her purse. She fumbled around in her wallet and pulled out a weathered, wrinkled piece of paper folded small enough to fit in the pocket of her billfold. She handled it gingerly, almost reverently, Casey thought, as she unfolded the small sheet of note paper. "... He gave me this." Casey's heart pounded as he could see she was holding back deep emotions as she continued, "No one has ever seen this

Steve Davis

before ..." she said, as she slid it across the desk, "... but it might ease your mind about him and me."

> Syl;
> I want to apologize for my actions the other night. I should have explained myself before I left you. You are a beautiful and intriguing woman, and I'm flattered that you were interested in me. I was very willing and ready for you.
>
> In fact, I had thought about you before, but in the end, it's too close to home, and I couldn't do that to my family. If I ever was going to be unfaithful, I hope it would be with someone just like you. I will always smile at what might have been.
> Sonny

Casey looked up and saw tears in Sylvia's eyes as she was mouthing the last four words from memory as he read them. After a few seconds, she said in a broken voice, "It cleared the air so we could work together after that," she said in a broken voice, "But I never got over him. Then ...," in a barely audible whisper, she said, "...two months later, he was ... dead."

Casey reached across the table and held her trembling hand. As he held it, she began to cry softly. After a few moments, he wiped his own eyes and pulled himself together long enough to say, "I guess, maybe, we are the two who miss him the most."

"Please don't get in over your head on this, Casey. Promise me you won't get hurt chasing shadows. I know Sergeant Regan has worked his tail off to get the killer, and now the killer has come after you."

"I can't promise, but I'll try."

"Please let Sergeant Regan take the lead now. Don't get hurt or killed. I see too much of Sonny in you to see that happen again."

Before he could respond, the sound of the rear door opening and closing meant his partner was here, so he got up, wiped his eyes, and shared a last glance as he started to leave the room. As he got to the door, he turned and said, "Sylvia, you wouldn't lie to me about … you know … after the note, would you?"

"It is true, Casey. But if it weren't … yes, I'd probably lie to you about it, anyhow."

He smiled and left the room.

Section Thirteen

Attack on Bonnie Tyler
February, 1988

"Sheriff's emergency line ... what is your emergency?" Humboldt Sheriff's Dispatcher Kevin Oswald said as he put down the book he was reading.

"This is Walter Johnson. I just heard some gunshots fired over at my neighbor's house ... on Walnut Drive. She lives alone and it's pretty late. I think she must be in trouble."

"What's the address on Walnut Drive?"

"5590 something ... Let me think. No, we're 5588, they must be 5600. She's the widow of that CHP Officer who was killed about 15 years ago. I can't imagine she'd be shooting unless it is an emergency. Can you send someone there to check on her safety?"

"Yes, sir, we will have someone there as soon as possible. Please hold a moment." Turning around in the seat, Oswald spoke into the microphone on the radio console behind him, "7-18, Control 1."

"Control 1, 7-18, go ahead."

"7-18. Neighbor reports shots fired, unknown circumstances, at 5600 Walnut Drive."

"Control 1, 7-18 en-route, Code 3."

Turning back to the caller on the phone, Oswald said, "Okay, Mr. Johnson, I need your … Excuse me again, sir, hold on. I have to get the other line."

"Sheriff's emergency line … what is your emergency?"

There was the sound of heavy breathing and panic in the voice on the line. "I need help," the voice pleaded excitedly; "My name is Bonnie Tyler. Someone's trying to kill me." *Click.* Oswald recognized the sound of a sudden, unexpected disconnect. The phone line was dead. "Hello. Hello? Mrs. Tyler?" There was nothing but dead silence on the line.

Quickly, he spun around in the chair and keyed the radio microphone. "All units; hold for emergency traffic only. Unit 7-18 and other units responding to 5600 Walnut Drive; the female resident just called for help and was disconnected. No further contact. This is the home of Bonnie Tyler, widow of the CHP 187 victim back in the seventies."

Picking up the phone, he again addressed the neighbor, who was on hold. "Okay, Mr. Johnson, tell me, can you hear anything else?"

"Where the hell you been? I have been yelling for you." Johnson yelled, "Hell yes. I heard her screaming at someone and the dog barking in the house. I couldn't hear what she was saying, and then another shot, then nothing."

"We've already got several units en-route, sir. I've been telling them what is going on. Now, I'm going to stay on the line, so let me know if you can hear anything coming from the Tyler home."

With the phone pinched against his right ear, he spoke into the radio mike. "Units responding to Walnut Drive, neighbor heard screaming and another shot fired; then nothing since. Use extreme caution."

After an agonizing wait of 11 minutes, Oswald could hear the sound of a siren through the open phone line.

Mr. Johnson said, "I think he is here, the siren sounds like a block away."

"Thank you, Mr. Johnson. I've got to go now," Oswald said before hanging up the phone. "Thank you for your help."

As Sheriff's Deputy 7-18 approached the address on Walnut Drive, Deputy Vaughn Collins slowed abruptly, turned off the siren and headlights, and approached slowly from the north. Other sirens could be heard in the distance, and Collins estimated they were still three or more minutes away. He stopped short of the driveway entrance, rolled down the windows and listened for a moment to the silence, broken only by the distant sirens.

"Control 1, 7-18 is 10-97 on Walnut," he said.

"7-18, copy you are 10-97."

Sensing Bonnie Tyler's life was in imminent danger, he felt that he couldn't wait for the backup units to arrive, so Collins crept toward the driveway clearly marked '5600'. As he turned into the tree and shrubbery lined driveway, the sound of his tires rolling on loose gravel gave away any chance of sneaking up on anyone. He could barely make out the outline of the darkened residence behind the thick shrubbery. He turned the headlights onto high beams and activated the alley lights which illuminated the sides of the driveway as his eyes darted left and right looking for any movement or suspects lingering in ambush. Seeing nothing, he continued to a point where he could see the front of the house, and the entire north side of the house was also illuminated.

He turned the spotlight toward the closed front door. He could see visible damage to the door in the vicinity of the door handle, and at least three bullet holes in the door, and wood splinters lying about the front stoop. A potted plant was lying on its side, having been knocked off the small front porch stoop. A few feet away, there was a four-foot-long four by four fence post, painted a redwood color, heavily splintered on one end.

As Collins panned the spotlight along the north side of the house, his eyes stopped at the frightening sight of the telephone lines to the home; clearly ripped from the connector box on the north wall.

"Control 1, 7-18. Bullet holes visible in the front door and phone lines have been cut. I'll be checking perimeter and will wait for backup to make contact inside.

Tell backup to come on in, it looks quiet and the suspect appears to be gone."

"7-18, Control 1. 10-4."

Collins eased out of the unit and drew his weapon. Using a redwood tree and landscaping for cover, he walked along the north side of the residence, where he could watch the driveway, the rear entrance, and the north wall. He took up a position behind a tree near the rear porch and waited.

"Who is out there?" Bonnie Tyler called out from behind the closed back door.

"Deputy Collins, Humboldt Sheriff," Collins responded. "Are you okay?"

"Yes. Is he still out there?" Bonnie asked.

"No, I don't think so. For both of our safety, open the door and come out with your hands in sight."

"I hear sirens coming. I'm scared. I'm going to wait until the sirens get here, then I'll come out."

"Okay," the Deputy said.

Within a few moments the first of a half dozen patrol cars approached the residence and pulled into the driveway. After the scene stabilized, Bonnie Tyler opened the rear door and walked outside, where Deputy Collins met her and hustled her out of the crime scene and over to his patrol car. Two uniformed Deputies hustled into the front door with their guns drawn.

"I'm so scared," she said as she wiped tears away from her eyes. "Will you please call my son, CHP Officer Casey Tyler, and tell him what happened, and have him come right over."

"Yes, ma'am, he's been called already," Collins said.

A young Sheriff's Deputy stuck his head out of the door, and said, "It's clear inside."

Deputy Collins said, "Let's go back into the house where you'll be more comfortable, and I'll get a statement." He escorted her carefully through the crime scene and into the living room of the residence. He glanced back and saw Ty Randolph, the Evidence Tech, approach from the driveway, looking like a ghost emerging from the darkness in his white lab coat.

Turning toward Bonnie, he said, "Tell me what happened from the beginning."

"I was home alone, and Ralph, my dog, started barking at the front door. I went to the closed door and saw it was unlocked. I locked it and heard a noise outside. I thought it might be Casey so I said, "Who is out there?" Suddenly, someone tried to open the door, but I had just locked it. I screamed and said, "Get out of here. Who are you?"

"The person yelled something like, "I'll kill you, you… crazy bitch." Then a few seconds later he hit the door with something to try to knock it down. The whole door shook, but it didn't open. He hit it again, while he was yelling, "I'm going to kill you, bitch." I ran to the kitchen where I keep a gun, and I went back to the door and said, "Get away from here, or I'll shoot." He hit it again and it made the whole house shake. I fired twice through the door; I'm sure I must have hit him. I had to hit him; I shot right through the door."

Bonnie was hyperventilating and sweating from fear. "I'm sorry," she said, "but I'm still scared. What if he is still here, hiding and watching for you to leave?"

"Take your time, Ms. Tyler. Your son is on his way, and I'm sure he will see to it that you are safe tonight. Tell me what happened next."

"Okay. Oh, yes. It was quiet for a moment, so I ran into the front room and called the emergency number. As soon as the dispatcher answered, the phone went dead. I was really scared then, and I turned off all the lights and waited by the door for him to break in so I could get a good shot at him. He hit the door one more time, and again I yelled and shot through the closed door where I thought he'd be."

Bonnie took a deep breath and wiped another tear from her right eye. "I didn't hear anything else, and I thought maybe he was dead. I hoped he was. I just stood in the dark with my revolver aimed at the door waiting for the next move, and then your first patrol unit showed up."

"Did you ever see him or the vehicle he arrived in?"

"No, I never saw him, I was afraid to look out the window. That's curious, I was standing perfectly still and listening intently, but I never heard a car leave. If he's not there, he must have run off on foot. There's no blood? I thought sure I'd hit him."

"No. No blood. Anything unusual about the voice?"

"Well …, I can't say for sure, so I hate to say anything, but I'd have to say it sounded like Alden Snider. I hear him on the radio. I don't want to officially accuse him though; I'm not a hundred percent. Maybe there will be some other evidence to link him."

"I know who Alden Snider is. Most people think he killed your husband. If you could identify the voice for sure, we could bring him in for questioning. Doesn't he live close by here?"

"Yes, just around the corner on Redwood Trail. It's a private road off Walnut."

At that moment, the Evidence Tech stuck his head in the door and called for the Deputy. Deputy Collins excused himself and went outside to the crime scene. "What've you got?" he asked.

"Not much, the ground is covered with gravel and redwood bark, so there are no footprints. However, the ivy in the front looks disturbed as if someone ran from the porch through the ivy to get to the road."

"Really? Almost as if the intruder walked here, huh. You know, Alden Snider lives just around the corner. I think we'll pay Mr. Snider a visit."

"This might help. The four-by-four post he used to try to knock down the door doesn't look like he picked it up here. I looked around the house and in the woodpile, and nothing else has that same redwood paint on it."

The conversation was interrupted by the arrival of Casey, who ran breathlessly up the driveway past the police vehicles blocking the driveway. "Mom, are you alright? They caught me just as I was leaving for work."

Bonnie didn't answer, staring at him with contempt.

Turning back and forth between the Deputy and his mom, Casey demanded, "Somebody tell me what happened."

Deputy Collins told him what had transpired, with details interjected by Bonnie. After the story was told, Bonnie turned to Casey and said, "Is this what you wanted, Casey? I'm lucky to be alive. You almost got me killed. Someone's going to get killed, and it will be your fault. Is it going to be worth it?"

Casey looked at the ground and didn't answer.

"Well ..."

Deputy Collins interrupted the exchange to take the pressure off of Casey. "Casey, you'd better take your mom somewhere safe for the night. We've got a call in for Sergeant Regan, and we'll be paying a visit to Alden Snider tonight. We may need your mom to come down to the office if we pick him up, Okay?" Turning toward Bonnie, he said, "We may get this all taken care of tonight, ma'am."

Deputies Arrest Alden Snider

The Alden Snider home was dark shortly after 11:00 pm, when three Sheriff's vehicles eased into the driveway without lights and parked facing the house. Deputies quickly and quietly exited the vehicles and took up positions from which they could see both doors to the house.

Sergeant Regan and Deputy Collins advanced to the front door and positioned themselves on each side of the front door and waited for other Deputies to declare themselves in position.

Then Regan reached out and pounded on the door. A light came on from the rear of the house, then another closer to the front door. "Who's there," Snider called out from inside.

"Sheriff's Department Snider, open up."

"What the hell do you guys want? What are you doing out there?"

"Just open the door or we will," Regan called out. "Open the door with your hands in sight where we can see them.

"What the fuck do you want?"

"We aren't kidding, Snider. Do what I'm telling you or you can get hurt really bad, if you know what I mean. Now, open it now!"

The front door opened slowly and Alden Snider first showed his hands, and then slowly swung the door fully open. "I didn't do anything to warrant this harassment. What do you assholes want?"

"Shut up for now. Anyone else in the house?"

"Fuck you, until I know what you're here for."

"Suit yourself." Regan motioned to the two Deputies, and they advanced toward the front door, ready to enter the home in a 'ready fire' position. Snider looked at them and said, "Shit. You guys are serious. Okay, okay. My girlfriend is inside. Name is Nancy." Calling out toward the back of the house, he said, "Nancy, come out, but be very slow, these guys want to shoot someone."

With that a statuesque blonde female emerged, dressed in blue jeans, unbuttoned at the top, and a half T-shirt. She raised her hands, which revealed her bare midriff and the bottoms of her breasts. Regan said, "You can put your arms down, Nancy, there's obviously no weapons there.

Two Deputies quickly searched the house declared it safe. At that moment, another Deputy who had been watching the back door walked up to the others and, holding out a redwood painted four-by-four fence post, said, "Look what I found alongside the shed over there. Must be a half dozen of them over there. Looks like a perfect match to the one found at Bonnie Tyler's house."

"Bonnie Tyler? I should have known that bitch was involved. What's she say I did now?"

"This four-by-four matches the one you left at her house where you tried to kill her tonight. You are under arrest for assault with a deadly weapon, and attempted murder. You have the right to remain silent …"

"What? Attempted murder? Whoa. You got the wrong man. I've been here all night with Nancy." Motioning with his head in Nancy's direction, he continued, "You think I'd leave something that fine to go mess with that crazy bitch?"

"Save your alibi, Snider. You are going to have to explain the four-by-four you left behind."

"That's a no-brainer. She obviously came up here and stole it so she could frame me. You guys aren't that stupid. You obviously don't know her. She's evil. She's made this all up."

"So, let me get this straight. Your defense is that Bonnie Tyler went to all the trouble of committing a burglary of your house, stealing the four-by-four so she could shoot up her own house, and accuse you of trying to kill her."

"Yeah, I guess."

"Why? Why would she do that, Snider?"

"She's fucking crazy. She's had it in for me for years."

"Really? Seems more to me like you've had it in for her; and Sonny, remember him."

"You guys never quit. It's been over fifteen years and you're still trying to pin that one on me. Just get me to jail so I can call my lawyer."

"I can hardly wait to hear you try to sell that bullshit to a jury, Snider."

As they loaded Snider into the back seat of the patrol car, Evidence Tech Randolph came running up to Sergeant Regan, out of breath. "Sarge, come here. Quick. I've got something to show you in the workshop. The Tyler murder. We hit the mother lode."

Regan glanced down at Snider. "Any idea what he's talking about, Snider?"

"Nothing you'd be interested in, unless your boys planted it."

"Take a good look at that," Randolph said, motioning toward a calendar of a naked woman hanging on the wall.

Regan glanced at the calendar, dated August, 1978, and looked back at Randolph, quizzically.

"Are you kidding me?" Randolph said, "You don't see it?"

"I've seen better tits than that, tonight, Ty. Tell me what she's got to do with the Tyler murder."

"Look behind it."

Regan took another closer look and could see the corner of a black and yellow California license plate protruding from behind one edge of the calendar. He stepped up to the calendar and reached up with his pen and swung the calendar aside, and there, hanging on a nail, was an old style black California license plate with yellow letters, ARM 601, with a 1964 sticker attached!

"Holy Shit! That's it!" Regan exclaimed. "That was the rear plate that was on the car Sonny stopped when he was killed. Ty, you've just found the Holy Grail."

He carefully lifted the calendar and the plate into plastic evidence bags, and Regan carried them directly to the patrol car. "Snider, for seventeen years, I've waited for you to screw up and give me the one piece of evidence that would put you away for Sonny Tyler's murder, and now, finally, the wait is over. You really screwed up, pal," he said, as he triumphantly pulled the plastic baggie with the license plate out and showed the plate to Snider."

Snyder looked at the plate in Regan's hand without emotion, "What the fuck is that?"

"It is the evidence that will put you away, my friend."

"Whatever it means to you, you planted it. I've never seen it before." Turning to Collins, he said, "Let's go. These handcuffs are starting to hurt and I want to talk to my lawyer."

Regan motioned for Collins to take Snider to jail. "He's good. Very good," he said as he turned back toward the shed. But he couldn't hide his surprise at Snider's lack of emotion at the sight of the plate.

The Next Morning

It was just after 9:00 am when Casey walked into Sergeant Regan's Office the next day. As he entered, Regan jerked his head up, startled from having dozed off while poring over the files that lay on the desk in front of him. "Wha ...! Oh!" he said. "Casey, ... you startled me. I guess I dozed off."

"Yeah, I sure did. Sorry." Shifting the conversation, he said excitedly, "Congratulations, Don. I knew all that hard work would pay off someday. Thanks for the call last night. I can't believe it is over, and that bastard will finally fry for killing my dad. And we've got him on both charges, trying to kill mom last night and dad's murder. This is great."

"Yes, I suppose so, Casey, but I've been poring over this all night, and we've still got some work to do to tie this up. We've got lots of unanswered questions."

"Like what, Don?"

"Like why didn't we find the license plate when we searched the same shed seventeen years ago? And it didn't have seventeen years of dust on it. Why would he keep such an incriminating piece of evidence around for seventeen years? And why didn't he even wince when we showed it to him? Nobody's that good. He acted like he never saw the plate before, and I'm sure he didn't understand its significance when he saw it."

He continued, "And what about the Plus P ammo? Where does that fit in with Snider? And … why would he hire someone to kill you instead of doing it himself, like he did with your mom … and your dad?

"Maybe he hired someone to kill dad, too."

"Well, if you figure he hired it done, fine. Now we have a whole new set of questions. Like why did he loan the killer his car, or one like it. Eduardo fits the description of your dad's murderer, all right, but what's Snider's connection with Eduardo Corona?"

Before Casey could respond, he continued, "If he hired someone to kill your dad, and you, why would he try to kill Bonnie last night, after seventeen years, all by himself? He could have had her killed anytime. And why did he do that last night of all times, if he and that HOT babe were watching movies at his house all night. He's right. I'd never leave her just to go harass Bonnie? And his clumsy attempt to kill her was too wild-eyed and disturbed; more like a drunk or stoned person. He was sober when we arrested him. I'm thinking someone tried to frame him for the attack on Bonnie, knowing we'd find the license plate."

"Who could that be?"

"Well, I've been wondering the same thing. When you get down to it, the evidence points to Randy Allen as much as Snider. How about this scenario. Randy was apparently involved in the arrest of Eduardo Corona, wasn't he?"

"The initials R. A. on the arrest report. Okay."

He hires Eduardo to kill your dad to save his job. The heat was off for seventeen years, and then he reads you are reopening the case, and he starts getting worried. Decides to scare you off by threatening Andrea, your mom, and then hires Eduardo again to kill you. When that didn't work, he decides to give us the evidence we need to put Snider away, case closed, and he walks. Oh, and don't forget the old batch of Plus P ammo."

"Okay, Don. I get it. We've got work to do. Shit. We've been trying to get the evidence on Snider for seventeen years and now we've finally got it, and we're back at square one because it doesn't 'feel right.' Where do we start? Bring in Randy for questioning?"

"Not yet. We may not want to tip our hands just yet. He's already lawyered up, so we can't question him. I think we're only going to get one chance to confront Randy Allen, and I want to have all I need in front of me at the time."

"Then what do we do next?"

"I'm going to need to think on that. I'm NOT sure of more things than I AM sure of right now. The Evidence Tech is out at Snider's house now, looking for more evidence. I told him to dust everything for prints. If we can put one Randy Allen fingerprint in Snider's shed, he'll never be able to explain it away."

"That's brilliant, Don."

"I'm beat. Snider isn't going anywhere till at least Monday morning in court. Let's see what the Evidence Tech turns up. I'll be here Monday morning at 10:00 am and go over evidence, statements and alibis from seventeen years ago from the 'Randy Allen' perspective, and try to answer some of these questions. By the way, how did your night go with Bonnie at your house?"

"Don't ask. I got an ear full for several hours, then after you called and told her Snider was in custody, she was relieved and went back home. Said she could protect herself better than I have been doing. That's cold."

"Yup. I figured you were in for a long night. All right, Casey, I'll see you Monday. Lock up when you leave."

He left Casey sitting at the desk contemplating the scenario he just outlined, as he walked out of the room, shaking his head.

Alone in the room, Casey took out his journal and began to write down the apparent inconsistencies in the case against Snider that Regan had just outlined. In order to discount the evidence against Snider, they would have to assume the whole event last night was staged by someone else, just to set up Snider for the crimes. The whole scenario seemed preposterous.

"The threats, the intruder, the attempt to kill me, and the attack on mom; the whole scenario was getting bizarre. If the murderer was not Snider, only Randy Allen could have staged the whole scenario just to frame Snider? I think Don is on to something. It always seems to come back to Randy."

He closed the ledger and stared at the words he'd inscribed on the back cover four months ago when he started his quest:

> The Investigator's Mantra:
> Don't Assume Anything --
> Don't Overlook the Obvious.

He sat back in the chair and contemplated how Randy Allen or a hired killer might have staged the attack, and marveled at how great a chance the attacker took when Bonnie started firing bullets through the door while he pounded on it with a 4x4 wood post. *"Pretty stupid, knowing that Bonnie would likely be armed and might fire at him. Then, after she fired two shots through the door, they still pounded on it with the 4x4. Only a drunk or an idiot would do that."*

Nothing else makes sense. He held the ledger in his right hand, and lightly slapped it against his open left palm.

A lingering thought kept pushing itself into his consciousness. *"Mom?"* he questioned.

He had to acknowledge that it was possible for her to have staged the attack on herself, but why? For attention? Revenge? Sure, she hated Snider, but would she go through all that to frame him for the murder? Perhaps she was attempting to accomplish what she saw as a failure of the 'system' to deliver justice in seventeen years. *"Whoa, wait a minute. If the attacker wasn't Snider, or Allen, the person who did this had to have had access to, and planted the old license plate from the murder vehicle, to frame Snider with."*

Whoever it was, the implications were astounding; it would implicate them in every crime all the way back to his dad's murder in 1970.

"How preposterous is that?"

Shaking his head, he picked up his notes and headed for the door. However, before he left, he wrote a message on the desk of Evidence Tech Ty Randolph:

"Ty;
Please keep Monday after lunch open.
I will explain then.
Casey"

Ballistics Tests on the Tyler Guns

Over the weekend, he went over and reconsidered all the evidence in the case, and reached the only logical conclusion that Randy Allen, or his hired killer, was the only viable suspect in the cases. Still, he couldn't discount the outside chance that his mother was a potential suspect in framing Alden Snider for his dad's death. He convinced himself he was only doing what a good investigator would do, namely, don't assume anyone is innocent, especially if there was financial gain involved, which he had to admit there was, and the best way to rid his mind of these thoughts was to prove them false as soon as possible. It would be simple enough. He knew every gun Bonnie had in the house, he would just have them all checked for ballistics, and she could be cleared and he could get that nonsense out of his mind and refocus on the investigation. He decided he'd look amateurish if he mentioned his thoughts about his mom to Sergeant Regan at this time.

Monday morning, he called Sergeant Regan and told him he wouldn't be in 'til afternoon.

"No problem, since they released Snider from jail about an hour ago on bail."

"I'll tell mom he's out again when I meet her for lunch today."

Then he called his mom and apologized for questioning her wisdom and offending her over the past weeks and invited her to meet him for an early lunch to make up for it, at her favorite seafood restaurant, The Seafood Grotto, in Eureka.

He knew she would have to hurry to be ready on time, and, as was her norm, she would be complaining about her hair, or at least he hoped she would, because that was now part of his plan. Sure enough, not two minutes into the lunch meeting, she complained that she was a little depressed because she "couldn't do a thing with her hair this morning."

"It looks fine to me, mom."

"You don't know about women's hair, Casey."

"You're right, I don't." He paused a moment, then said, "But, I'll tell you what. I've got an idea. Out in my car, I have a gift certificate that I bought Andrea months ago that I would like you to use to get your hair and nails done. Let's try to get an appointment today, and you'll be beautiful for the week."

"Men. You are clueless. You can't just call and get an appointment for today. It takes months to get in. Plus, I have my own favorite stylist, Sonia."

"Who you introduced Andrea to ... remember? It's for your salon, mom. But, you're right, I don't know anything, but it was worth a try. It's probably expired anyhow."

"Expired? When does it expire?"

Casey knew it was not even close to expiration, but he said, "I don't know. I just thought since you said you weren't happy with your hair, it might work for you today. I guess I'd better hook up with some girl soon, or it will expire for sure. It was just an idea. Forget it. Let's see what we're going to order."

"Hair and nails, huh?" she said as she looked at her fingernails. "I'll tell you what. I'll go call Sonia, and see if she has a spot available, but I doubt it."

Sure, if you want to try. I'll get us both a bowl of chowder while you make the call."

"Okay." Bonnie got up and made her way to the phone, Casey laughed at the thought that after all these years of being manipulated, once in a while he could turn the tables on Bonnie.

"I can't believe it," Bonnie said on her return to the table. "Sonia has an opening at 1:15, and I can get my nails done right afterwards. I'll do it, Casey." She reached across the table and patted his cheek. "Thank you for being so thoughtful."

"You are welcome."

As they finished lunch, Bonnie said, "Casey, honey, I left in such a hurry this morning, and Ralph was asleep when I left, so I didn't get to feed him. Now, I barely have enough time to get to Sonia's for the appointment. Would you please go by the house and feed him on your way home?"

"Be happy to." "This will not be a problem," he thought, "since I'll be going there anyhow."

"He gave Bonnie the Gift Certificate and they parted ways, and as she got to her car, she waved back at him like a schoolgirl waving goodbye to her benevolent daddy who just gave her the keys to the family car.

Steve Davis

When he got to the Tyler home on Walnut Drive, he greeted Ralph and fed him. The old dog's arthritis was getting the best of him, but he still had good days occasionally, and neither Casey nor Bonnie had the courage, at this time, to consider letting him go.

After feeding Ralph, Casey went to the drawer in the kitchen and retrieved his father's .38 snub nosed off-duty revolver, which had been fired at the intruder two nights earlier, and carefully retrieved another .38 revolver Sonny had worn on duty very early in his career from the shelf in the closet, without disturbing anything else. He carefully closed the closet door to within one inch of the door jamb, just as it was before.

He locked up and went straight to the Sheriff's office with the guns in a paper bag. At the office, he entered through the back door and quietly made his way to Ty Randolph's office, several doors down from Sergeant Regan's office, the door of which was closed.

Randolph always had country music just a little louder than needed, and when he saw Casey, he reached up to turn the volume down, but Casey stopped him.

"Hey, Casey, I got your note. What can I do for you?'

Casey leaned over to be clearly heard with the music in the background. "Ty, I need a big favor right away. And I need it done on the QT for now. In this bag are two .38 revolvers. I need you to do a test fire on them and compare them later to the slugs from my dad's murder. I need the guns back in two hours max. Don't ask for any more info unless, of course, they match. I don't expect them to, so it won't matter whose they are. Okay? Favor? Just between you and me. I don't want Don to get implicated in the deal. Will you do it?"

Randolph held his finger up to his mouth in a gesture of silence. He scooped up the bag and walked out the door and down the hall to the elevator to go down to the weapons testing facility in the basement.

Casey went the other direction in the hallway, and entered Sergeant Regan's office. He could see he slightly startled Regan again, who was poring again over the case files on his desk.

"Startled you again?" Casey asked.

"Yes, I always get a little jumpy when I'm close to closing a case and looking for that one last nail in the coffin," Regan said.

"Sounds good. What do you have in mind?"

"Randy Allen. If it's not Snider, then the attack last night was staged to frame Snider. If the attack on your mom was staged, then Randy Allen is the only known suspect who could have pulled it off, planted the 4x4 which gave us the right to search Snider's shed, which led to the discovery of the murder license plate. Do you still talk to that Officer who keeps in touch with Randy Allen? I'd sure like to know where Randy was on that night. Think he'd be able to inquire surreptitiously?"

"Sure, I'll try."

Regan continued, "We dusted the license plate for prints and found several on it. We forwarded them to the Department of Justice crime lab for identification. We put a 'homicide' expedite request on it so they should come back soon. Maybe we'll get lucky and find Randy's prints on them. He could never explain that away."

"I need your help on another thing, Casey. We need to know what connection Randy Allen had with the arrests of Eduardo Corona and Tony Garcia. Remember his initials were on the arrest reports, we need to know why."

"Okay, Don, I'll work on it."

"When I left Friday night, you were engrossed in the files. Did you find anything interesting?"

"No, not really."

"Not really? That's not very convincing."

"Just a thought I had. I'll tell you about it later. I need to get on the Randy Allen-Eduardo Corona connection."

"I'm not fond of secrets …"

Casey's end of the conversation was saved by a tap on the door, and Ty Randolph stepped in and said, "I thought you might be here Casey. I have that old lab coat you asked for in my office. Stop by on the way out."

As Randolph turned to leave, Casey got up and said, "Okay, Don, I'll keep you posted," as he quickly exited through the closing door.

He followed Randolph to his office and closed the door. "Thanks, Ty. When do you think you will know the results of the comparison?"

"Just because you're new in this office, rookie, doesn't mean I am. What do you think I been doing while you two were chit-chatting?" Turning serious, he said, "The guns don't match the murder weapon, so you don't have to worry about her any more.

"Her?"

"Yeah, or whoever." He winked and smiled at Casey's obvious relief. "By the way, I hope your mom's feeling better after her ordeal."

"Yes, she is. I'll pass on your good wishes." He sheepishly held his finger to his lips."

Casey was not fully relieved until the guns were replaced at his mom's house, and he was gone before she returned from the beauty salon.

When he got home, he called back to Bonnie's house and was relieved to hear the answer machine kick in, because he didn't want to get an earful of his mom's reaction to Alden Snider's release. "Hey, mom, this is Casey, I just wanted to let you know that Alden Snider has been released from jail on bail. Be careful, and give me a call when you want to."

Though pleased he had pulled it off, he scolded himself for considering his own mother a person of interest. "At least now I can concentrate on Randy and Snider, and not have that nagging at me."

Section Fourteen

The Fingerprint

The next day Casey was scheduled to work the afternoon shift on the CHP. When he walked into the briefing room, everyone began asking questions about the attack on Bonnie, the arrest of Alden Snider, and the license plate evidence connecting Snider to the Sonny Tyler murder. He was surprised they already knew so much about the incident. He also couldn't bear to reveal that, after seventeen plus years of trying to get evidence against Snider, he and Sergeant Regan were starting to question Snider's guilt, so he just said they were looking at clearing up some loose ends and hoped to file murder charges soon.

The shift Sergeant entered the room to start the briefing and handed him a phone message as he passed. "This just came in. Sergeant Brown said it was urgent. Let me guess. Looks like we'll be short-handed again tonight," he said, not even attempting to cover his growing impatience about too many missed shifts by one of his officers.

"Sorry, Sarge," Casey said, as he excused himself and stepped out of the room. He didn't call Regan, but instead drove immediately to the Detectives' office.

Upon arrival, he was directed to the Sheriff's conference room, where Regan, Ty Randolph, and other detectives were busily perusing case files spread across the huge conference table. A makeshift barrier across the table divided two separate case files.

"This looks big; what's up?" Casey asked.

"This." Regan responded, handing Casey a piece of paper. "The Department of Justice Report came back."

Casey quickly scanned down the page until he got to the FINDINGS section. He paused in disbelief at the name that jumped out at him. "Holy Shit!"

"Not exactly what we expected, was it?"

"Tony Garcia? Tony Garcia's fingerprints were found on the license plate?"

"Yep. I wouldn't have been surprised if Eduardo Corona's prints were there, but I never expected Tony Garcia's"

"If Tony Garcia handled the plate, he obviously was the one who cold-plated the white Chevy my dad stopped. He wouldn't have known an 'A' series license plate would be wrong on a late model car. He had to be the killer, only to be killed himself an hour later."

Regan mulled the new possibilities, "We know Garcia was killed south of town an hour later selling drugs. Maybe Sonny found the drugs on Garcia, who got the jump on him and killed Sonny north of town and then got himself killed dealing the same drugs an hour later south of town. Your dad must have found the drugs on him that he was en-route to sell."

"Why would he be driving north when he was stopped, then shot south of town an hour later? Doesn't make sense."

"Maybe he was driving north to get the drugs to sell?"

"If so, why shoot my dad if he was clean at the time?"

"Maybe he was afraid he'd go to jail for some other reason. Maybe Sonny asked him about the plates and he knew he'd get busted. Maybe your dad saw a gun or some other contraband?"

"I don't think so. Dad never had a chance to even talk to him. The footsteps at the scene seemed to indicate it was a deliberate, premeditated act; at least once he was stopped. The killer knew he was going to kill my dad, and he wasted no time doing it. Remember? The killer walked directly up to dad and shot him point blank. But why?"

"Remember, your dad had arrested him once before. Maybe he just snapped."

"And here's another thing. What happened to the white Chevy? Wasn't Garcia driving his wife's car when he got killed an hour later? And where is the murder weapon? Wouldn't it be with Garcia? Neither murder weapon has ever been identified."

"Maybe Snider put him up to the murder. Snider gives him his car, he kills your dad, and Snider kills him an hour later and gets his car back. Never mind that. No way. Forget it. That would be too stupid, even for Snider. Hire a hit man and let him drive your car for the hit? And then keep the cold plate for a souvenir. No way."

"Maybe Randy Allen hired him, and then killed him an hour later to cover the crime."

"That makes more sense. A lot of planning went into this murder, yet your dad was killed immediately after making the stop, like it was intended all along. I knew Tony Garcia, and he wouldn't have gone to that much trouble to shoot someone. He'd have just done it. The other crimes are more sophisticated. This has the earmarks of a mastermind murder for hire."

"The person who hired Tony knew dad would stop the car for the license plate violation. Allen would know that any good Chippie would immediately know the plate didn't match a late-model Chevy. All he had to do was get dad to follow the car."

"The phony accident call!"

"Exactly. Dad goes to the location of the phony call. Soon as he calls it in as GOA, the white Chevy drives by in front of him. Dad follows him and makes the stop on a deserted road the driver has lured him to. No conversation, and the killer meets him between the cars and pulls out a gun and shoots him just above his vest; as if he had been told Sonny would be wearing one."

"Garcia wouldn't know Sonny's schedule, he wouldn't know about the license plate thing, or the vest, or how to make it look like a traffic stop that went bad, but Randy Allen sure would."

"Randy had easy access to Plus P ammo, knew dad's schedule, knew how to call in a phony call, knew Sonny wore a vest, and that he would stop the car for the license plate violation, and he knew the old plate would be untraceable."

"And, above all that, he is the only person who had a motive; to save his job. Casey, you've got to go over those arrest reports again and run them by your office and find out how Randy Allen's initials got on those reports in the 1960's. That is a critical piece of information to link Allen to Garcia and Corona."

"Oh Shit! … Shit!" Their conversation was interrupted by Ty Randolph, behind them, who had been perusing the two now-connected cases spread out on the conference tables behind them. "You are NOT going to like this, Don." He handed Regan a photo from the Tony Garcia murder case files.

Regan grimaced as he looked at the black and white photo Randolph handed him. "Oh. No! This was in the Garcia case files? All along?"

"Yes. I was looking through ... there must be a hundred photos in the envelope ... and there it is. It just jumped out at me."

"What? What?" asked Casey.

Regan handed the photo to Casey with a heavy sigh. "This is the left boot of Tony Garcia; taken at his murder scene, an hour after the same boot left a print at your dad's murder scene."

"Oh, Crap."

"That about says it all," Randolph said. "Right downstairs in front of us all this time."

As the significance of the find sunk in, Regan sat down in a nearby chair, and said, "Shit! All this time. ... seventeen fucking years under our noses. They were connected all along. I've been through these files a hundred times. How could I have missed this photo? This changes EVERYTHING. Now I've got to tell the world how bad we screwed up seventeen years ago."

The Press Conference

The local media were assembled the next morning, including Times-Standard reporter Jeff Olsen for the highly anticipated news conference hastily called by Humboldt County Sheriff Scott Crawford to discuss "New evidence in two seventeen-year-old cold murder cases, including the murder of CHP Officer Sonny Tyler."

The din of the conversations stopped immediately when Sheriff Crawford and CHP Commander Jerry Webster entered the room, accompanied by Sergeant Regan and Casey. Sheriff Crawford approached the microphone. Although Regan and Crawford knew the revelation would be an embarrassment to the Department, they knew the Tyler case was too big, and the information too important, to think they could stall or avoid the humiliation that they would receive.

"Thank you, ladies and gentlemen, for coming here today," Sheriff Crawford began. "We have some exciting news regarding the seventeen-year-old unsolved homicide of CHP Officer Sonny Tyler. Tonight, we are prepared to reveal that we have identified the person who shot and killed Officer Sonny Tyler in 1970. Detective Sergeant Don Regan is going to fill you in on the details. Sergeant Regan?"

The small group of newsmen jostled for position as Sergeant Regan stepped to the podium and got straight to the point. "Ladies and Gentlemen, many of you are aware that on October 15, 1970, CHP Officer Sonny Tyler was brutally murdered on a traffic stop on Greenwood Heights Drive, north of Eureka. Some of you might recall that on the same date, about an hour later, a second murder occurred in Sequoia Park south of town. Tony Garcia, a known gang member was gunned down in cold blood behind the snack bar. Both murders were investigated by separate homicide investigation teams, who shared information and determined, at the time, that they were unrelated. Until yesterday, both murders were unsolved and believed to be unrelated."

A murmur of anticipation filtered through the media as he continued. "That changed yesterday. Last week, as you know, we arrested Alden Snider for an unprovoked attack on Bonnie Tyler, the widow of Officer Tyler. During that investigation and arrest, we uncovered a license plate at Snider's home that conclusively linked him to the Tyler murder scene.

Yesterday, we received the lab report from DOJ who analyzed the fingerprints found on the license plate. Those prints have been positively identified as being from Tony Garcia, the second murder victim that morning.

Also, yesterday, in reviewing the files with this new evidence in mind, we found that crime scene photos of Tony Garcia's left boot appear to identically match the boot prints found at the Tyler murder scene.

"If you are skeptical, as we were, as to how this might have occurred in such a short time frame, I have prepared these point by point comparison photos from the plaster casts at Officer Tyler's murder, and the boots of Tony Garcia. You will have to agree this appears to be an exact match."

He paused to let the effect of the photos sink in to the media assembled. Just as one reporter started to ask a question, "So, Sergeant, …"

Regan continued, "So far, it appears that Tony Garcia, wearing these boots, murdered Officer Tyler, northbound, north of Eureka, at about 5:52 am, and then he, himself, was murdered in Sequoia Park at about 6:40 am, still wearing these boots. Driving time between these points is about 20 minutes, so there was enough time to get from one place to the other with about 25 minutes to spare. The good news is that we have apparently solved the 'who, what, when and where' of Sonny Tyler's murder, but the bad news is we still don't know the 'why', and that may be the most important factor in his murder, and perhaps will lead to the identity of the murderer of Tony Garcia, also."

We will continue to review both cases and see if there is any other thread of connection between the two. We have theories we will pursue, and we hope to gain information in the coming weeks as we aggressively pursue these new leads. This is, nevertheless, a giant break in the investigations and we knew you would want to know. We will attempt to answer your questions now, if it doesn't compromise either investigation."

"Does this mean that Alden Snider has been cleared of the crime after all these years?" a reporter asked.

"Actually, no. Mr. Snider remains a suspect, until we can explain how the license plate from the murderer's vehicle was found in Snider's shed."

Steve Davis

"So, you think Snider and Garcia acted together to kill Tyler?"

"I didn't say that. I am just reporting a new revelation in the case. We are looking at numerous possible scenarios, including the possibility that Garcia acted alone, or that he was hired to kill Officer Tyler and was then murdered by the accomplice."

Jeff Olson had been waiting for this day for seventeen years. He had never forgotten the manner in which Sergeant Regan embarrassed him at the scene of the first murder. Now, it would be his time to turn the tables on the Detective. "Sergeant Regan, are you saying that the very evidence you are now showing us has been sitting on a shelf in your basement next to each other for seventeen years, and it took until yesterday to notice?"

Casey, Sergeant Regan, and Sheriff Tatum winced at the manner in which Olson had struck for the jugular. Before they could respond, Olson continued, "How could it be that the two homicides were being investigated at the same time by the same Department, and no-one ever compared the cases for a connection?"

Regan stepped back up to the podium and addressed Jeff Olson directly without hesitation. "I'll tell you what I know about that, 'Jeffrey'." He intentionally used the reporter's full name, parenthetically, because he knew Olson would relate it to his earlier career, and the incident when they first met at the murder scene, and he wanted Olson to know that he, Regan, was still not to be trifled with.

"I am more than a little embarrassed at that myself," Regan continued, "I will tell you what we think happened, Jeffrey. We had a small detective squad in 1970, and the CHP slaying was the biggest case we had ever seen. It got the majority of the attention, from our homicide team, and the media as well. I'm sure you recall that, don't you Jeffrey? In fact, as I recall, you were there, at the scene, weren't you?"

"Yes, sir." Olson responded, rather sheepishly compared to a moment before. Somehow, he was now on the defensive, and he hoped Regan wouldn't mention how he threw up at his first homicide. He decided then and there not to attempt to embarrass Sergeant Regan again … ever.

Sergeant Regan sensed his point had been made with Olson, and continued. "We threw ourselves into the case and worked it twenty-four hours a day for weeks and for months thereafter. We assembled a second homicide

-- 377 --

team to work the Garcia murder, which appeared to be a clear-cut drug murder. Investigators compared the cases for a connection, but due to the unique locations and circumstances of each case, we also speculated that it was too close in time, too far in distance, and too dissimilar in nature, to be logically connected. The other team never inspected the plaster casts from our scene, and they went back to their regular assignments after they finished their investigation. Later, I looked over their files, but I just never noticed the detail of the boot on the photo of Tony Garcia. I still find it incredible that they are related, but these photos don't lie."

Another reporter stood up and introduced himself as a representative of Channel 6 TV. "Before I came here this morning, I looked though our files from 1970. The cases still seem unrelated to me. The Tyler murder just seems like a traffic stop that went bad. Wasn't the killer driving a white Chevy? It was noted at the time that Garcia didn't own a white Chevy. What happened to the white Chevy? How could Garcia have killed the Officer northbound north of town driving a white Chevy, which he didn't own, and end up dead south of the city in another car less than an hour later? Our notes indicated a witness, a homeless man, who described the drug deal in detail. I'm not convinced they are connected, Sergeant Regan."

"We have asked, and will continue to ask, those same questions over the next months. But let me assure you, these photos don't lie and the boots appear to have been on Garcia for a while."

"That is all we have to share at this time. If further information is to be revealed, we will issue a press release. Thank you." They walked out of the room together, and left the reporters talking excitedly among themselves.

Back in the Detective's Office, Captain Webster congratulated Regan and his team for clearing up the cold case murder.

"I'd like to say I'm proud, Captain, but we just changed the game, that's all. For seventeen and a half years we had no solution to the crime, then two days ago, we figured out Snider was our killer, then I thought it was Randy Allen, and the next day, we prove El Gato was the killer. Now I think Randy Allen hired Garcia to kill Sonny. We are starting to look like a bunch of Inspector Clouseau's. We still have another daunting task. Who killed Garcia? Was he hired by Randy to kill Sonny? And where are the murder weapons? We just changed the focus a little, and maybe not that much at all. Someone still wanted Sonny dead; we need to find out why."

"Well, everyone on the CHP, right up to the Commissioner, knows now that I assigned Casey to the team, and no-one has directed me to remove him, so let's just keep going until I'm told to put him back on the road."

"Great, Captain. Thanks. We'll try to get some answers soon. This puts a lot of pressure on the killer. I have an idea we will hear from him again, soon."

Section Fifteen

March, 1988 - The Parolee and the Big Gun

The chipped bark and wood chips crackled under the weight of the tires as the car turned off the highway and into the abandoned forest log deck. The entry gate, a steel beam on a pivoting steel post, was swung wide open, and a quick glance on the ground revealed the intact padlock and broken chain discarded alongside the post, just as the driver had left them several hours earlier. The driver paused briefly at the entrance and let the headlights slowly play across the emptiness and onto the small remaining pile of logs at the back of the clearing. As expected, another set of fresh tire marks were clearly visible entering the large, now-abandoned log clearing.

The driver of the vehicle took a quick glance backward to be sure they he was indeed alone, then steered toward the log pile, and stopped about 40 yards short, and turned the headlights off. The door opened without delay, and a slightly built shadowy figure slipped quietly out of the car and stood by the left front fender. The macabre figure wore black clothing topped by a dark hooded sweatshirt tied loosely, close to the face.

After a few moments, another person emerged from behind the log pile and slowly walked toward the car. A huge dark-skinned black man, he was dressed in black loose-fitting clothing that blended naturally with the night. Instead of directly approaching the first figure, he walked toward the passenger side of the car and looked inside as if he expected to see someone else. He completed his circle of the car and asked, "You Snider?"

"Yep," said the smaller of the two.

"You alone?" the big man said.

"I said I'd be alone. Let's cut the crap. You got it? Or are we going to stand around and chit chat all night?"

"Easy, man. Ain't no need to get all uptight and all that. We gonna do some business, but first I gotta make sure I ain't gonna get burned or nothin'. You know what I mean?"

"Yeah, yeah, but I'm kind of in a hurry, if you know what I mean."

"You kinda mouthy for a small man, all alone out here in the middle of nowhere, tough talking to a big parolee. Now we both know I got a big gun," he said as he pulled a huge .44 caliber revolver from his waistband, "and we know you ain't got no gun or we wouldn't be doin' business out here."

He began to wave the big gun around as he spoke. "And, now I gotta ask myself, 'Why is this guy, with no gun, talkin' shit to a bad ass like me, who does got a gun'. You know what I think? I think you got a lot of help around the corner. I think maybe you're a cop, or you're working for 'the man', and you're wired or something."

"Okay, Okay. Look, I'm kind of nervous. I'm no cop, and I'm not working for no damn 'man'. Like I told you on the phone, I just need a gun to kill my wife. Maybe we should forget the whole thing. I think I should go now."

"Why you want to kill your wife, Mister Snider?" he sneered, "You catch the bitch fucking someone else?"

"I don't think we need to go into all that."

"You think you actually got the balls to shoot the bitch, Mister Snider?"

"Look. You going to sell me a gun or not? Cause if you aren't going to sell me a gun, forget it, I'm out of here!"

"Easy, buddy. I didn't come all the way up here to just 'forget it'. We got business to do here. Show me the money, $1,000, like we agreed."

"Okay, that's better." He reached into the car and pulled out a brown McDonald's paper bag. "Here is the money; small bills, like I promised."

The large man looked into the paper bag at the bundles of fives, tens, and twenties. "Man, Snider," he said as he began to wave the gun around in the air. "You're either a snitch or the dumbest mother fucker ever, meeting a big ex-con with a gun out here in the middle of nowhere with a bag full of money. You're a dumb shit, either way. What makes you sure I won't kill you and take the money and leave you out here to rot?

"You ... You wouldn't do that, would you?"

"Hell yes! I wouldn't even blink an eye doin' it. You thinking I'm a nice guy? You know I just got out, how the fuck you think I got into prison?"

"I think I better go."

"Yeah, I think so. And hey, Mister Snider, maybe you should leave that bag of money on the ground, or else something might happen to you on the way home carrying all that money."

"You're going to rip me off, aren't you?"

"Uh … Hell, yes. You're too god damn stupid," the big man laughed out loud, "The only reason I ain't gonna kill you is you need me. Let's consider this a down payment for the job you need done. You ain't got the balls to kill your bitch, Mister Snider, so you ain't gonna need no gun. But I'm gonna need the gun to kill the bitch for you, so call me when you get some more money and we'll get the job done. And you won't even have to get your hands dirty. Have a nice night, Mister Snider."

With that, the big man picked up the bag at his feet and turned back toward the log pile. "Too fuckin' stupid to live, too fuckin' stupid to kill," he muttered to himself as he walked away.

He hadn't taken three steps when the smaller man calmly drew a hand gun from under the parka and holding it with a two-handed grip, fired two rounds directly into the back of the big man, just above the shoulder blades. The impact knocked him forward, dropping the bag, staggering, but he didn't fall. As he started to turn slowly back toward the shooter, straining to raise the gun in his hand, the shooter fired another bullet into his chest, which caused him to stagger back one step. His eyes rolled back, and he staggered forward, as he tried again to bring the gun up to fire it, the shooter fired one last time, hitting him between the eyes. His knees immediately buckled and he crumpled to the ground, hard and fast with a thud.

Without a word, the smaller man stood over the fallen man, took aim at his head and began to squeeze another shot, then thought better of it since the big man was obviously dead. He reached down, scooped up the handgun and the bag of money, and stepped backward away from the body.

In the distance, the crackle of wood chips from near the log pile caught his attention.

"Who's there?"

There was no answer, only silence.

"Come out, now, or I'll come get you," he ordered, even though he had no intention of doing so.

His bluff was immediately answered by a gunshot in his direction from behind the log pile, the projectile whizzing by his head, narrowly missing him.

"Holy Shit." Ducking down behind the fallen big man, he fired the final two rounds from his own weapon toward the location where he thought the shots had come from. Seconds later, he fired two more, much louder gunshots from the weapon taken from the dead man.

Those shots were still ringing through the night air, when they were answered by two more shots from the woodpile, then he heard footsteps running from the log pile across the open area and into the forest behind the log deck.

The killer got quickly to his feet and ran to his parked car. Starting the engine while lying across the seat, he sat up and cranked the wheel hard left and skidding in a half circle, he bolted through the open gate onto the highway, and disappeared into the night.

Murder Déjà vu

"16-21, Humboldt."

"Humboldt, 16-21, go ahead."

"16-21, 10-19 the Sheriff's Office. See Sergeant Regan, A.S.A.P."

"Humboldt, 16-21, 10-4, advise the Sergeant and adjacent units I'll be away from my beat for a while."

Whenever he got a call of this type, Casey's heart would race, knowing that it meant some new development in the old homicide case. Sometimes it was big news, and sometimes much less, but always a new development of some type. But today … today was Sunday. It would be unusual for Sergeant Regan to be in the office on a Sunday. Whatever he wanted, it had to be important. He turned the big Dodge through the highway divider and gunned it for the Sheriff's Office in Eureka.

When he walked through the door of the Detective's office, Sergeant Regan was sitting in the chair with his feet on the desk, talking to another Detective. Casey could see from the smile on Sergeant Regan's face that this had the potential to be a big development.

"It must be something good to get you down here on a Sunday, Don."

"It just might be, Casey. Listen to this," he said, "We had a new homicide last night. According to the report, our victim, a male black named Big Mike Owens, is a parolee up from the Bay Area who gets himself snuffed on a deserted log deck up past Blue Lake. Our Deputies respond to a 'gunshots fired' call and find the victim shot twice in the back, once in the chest, and a coup-de-gras between the eyes for effect. Then, another parolee, guy named Chaka something walks out of the woods and tells the Deputies a wild story about how he and his buddy drove up from SF to meet some guy to sell him a gun to kill his wife."

"I don't understand what that has to do with my dad's case."

"I'm getting to that. This gets good. Big Mike is supposed to be alone, but he brings this Chaka guy along, and they decide to double-cross the guy and take his money, since they have guns and he doesn't have a gun.

Steve Davis

But the local guy <u>does</u> have a gun, and he double-double-crosses them, and kills Big Mike. Cold blooded. Shoots him in the back, then a head shot, then he steals the gun and steals his money back."

"I'm still drawing a blank on the connection."

"Oh, you will, Casey, my man. Now, think about it a second and see if this doesn't start to sound familiar. A local thug, wearing a black hooded sweat shirt or parka, solicits a dirtbag parolee to sell him a gun. They meet in a dark deserted place, and when the parolee tries to consummate the deal, Bam! He gets blown away for his trouble, cold blood, bang, bang. The local thug takes the gun and the money and splits. Sound familiar?"

"The Garcia murder?" Casey said with subdued excitement, as the facts slowly began to sink in.

"Exactly. It's the gang banger murder all over again. I'm not sure how this all fits in, but it's too close not to fit in, and it gives us the first real <u>live</u> lead we've had in a while. Oh. And here is the best part. The victim only knew the guy by his name: "Snider.""

"Snider? No shit, Alden Snider?"

"He didn't hear a first name, but he definitely called him 'Snider'."

"So, where is this witness?"

"He's in the jail right now. Crime scene, dead body, one survivor, gunshot residue on his hands, violation of parole, plenty of probable cause. He can't wait to talk to us. I thought you might like to help me interview him?"

"Beautiful! Do I get to be the black hat or the white hat?" Casey laughed as they walked out of the room.

Chaka Andrews was already seated all alone at the grey metal table, looking forlornly at the floor, when Casey and Sergeant Regan entered the interview room. As they introduced themselves, Andrews said, "Look, man, I didn't shoot Big Mike. I ain't never shot a gun at no-one till last night, and that was just 'cause the other dude was shootin' at me. Check it out, I'm not a violent person, that's why I keep Big Mike around. It was that 'Snider' dude. That bastard shot him in the back."

"Whoa a minute there, partner," Regan said, "You are getting ahead of us. First we've got to advise you of your rights."

"Don't need to man, I <u>want</u> to talk about it"

Casey smiled imperceptibly. They weren't going to need the good cop – bad cop approach with this guy, he was singing like a canary and they hadn't even started yet.

"I do need to," Regan persisted, "Those Supreme Court wackos say we have to, so just bear with us. You have the right to remain silent. Anything you say can and will be used against you in a court of law. You have the right to have an attorney present anytime you are being questioned, and if you can't afford an attorney, one will be appointed to represent you free of charge. Do you understand these rights that I just explained to you?"

"Yeah, man, like I said, I didn't….."

"Not so fast, my friend. Having those rights in mind, do you want to talk to us now?"

"Yeah, man. Like, when do I get to tell you my side of the story?"

"Right now. Tell us what happened."

"OK. Big Mike just got out of the joint about a week ago, and me and him was hanging out at his girlfriend's in Hayward, and Mike gets a call from another brother who says someone wants to buy a gun. Mike says he has a piece and he'll sell if for a grand. A little later the phone rings and it's this guy who calls himself 'Snider'. I can only hear Mike talking, but he repeats everything so I know what's being said. Anyways, this 'Snider' dude tells Mike he needs a gun to kill his wife."

"Did you hear, or did Mike tell you Snider's first name?"

"I'm not sure, I just heard Mike calling him by the last name."

"What's the other man's name who called Mike?"

"You kidding, man? I tell you that and I'm a dead man. You couldn't protect me. A fuckin' dead man is what I'd be."

"You fall for this murder, and you might be dead anyhow. Who was it?"

"Screw you guys, man. I might be dead if I don't tell; and I'm 'for sure' dead if I do. No way. You want to hear the story, or not?"

"Okay. Go ahead with the story."

"Somehow, this Snider guy knows that Big Mike just got out of the joint and says he'll pay the grand for the .44 magnum if Mike comes up to Eureka and delivers it exactly as directed. Says to go to the McDonalds in Eureka and look at the base of the trash can for a Burger King bag and follow the directions inside." Casey and Regan exchanged glances at the mention of the McDonald's and Burger King bags.

Willie continued, "Me and Mike drive up there and he lets me out before he goes to the McDonalds, in case we was being watched. He finds the bag and it has a map and says to meet Snider at this old log fuckin' place out in the middle of nowhere at like 9 p.m. We got there real early, and it's dark as shit and I'm scared. I just knew something was going to go real wrong. Mike laughs at me and calls me his 'little bitch', but I knew; I just knew. I hid in the car while Mike pulled around and parked behind the logs. We waited about an hour and then this car pulls in to the area and stops."

"What kind of car was it?"

"I don't know. It had bright lights, but then they went out and we couldn't see anything. I was hiding so he wouldn't see me and I barely saw him, but I could hear them both.

"What did Snider look like?"

"Me and Mike almost laughed when we saw him. He was a frickin' pussy; a wimp. He was about the size of my girlfriend, Tisha, but he talked real big."

Casey passed Regan a note that said, 'Doesn't sound like Alden Snider,' to which Regan nodded.

Andrews continued, "Big Mike got out while I hid, and met him at his car. Next thing, the guy gets mouthy with Big Mike and starts talking tough. Mike stops him and says, "Screw you, you fuckin' little mouse." Mike takes the bag of money from him and keeps the gun and tells Snider, "You little pussy. Call me if you want your old lady snuffed, 'cause you ain't got the balls to do it yourself." Mike turns around to come back to the car, and Snider pulls out a gun and shoots him twice in the back, then one more time, and then in the face, real cold like. What'd he need a gun for, if he already had one? I'm like real scared, man, and I must have moved or made a noise or something, 'cause Snider turns to where I'm hiding, and starts to shoot at me. I had another piece that Mike gave me, just in case, and I shot at him to scare him off. Then he shoots back at me with a really big gun, I think it was Mike's gun, -- that sucker was loud – so I ran into the forest until the cops got there and I gave up."

"Where's the note?"

"I don't know. It must be in the car."

"Whose car is it?"

"Hell if I know. Mike just lifted it for the ride."

"Glad none of us stopped him en-route," Casey muttered to Regan.

After the interview, Regan and Casey returned to the Detective's office. Both men were deep in their individual thoughts, when Casey broke the silence. "McDonalds and directions in a bag," he said resolutely. "Where have I heard that before?"

"Well, it doesn't sound like Alden Snider, but Snider may have paid for the hit, or the killer wants us to think its Snider, if Big Mike gets caught."

"The guy is good. Three murders and a dead hit man, and we don't have squat. They're all related, but we can't figure out how. The more we try … the closer we get, the more people end up dying."

"If we are right, the killer last night is the same guy who killed Tony Garcia, who killed my dad."

"McDonalds. Note in a bag. Not to mention the same guy who hired Eduardo Corona to kill you. They are all connected. We've got to find the common thread, and keep working it until we get our man."

Casey looked at his watch. "Let's get going on it tomorrow morning. Oops, make that Tuesday morning; I told the office I'd work days tomorrow. They're shorthanded."

"Okay, Casey, see you then. I'll be working on it till I see you. Oh, by the way, what'd you find out about Randy Allen's whereabouts on the night your mom was assaulted?"

"Interesting. My mutual friend said that Randy was in Sacramento with his family. Sound familiar?"

"Yes. Sacramento family seems to call for him every time someone gets assaulted or killed in this case. I'll bet he was probably in Sacramento last night, too. How are you coming along on the Garcia-Corona-Randy Allen connection?"

"I'm working on a possibility. Tracking down an old timer who was with dad on one of the arrests. I'll let you know what I find."

Section Sixteen

The Secret Code

It was two days later before Casey was able to track down retired Officer Brice Tomlinson. He hoped Tomlinson, who assisted Sonny Tyler on the Eduardo Corona traffic stop in 1967, might recall the case and provide information on Randy Allen's role in the case. Tomlinson retired about fifteen years earlier and lived quietly just outside of Orick, about 40 miles north of Eureka. Casey drove up to the clean, nicely landscaped home on a side street about a quarter mile east of Highway 101. Casey reached inside and opened the white picket gate which provided access to the sidewalk which led to the front door. He could hear a small dog barking inside as he rapped three times on the front door and waited.

He was about to knock again when he heard the door being unlocked from inside. Seconds later the door opened and he was greeted by the much older, but still recognizable, face of the man who Casey remembered as old when he met him several times as a child. The man looked at the young uniformed Officer standing in the doorway stoop and frowned. "What can I do for you, young man?"

"Hello, Officer Tomlinson. I'm Casey Tyler. My dad was Sonny Tyler. You used to work with him before he was killed. That's why I'm here."

"Hello, Casey. I think I read somewhere that you were in the area looking for your dad's killer. Any luck?"

"Yes, and no, sir. The newspaper kind of blew my role in the investigation out of proportion. But I'd like to ask you some questions that came up, if you don't mind."

"Come in, Casey. I remember you as a child. I'll never forget seeing you at the funeral and wondering what would become of you without Sonny's influence. He was a good cop, although I didn't like him for a while after he got here. He worked so hard, making arrests and stuff that we all had to work a little harder, and I had gotten pretty lazy up here. There wasn't much in the way of expectations for a Chippie back then."

He directed Casey into a small but well-furnished living room. Well-furnished if you liked the semi-antique furniture of the 1940's and 50's. The once overstuffed couch, now sagging, had a strip of walnut trim accentuating the curving top, with matching wood trimmed armrests. Reprints of classic old paintings adorned the walls as they had during the era.

"Make yourself at home. He motioned to an empty Queen Ann chair opposite the couch. He instinctively reached for and turned on a glass lamp base with a frilly tiffany lampshade. The room looked like, other than dusting occasionally, it hadn't been rearranged in twenty years.

Seeing Casey taking in the furnishings, he added, "The place looks just like it did in the 1970's when Ruth died. Never saw the need to change it. It's good enough for me and Daisy. There's just the two of us now."

"I'm sorry about Ruth," Casey said.

"Thanks. We'll be together soon I figure. Say, didn't I read recently where they think the other fellow that got murdered that morning was actually the killer of Sonny. Is that true?"

"Yes, it is. But we still don't know why, and there are a number of things that just don't quite fit, so we're still digging for more information, which is why I'm here. Can I ask you some questions?"

"That was a long time ago. Actually, I was off that day, so I wasn't involved in any way."

"I know, sir, but I'm hoping you can shed some light on another arrest by my dad that happened three years earlier. You assisted him on the stop."

"Three years earlier? I don't know. I have a hard time remembering to take my pills, much less a traffic stop I assisted another Officer on twenty years ago. But if it will help, I'll try. Do you have a name or location to refresh my memory?"

"Better yet, I have a copy of the report. Here it is." He pulled the report from the file that he carried, and handed it to the old man, whose hands quivered as he took the papers. "Can you hand me those glasses on the table behind you?"

Casey handed the glasses to him, and he put them on one handed, almost poking himself in the eye with the temple. "Damn eyes. Can't see a thing anymore without these coke bottle lenses. Did I mention I have Glaucoma?"

"No, you didn't," Casey answered, hoping Tomlinson wouldn't go on about it. Luckily, Tomlinson began to read the report and didn't expound on his medical condition.

Casey looked around the room as Tomlinson read the report very carefully, pausing to flip the pages back and forth as he refreshed his mind. On the buffet table behind the dining room table, he could see a shrine of photos of a woman he thought he recalled seeing maybe once at a picnic in the late 1960's.

"It just isn't ringing a bell, Casey. I do remember it, vaguely, but pretty much everything I remember is what the report says. Why is this arrest important? Is this the guy that got killed that same day?"

"No, he is another individual involved later in the case."

"One other thing, if you remember, what did Randy Allen have to do with this case?"

"Randy Allen? Nothing. I stayed away from that guy at all times. He was bad news. No, I remember standing there watching the Mexican while your dad searched the car and found the bag of stolen jewelry. I stored the car for Sonny, who took him to jail. Randy never was there."

"Are you certain? See on the report, here, next to dad's signature, just above the 'witness' line, above your name, the initials R.A. for Randy Allen."

"No, that's not what that means. R. A. was a code the prosecuting District Attorney wanted on the report to indicate that you had a ride-along with you at the time. I guess it was because they didn't want any surprises in court and wanted to know all the witnesses. Then they could decide if they wanted them subpoenaed. So, we'd write RA on the signature line and remember who was there if it was needed later."

"R. A. means ride-along? Dad had a ride-along with him on the stop? Do you remember who it was?"

"Sorry, Casey. Maybe a few years earlier I might've remembered, but I can't recall now. If it weren't for Sonny's notation, I wouldn't remember it at all."

Casey realized the importance of the name of the ride-along, and excused himself quickly after pleading with

Officer Tomlinson to devote a few days to try to recall who was on the ride-along that night. "It's very important, Sir. Very important."

"Okay, Casey. I'll try."

As he drove back to town, the reality of the information was clear in his mind. Whoever, was on the ride-along that night, very likely may have been the same person who was a ride-along when Tony Garcia was arrested by Sonny. Now there was a possible connection not only between Sonny and the assassins, but possibly between the ride-along and the murderers. Again, he was baffled. *"Who would have been close enough to ride with Sonny on patrol, but would want him dead just two years later. It still might be Randy Allen."*

His thoughts were soon interrupted by the CHP radio. "7-11, Humboldt, I have a telephone request from a private party."

"Humboldt, 7-11, go ahead."

"7-11, 10-21 retired Officer Tomlinson at you earliest convenience. He says you have the number."

"Humboldt, 7-11. 10-4, and affirmative on the number."

Casey's mind was racing as he drove the next fifteen minutes to the nearest pay phone, at the Chevron station in Trinidad. He stopped his patrol car next to the phone booth and fumbled through his pockets for the change to make to local call. He pulled out a nickel and several pennies, but not enough to make the call. The whole case just might balance on the information he was about to receive, and he didn't have the change to make the call. He ran to the gas station and asked the attendant for change for a dollar.

"Sorry, Officer, the boss says we don't give out change," said the overweight, middle-aged woman behind the counter. "You'll have to buy something."

Casey looked at her incredulously for a moment, then grabbed a Snickers bar next to the register and pushed it across the counter. When he got the change, he pushed the Snickers bar back across the counter toward the woman. "Tell your boss to put this where the sun doesn't shine."

He sprinted back across the parking lot to the booth, and closed the door. His heart was pounding as he nervously dialed the number, and waited. One ring. Two rings. Three rings. On the fourth ring the answering machine kicked in, but he could hear Officer Tomlinson pick up the phone. As the recorded greeting of a young woman expressed regret that the call was missed, he could hear the old man cursing the device, "Hello? What? Hold on while I figure out how to turn this damn thing off." Casey could hear him pushing button after button as the recording droned on. "Worthless piece of crap. I don't even need this damn thing." As the recording finally stopped, he repeated, "I don't even need this thing, but my daughter in Antioch says I need it. Who's there?"

"It's me, Casey Tyler, Officer Tomlinson. Did you remember who the ride-along was?"

"Oh, yeah, Casey. Sorry about that damn answering machine. I didn't even want it but my daughter insisted …
"

"The ride-along, sir, who was it?" Casey interrupted.

"I remembered it just now. It was your mother. It was Bonnie."

The words hit him like a baseball bat in the chest. "Mom?" he asked incredulously.

"Yup! She sat in the car and never said a word. Of course, that's what they are supposed to do; shut up and say nothing. Be invisible. That's what she did, alright."

Casey thanked Officer Tomlinson and hung up. He walked slowly back to his unit and sat in the seat, staring out the windshield. Then he buried his face in his hands, pondering the unthinkable.

Could it be possible that his own mother contacted Tony Garcia three years later and arranged for Sonny's murder? "Why? It was preposterous. Then who killed Tony Garcia? And why? Could his mom actually be capable of double-crossing, and killing someone like Garcia in cold blood? Preposterous! What on earth could have been the motive for such a heinous crime? Then did she contact Eduardo Corona seventeen years later to kill me? And, a week ago, could she have repeated the act by killing Big Mike cold-heartedly, just to get another gun? Why would she need another gun? She had several at her disposal." The thoughts were outrageous, and he intermittently scolded himself for even thinking them.

When he got back to Eureka, Casey headed straight for the bar at the Eureka Inn, ordered a Jack and Coke, tall, and sat in a corner by himself, trying to make sense of it all.

Not normally much of a drinker, he had had his fill of reality for the day. Several hours and a half dozen cocktails later, Casey stumbled out to his car in the parking lot. Wisdom prevailed, and he turned away, left his car at the Eureka Inn parking lot, and walked the mile and a half to his home.

Half way home he remembered why people don't walk long distances at night in early March in Eureka. The cold, fresh, damp air sweeping in off of Humboldt Bay chilled him to the bone, so that when he got home, he threw a log on the fire, poured another Jack and Coke, this time heavy on the Jack and light on the Coke, and slumped into his recliner.

He stared into the fire as it began to warm up the room. With an awkward sweep of his hand, he hit the light switch, leaving the room totally dark except for the light from the fire. His mind raced back and forth reliving his simple question and Officer Tomlinson's totally unanticipated answer. What had begun as a quest for the truth, and justice for his father, had now brought him face to face with more truth than he could fathom.

The Revelation

It was 1 a.m., but sleep was still not forthcoming, even with the alcohol he'd consumed. He locked the front door, then went to the tall cabinet near the fireplace, and pulled out the journal he had kept since he began the investigation. He sat back in the recliner, and turned on the reading lamp over his right shoulder. He took a long drink from the now-diluted cocktail, and put it on the floor next to the chair. He opened the journal, and began at the beginning, looking for every possible scenario that didn't point to his mother being involved in his dad's death seventeen years ago.

Somewhere around page 21, the "Summary of the Facts on Alden Snider," he began to nod off. By the middle of the page, the book slid down his chest and he fell fast asleep in his favorite chair.

In what seemed like just moments later, his sleep was interrupted by movement in the room. He aroused, and in the dim glow of the embers in the fireplace, he could make out the presence of a shadowy figure moving toward him from the front door. He squinted to see the details of the stranger, but, in an instant, the black-hooded figure moved directly in front of him and raised both hands, holding a gun. Casey saw the barrel of the gun, a big gun, with a long barrel, which was now aimed at his chest. Suddenly three shots rang out; two in quick succession, and then a third, almost point blank. He saw the muzzle flashes directly in front of him.

He instinctively rolled out of the chair to his left, and scrambled across the floor on all fours. He was surprised that he was still alive and able to move. But he had to keep moving before he could be shot again, so he scrambled behind a nearby dumpster. *A dumpster? Where did that come from? He looked down at his chest. Where's the blood?* The shots had been almost point blank, and yet he didn't see any blood or feel any pain. "*A gun. I need a gun. Where's the closest gun?* The closest gun was on the fireplace mantel, his dad's CHP Commemorative Revolver, in its decorative wooden display case just 8 feet away. *Why is the fireplace mantel in this alley?* There was no time to think, he had to act fast. *Could he get to the gun before the shooter fired again?* He tried to lunge toward the display case to get the gun, but his legs wouldn't respond to his mind's urging. *Oh my God, my legs were shot! I'm paralyzed!* He began to pull himself toward the fireplace, but he could barely drag his feet. Everything was in slow motion as he pulled himself across the room toward the gun on the mantel. *Why can't I move? Why can't I think faster?"*

Slowly, he pulled himself up the fireplace and opened the wooden gun case, reaching inside for the gun, but the gun was gone! Total despair overtook him as he realized that he was going to die at this moment, at the hands of his assailant.

He turned to meet his inevitable fate, but the black-hooded attacker was gone. Quickly, although much too slow for his comfort, his stream of consciousness returned, and he realized that he was on the floor in his living room, not in a deserted alley as he recalled from a moment before. Gone were the dumpster and the shadowy figure which had just tried to kill him. Only then did he fully realize that the whole episode was a dream; albeit it a very real, and very frightening, dream.

Sweating profusely, he was euphoric that he was alive. The dream seemed more real than any he had ever had, and now he was just glad to be safe. Nevertheless, the dream became even more disquieting as he realized he had just relived the nightmare of his father's death. He sensed the very real fear his father must have felt when he realized he was about to die.

As he regained his composure, he sat back in the chair, trembling, with his head buried in his cold clammy hands. He began to sob as he relived the dream in his mind, his hands shaking as he remembered the details. Perhaps it would be important someday, but for tonight, all he could feel were the sordid details and the stark, hopeless mixture of fear and euphoria he had just felt.

As he relived the nightmare step by step, he was puzzled. He was so utterly familiar with the circumstances of his father's murder, he wondered why he dreamed it differently. Why were there differences? Why were there three clear and distinct shots in the dream instead of two, and why was he in an enclosed alley, instead of along a rural highway.

Was it a premonition of how he, himself, might die someday? In an alley; point blank; by a hooded figure, perhaps even by the same person who had killed his father? After all, he was dealing with a cold-blooded killer who had shown that he would not hesitate to kill again to keep from getting caught. The answers were not forthcoming, but the questions were overwhelming.

He picked up the overturned drink glass and cleaned up the spill. *"What an eerie and frightening week,"* he pondered.

He stood up next to the mantel and looked at the display case containing the Commemorative .357 Revolver, and was relieved to see it was, in fact, still in the case and wasn't missing as it was in the nightmare. *"Thank goodness it is still here. I wonder why I dreamed it was gone?"*

Casey retired to the bedroom and sat on the edge of the bed. Another hour of lost sleep as he relived the nightmare, until he eventually fell asleep from exhaustion.

The Dirty Barrel

He slept in till 9:00 a.m. the next morning, the first of two normal days off. When he awoke he was still pondering the very thoughts he was thinking when he dozed off. He walked into the front room and again picked up the journal and leafed through it. He stepped to the mantel and looked at the open box containing the Commemorative Revolver. To his knowledge, the gun had never been out of the display case. *Why was it gone in his dream?*

He picked it up and turned it in his hands, looking at it from all angles. He looked into the barrel and his eyes froze at what he saw. He snatched up a Kleenex from a nearby box and pushed it into the barrel about a half inch, then retrieved it and looked at it.

"That can't be!" he said aloud. *"It's been fired."* *"Dad would never have fired this weapon. By shooting even one round through it, the collector's value of it would have been significantly decreased."* Then, catching himself in mid thought, he stopped in his tracks. *"It can't be. I must be mistaken. I have to get to the office!"*

He hurried to shower and dress for a quick trip to the Sheriff's Office. As he opened the door to leave, the phone rang. He picked up the phone, hoping, as he had for the last month, that it might be Andrea.

"Hello. ... Oh, hi mom. Say, mom, I've got to go right now. I'll tell you later. I've got to get down to the Sheriff's Office."

"Casey, honey, I thought you were off today?"

Casey was sorry he had even mentioned the Sheriff's Office. Especially with the thoughts he was entertaining. "Well, I am ... sort of, but something came up and I've got to go in and talk to Sergeant Regan."

"Honey, you are starting to scare me again. I worry about you. Your fiancée almost got killed and now she's left you. You almost got killed. I almost got killed. Now, finally, Snider is finally going to have to pay for his crimes ... Don't you get it, Honey, it's over. We can finally relax and put this behind us."

Casey decided to divert the conversation and not arouse any more angst and suspicion than necessary. "You know, Mom. You may be right. It wasn't smart for me to jeopardize everyone's safety. I'm just glad it's over. Let's get together over my days off and celebrate. OK?"

"Now you are starting to make sense. Why don't you come over tonight for dinner? I'm so glad it is behind us and none of us got hurt this time. Honey, you were getting obsessed with this and I'm just glad Andrea and I didn't get killed by Snider. Let's have dinner tonight."

"Sure, Mom. I've got to go now."

"Okay," she said with reluctant resignation, "By the way, what is so important to get you to go into the Sheriff's Office today?"

"It's not that big a thing, mom. I'll tell you later tonight."

"Okay, honey. Be careful. See you later."

"Goodbye." He placed the phone back on the cradle and hurried out the door.

Bonnie Tyler slowly laid the phone back in the cradle and sighed. She knew Casey, and she knew he was lying. *"I just hope he knows what he's doing."*

Section Seventeen

The Ballistics Test

"Amarillo by morning, up from Santa Fe …" blared out the song from the radio on the lunchroom counter. Evidence Tech Ty Randolph was sitting with his back to the door, when Casey approached the employee's break room. He had his feet up on the adjacent chair, right hand holding an imaginary microphone and mouthing the words as he sang along with the song. On the table in front of him sat his morning cup of coffee. No one else was in the room as Casey quietly walked up behind him and said, "Excuse me, Mister Strait, can I have your autograph?"

Randolph jumped upright in the chair in surprise and embarrassment as he turned to see who had caught him in his fantasy. "Casey. I thought you were off today. I hoped I was going to get some things cleared up on my desk today, but if you are here at 8:00 a.m. on your day off, something is up."

"Yeah, it is. Don's not in his office. Is he around?"

"He is signed out to the range this morning. Quarterly qualifying. He should be back in an hour or so. Anything I can do?"

"Actually, yes, you can. I need you to do something for me. Just to clarify one last thing…" At that moment, three other employees came into the room and walked toward the coffee pot. "Can we talk in your lab office?" he said quietly.

"Sure." Randolph knew something was serious in Casey's voice, even though Casey was trying to act normal. Without further conversation, they walked briskly down the hall and into Randolph's tiny cluttered office, where he closed the door behind them. "What's up?"

Casey opened his briefcase and pulled the wooden inlaid Commemorative Revolver box from it. He opened it and pulled the revolver out of the velvet indentation and held it in his hands. "This may be a bizarre request, but I want you to check this weapon for me. Check it out to confirm it has never been fired." He handed the weapon to Randolph as he continued, "If it has been fired, I want you to test fire it and compare the round …"

Randolph looked down the barrel as he listened, then interrupted, "I can tell you right now with 99% certainty that it has been fired."

"I thought so, too. This is important, and it's a little embarrassing to even ask, but would you check it against the bullet that killed my father, like you did the other ones."

Randolph stood there for several long moments with his mouth open. "No shit? You think THIS gun …?" … his voice tailed off as he contemplated the significance of the request. He took a deep breath and slowly let it out. "Why do you think …?"

"Actually, it all started with a real weird dream, but the story is too long to tell right now. Can you do it for me? I'm sure it will be just like the other guns; negative. Do you still have the test firings from the other guns?"

"Yeah, right here in this envelope in my desk drawer," he said, as he slid the drawer open to show Casey. "I just held them here, since they aren't evidence or anything like that."

"Great. While you are at it, how about comparing all three against the Garcia murder rounds, too. I want to get this bullshit out of my mind once and for all."

"Sure. I know how hard it must be for you to even think …"

"Yes, it is," Casey interrupted him before he could even utter the thought aloud. "That's why I need it right away. This morning?"

"Of course. We need to eliminate it as soon as possible."

"Thanks, Ty. I need to go check out one last thing I just thought of at the Plymouth. I'll be back in an hour or so. There's a big new wrinkle in the case, and I'll tell Don all about it when I get back."

"The Plymouth?"

"Yeah, that's another long story." Casey said as he opened the door and exited.

Randolph stared at the gun in his hands as he contemplated the bizarre thought that Sonny Tyler's own Commemorative Revolver might have been used in his murder. "*That's inconceivable,*" he said to himself as he, too, left the room and headed for the evidence lab and the indoor weapons test area.

Section Eighteen

The Plymouth Reveals its Secret

With the inconceivable now conceivable, yet still unbelievable, Casey headed for Forest Circle, the cul-de-sac north of the Tyler house, from which he could make his way, virtually unseen, down to the old Plymouth. It was still midmorning when Casey pulled onto Forest Circle and parked at the curb next to the tarnished 'For Sale' sign that guarded the old trail, which led along the forest ravine parallel to Walnut Drive, and eventually intersected the trail from the Tyler residence to the Plymouth. This way, he could make his way down to the old car without being observed from the Tyler residence.

He felt extremely self-conscious as he opened the car door and looked around to see if he was being watched. He got out of the car and walked briskly down the path, turned left at the charred redwood stump and skirted along the ravine toward the deep forest behind the residences along Walnut Drive.

As he traversed the trail through the underbrush and deeper into the forest canopy of the tall redwood trees that blocked both light and noise, he replayed his thoughts over and over again. *"The murderer's license number, in 1970, was from a car that had been out of service for at least five years at the time. Off the road for five years in 1970! Then the rear plate from the murder vehicle turns up at Alden Snider's house; with tags that expired in 1964. Could they have been the old Plymouth plates? When dad and I originally found the old Plymouth in 1968, I'm sure there was an old license plate on it. But after the funeral, and for as long as I can remember after that, I don't recall there being a license plate on the rear of the old Plymouth. But the front of the car has never been uncovered, so I don't know if the front plate is there or not."*

The revelation from the night before that Bonnie Tyler was riding along with Sonny when Tony Garcia and Eduardo Corona were arrested certainly shifted his suspicions. *"Randy Allen had the ability to commit the murder, the opportunity, and a strong motive. Sure, some of the newest evidence did appear to implicate Bonnie, but there was no motive for her to kill Sonny."* This last curiosity, at the Plymouth, would resolve the one last nagging issue that might prove the case one way or another.

Five minutes later, he entered the clearing and stopped and stared at the old Plymouth. He flashed back seventeen years ago, remembering the days after Sonny Tyler's funeral, when he stood in the same spot and 're-discovered' the old Plymouth. Reliving it now through a grown man's eyes, wasn't it strange that the rear of the car was not nearly as overgrown as the front? He remembered reading the name 'Plymouth' in chrome just above where the rear license plate would have been. Why hadn't he noticed that before? Or was it just his over-active imagination getting the best of him? *"Please, God, let me be wrong. I don't ask for much, but this time let me be wrong."*

He walked to the back of the car, cleared away the fresh overgrowth and saw it again, just as he remembered it; the chrome Plymouth emblem, just above the rusted out bracket which would have held the rear plate, which, just as he remembered, was missing.

His heart was pounding loudly in his chest, but before he could reflect further on his discovery, while he was still bent over the back of the car, he heard a loud rush of crackling twigs and branches coming toward him from behind. He could hear the labored breathing of an intruder, charging toward him. He spun around to defend himself from the attacker, and was immediately confronted by the family dog, Ralph, who came running toward him through the bushes and across the clearing. Ralph's tail was wagging furiously and he let out a single greeting bark as he rushed to his side.

Casey gasped in relief, and held his hand to his chest. "Jeezus, Ralph, don't fricken' do that! You almost gave me a heart attack," he said as he sat back against the Plymouth. "That's twice you've scared the crap out of me down here. How'd you know I was here, boy?"

After petting him for a moment, he said, "Got to check something out, Ralph. Go play."

He returned his attention to the front of the car, while Ralph wandered nearby. Within two minutes, he had cleared his way to the point he could see the front bumper of the car. Bending down and looking at bumper level from the side, he was able to see that the front plate was still on the bumper.

Another few moments and he could reach down and touch the top of the plate. He could get just enough leverage to bend the corner of the plate back about an inch. He peeked into the opening, and he could make out the number '1' was the last letter.

He could feel his arteries in his throat pounding so hard he thought he might choke from the pulsing, and his hand was shaking as he grabbed the inch thick sapling and ripped it away from the grill. He was stretched across the hood of the car with his feet off the ground, looking down upside down at the plate until he could finally see the full plate. Raw emotion, the kind that occurs when dreams are shattered by reality, overwhelmed him, and his eyes teared up, as he looked at it and mouthed the digits; A – R – M – 6 –0 –1. He settled his feet back onto the ground and leaned onto the hood with his face buried in his hands.

He felt a cold shiver run down his spine as he gave up all hope for a reasonable explanation that didn't point to his own mother as being involved in the murder of his dad. "Jeezus!" He uttered as he faced the reality of the revelation.

'Crack-crack'. The sound of leaves and twigs breaking directly behind him commandeered his attention,

Steve Davis

but then he smiled, without looking, and said, "Oh, no you don't, I'm not falling for that one again, Ralph." Hearing his name, Ralph wagged his tail, and Casey's eyes slowly looked down to see the faithful dog sitting at his feet.

"*O-h-h, shit!*" he said to himself.

The Tangled Web Unravels

Ty Randolph had completed the test firing and leaned over to look into the comparison microscope when he heard Sergeant Regan coming down the hallway approaching the lab. "For god's sake, how can you listen to that twangy hillbilly crap," Regan said as he came in and turned George Jones off in mid-sentence.

Randolph moved away from the microscope and shuffled the papers on the counter next to it. "Morning Sarge," he said, turning to greet the Sergeant.

Regan hoisted himself up on the edge of the desk. "What has you so engrossed in your work this Monday morning?"

"Just a routine test firing," he offered meekly. He wasn't sure how much he should tell Regan about Casey's suspicions about the Tyler guns at this time, so he hoped the conversation could be diverted until he could complete the comparisons. "How did qualifying go? Are you still as deadly a shot as you always were?"

"Qualifying went good. It's over for another quarter. Noticing the light on the microscope, he said, "You never seemed to be interested in my qualifying in the past. You look like the kid who got caught in the cookie jar. What's up?"

Randolph cringed at his transparency. Sergeant Regan was simply too good at interrogation to pull anything over on. "Okay, Sarge," he said resignedly, "Just let me finish what I'm doing and I'll fill you in on the details, okay."

"All right, Ty. I'll be in my office. Don't take too long, you know I hate surprises."

Sergeant Regan left the room and walked toward his office at the end of the hall, but returned immediately. "Okay, Ty, let's hear it. I just walked by your office and I see an empty CHP Commemorative Revolver box on your desk. The only person I know who has one is Casey. What's going on?"

Randolph eased away from the microscope and leaned against the back of his lab stool. "I promised Casey I wouldn't say anything until I finished, but I'm sure he won't mind if I tell you. He just wanted to eliminate any possibility that this gun is involved in the murder of his dad."

"His dad's murder? His own Commemorative Revolver? Why did he think that might be involved?"

"Something about a dream he had and he wanted me to do this test and not tell anyone what he was thinking if it came back negative, which he expected it will."

"So how did it check out?"

"I don't know yet. I just got it set up for comparison viewing when you came in. I should know in minutes."

"Okay, I'll be in my office. Let me know as soon as you see anything, either way."

"10-4, Sarge."

Sergeant Regan paused in the hallway to pick up his message slips from his "pigeon hole" and was glancing at them as he walked toward his office, when Randolph shouted, "Sarge, come here, you've got to see this!"

Regan rushed back into the lab, where Randolph was standing next to the microscope and motioned for him to look.

He eased into the stool and looked into the microscope. The bullet from the murder was displayed on the left, and the test round from the Commemorative Revolver was on the right. Randolph had turned the finger wheel until the striations from the barrel of the shooting weapon, which had transferred to the shaft of each bullet during firing, lined up in a straight across pattern. The conclusion was unmistakable; both rounds had been fired from the same gun barrel."

"Oh … my … God," Regan said as he slowly stood up to the full length of his 6-4 height. "Any way there can be an error, or other explanation?"

"Not a chance. The scope doesn't lie and no two barrels will mark them the same."

"You're sure you got the right bullets?" Regan asked incredulously, knowing the answer before he spoke the words.

"Yep, right bullets. It is just hard to conceive, isn't it?"

"Shit! I was there when Bonnie gave this gun to Casey. Where's Casey now?"

"He said he'd be back. He had to go check something at the "Plymouth." He didn't say where that was or what that meant."

"The Plymouth? That's back in the woods behind the Tyler house. I've got to find him. He may be in danger." Regan rushed from the room, grabbed the gun off his desk and headed for the door.

The Confrontation at the Plymouth

"You just couldn't leave it alone, could you?"

The voice was familiar, but the tone was menacing and cold, unlike anything he'd ever heard from his mother. Before he even turned around, he knew he was in the gun sights of a cold, calculating murderer armed with a <u>big</u> gun.

He slowly turned around and found himself staring down the barrel of the largest revolver he'd ever seen from that perspective. He guessed it was a .44 magnum, like the one that Big Mike Owens brought to his own murder. He knew it would blow him into the next county if he didn't come up with a plan pretty fast.

The hands that held the gun, not six feet away from his face, showed no sign of trepidation. His own knees were shaking as he said, "Mom, put the gun down. You aren't going to shoot me, are you? I'm your own son." He knew the answer, but he was looking to stall for any time he could to come up with a plan.

"I have to, honey, you wouldn't give it up, and now, you know." Her voice was kind and motherly, but there was no mercy in her combat stance and the rock steady two handed grip on the gun. "Oh, I tried to save you, but you wouldn't listen," she said as she shook her hair out of her eyes. "I tried to scare some sense into you, but you just wouldn't give it up."

"Mom, others know, too."

"I don't think so. You just found out for sure."

"You … you killed my dad. Your own husband!"

"No, I didn't, Casey," she said sweetly. "You are wrong. I did not kill your father. In fact, I consider myself a hero. I killed the man who killed your dad!"

"El Gato. But … you hired him to kill dad!"

"See, there you go again. You are just like your father. You just can't see past your self-righteousness."

"Self-righteousness? We are talking about a cold, calculated murder!"

"He was going to leave me. I had no choice."

"What are you talking about?"

"See, I knew it. You don't understand. Your dad was not the saint you think he was. You should have seen the way she looked at him. And the way she carried on after he died."

"Who?"

"That dispatcher slut. I knew what she was up to. I looked at him the same way, years ago, and he fell for it. I could see she was going to steal him away from us. I couldn't let it happen."

"Sylvia? No, mom, really; you've got it wrong …"

"Shut up, Casey. I don't like this any better than you do, but you've left me no choice. Now I don't want the last thing I hear from you to be sticking up for that bitch."

Hearing the unfamiliar stressful tone in their voices, Ralph ran up between them and looked at Bonnie. He, too, sensed there was something different about this confrontation between mother and son. He growled at the gun in Bonnie's hand. "Shut up, Ralph, you are supposed to protect me. I'll deal with you later." The dog just stared back at her but didn't move."

"Well, then …" Casey continued to stall, "What, exactly, <u>do</u> you want to hear from me before you kill me?"

"I don't know. I have to admit it was easier when I didn't really know the dirtbags before I killed them."

Casey saw an opportunity to stall her while he formulated a plan. "Just tell me a couple things before you shoot me. I put a lot of time into this and I'd like some answers first. I know you were on a ride-along with dad when he arrested Tony Garcia, but how did you arrange for Tony Garcia to kill dad three years later?"

"That was easy. He went back to prison for a year, thanks to your dad, so it was easy to get him to ambush your dad for a thousand bucks, even without knowing who was hiring him. I even gave him the gun and the untraceable license plates. All he had to do was steal a white Chevy, do the job, and return the car to where he stole it. I guess he was a good car thief, too, because the car never even got reported stolen by the owner."

Casey could see that she was actually enjoying reliving the details of how smart she was in planning the murders down to the last detail. "And Eduardo Corona? The same thing, huh? You were with dad when he arrested Eduardo Corona, too. And you hired him to kill me, but it didn't work."

"No, honey. I wouldn't do that. I just hired him to scare you. He botched that job and got himself killed, but it worked out OK in the end."

Casey's mind was piecing it together at blinding speed. "The intruder at Andrea's, the attack on you, all bullshit that you staged!" he continued, incredulous that this woman he knew so well could contrive such deception, and fool so many for so long. "And the Plus P ammo. Of course. You used dad's own gun and ammo to kill him!"

"Why not. He always said it was good stuff."

At that moment, Ralph growled again at the gun in her hand. "Shut up, Ralph. We'll be done in a minute and then we will go plant the other license plate and this gun at Alden Snider's and wait for the action to start."

"Alden Snider. That's another thing. You were willing … No, you actually worked at it, to set him up to go to jail for a murder he didn't commit. Why would you do that?"

"He called me a 'bitch!'"

Casey gulped hard as he realized that his mom was far more disturbed and menacing than he ever dreamed she could be.

He readied himself for an opportunity to attempt to escape. From his training, he knew, statistically, that he had the advantage of surprise if he acted unexpectedly. It would only take about a half second for him to act, and it would take her three-quarters of a second to react to whatever he did. He knew he couldn't cover the six feet between them and get the gun away from her in that one-quarter of a second advantage. But, perhaps, just perhaps, if he could distract her, he could bolt for freedom into the depths of the surrounding forest. He hoped that she would miss with her first shot, and the noise and recall from the .44 Magnum might surprise and disorient her and offer his only possibility of getting out of her accuracy range. Young and in good shape, he knew if he could dodge the bullets that far, he had half a chance of escaping.

"How are you going to explain this to the cops?"

"I won't have to. If they don't miss you themselves, I'll just report you missing tonight. They'll find your car where you parked it, track you down here and find you. I'll make sure the trail is clearly marked right up to Alden Snider's, where they'll find this gun and other evidence at his house. Case closed."

She gestured with the gun to emphasize her point. At the movement, once again, Ralph growled at the gun in her hand. This time, the growl was followed by a bark and a step toward Bonnie. "I told you to shut up." She pointed the gun at the dog to emphasize the order.

Casey seized that moment of distraction. He quickly bolted to his left, toward the rear of the Plymouth. He heard the deafening boom from the big gun, and heard the bullet ricochet off of the roof of the car. But instead of the disoriented pause he had hoped for, Bonnie quickly found her target again and squeezed off another round. He felt the percussion of the second bullet as it passed close to his right ear and slammed the tree he was approaching.

He ducked around the rear of the Plymouth and dove into the underbrush as the next shot struck another tree next to him. *"That's three shots,"* he thought as he scrambled to his feet behind a small sapling for cover. *"I've only got to dodge three more,"* he reassured himself, as he headed for the density of the forest

After only two or three steps, he tripped over a vine and fell on his face. As he scrambled to his feet, he glanced back over his shoulder and saw Bonnie, who had stepped to the edge of the clearing and was again pointing the gun at him, in a shooter's stance, steadying it with both hands, from about fifteen feet away. He saw the muzzle flash out of the corner of his eye, and felt the bullet strike him in the middle of the back, just below the right shoulder blade and tear through his right arm. The impact of the .44 caliber round propelled him forward a full six feet and his momentum caused him to tumble about ten feet down the embankment where he came to rest at the bottom, stunned and unconscious.

Bonnie worked her way carefully along the thick, thorny berry vines of the clearing until she could see his motionless torso through the weeds and blackberry vines, lying at the bottom of the ravine in the creek bed. Blood covered his entire right side.

"I'd better not go down there. I'll get scratched up and have to explain it, but I'd better finish him off," she thought to herself, as she took careful aim at Casey's back and pulled the trigger one more time. The sound seemed even more deafening now that she was composed, and she heard the sickening "thump" as the bullet struck his still form, causing it to pulsate, then shudder and again lay motionless.

As she directed the weapon, and the last shot, at Casey's head, Ralph ran toward her, growling menacingly, and snapped at her gun hand. She turned the weapon on the dog and fired one round, striking the animal, which yelped once, and fell dead on the ground. "Stupid dog," she said as she turned her attention back toward Casey's still body. She inched closer until, from about fifteen feet away, she noted his entire right side was covered with blood. She carefully took aim at his head, and slowly squeezed the trigger one more time. CLICK.

"Damn." She said. She looked again at his still body in the underbrush. He didn't move, and she satisfied herself that he was dead or at least mortally wounded.

She turned toward the trail and headed back up the clearing toward the fork in the trail that led to her house, but when she got to the switchback that led to Redwood Trail, where Alden Snider lived, she set off on that path. But before she went far, she stopped to listen to a sound that caught her attention. In the distance, along the ridgeline path from where Casey had come, she could hear another person approaching loudly along the trail, although he or she was still quite some distance away.

She doubled back to an old tree stump from which she could see the convergence of the trails, and took cover, seated on a stump out of sight of the approaching and unsuspecting person. She reached into her pocket and pulled out six new bullets and quietly and deliberately loaded them into the gun. She nestled the barrel of the gun on a branch, making a tripod, and waited in ambush for the unsuspecting person.

The Rise of the Phoenix

Deeper in the forest, at the bottom of the ravine, Casey aroused from the shock of his injuries, and, moaning in pain, rolled onto his left side and eventually got into a sitting position.

'Shit!' he cursed, as he began to take stock of his injuries. His right arm was badly injured by the bullet wound it had sustained, but the bleeding stopped for the most part if he held it doubled up against his side. He used his left arm to pull up his shirt and was greatly relieved to see that his bullet proof vest had done its job and prevented the rounds from entering his torso, although the blue-black bruise covering his entire right side looked like it had been pummeled by a baseball bat.

Casey looked around, while he cleared his head and caught his breath. *"Shit! My own mother!"* He sat quietly for a few seconds as he regained his cognizance and recalled the events, and then he realized he had lost a fair amount of blood, and needed to get help.

He was eventually able to get to his feet, and climb back up to the trail.

He drew his .38 snub nosed revolver from his right pocket with his left hand, and held it awkwardly as it clearly felt out of place. It was no match for the big .44 magnum Bonnie had, but he was glad to have it just in case. He also took some solace in the fact that every month of his career he had to qualify shooting at least 6 shots using his left hand. *"Maybe the CHP knew what it was doing on that call,"* he thought.

As he began to advance up the trail to the clearing from which the shooting started, he saw the dead body of Ralph. He kneeled down next to the dog and stroked its fur. "Thanks, Ralph. Good dog." Not only did the dog save him by his diversion, the bullet she fired at the dog had caused the gun to be empty when Bonnie attempted to finish Casey off in the ravine.

"That cold bitch!" He wiped the tears away and headed up the trail, quietly as possible. He too, could hear the approach of the person on the trail far ahead, and, thinking it was Bonnie, possibly returning, he crept slowly and quietly, ever mindful of another ambush.

Steve Davis

After a few minutes, as he was nearing the trail convergence, the sound of the person was getting clearer, cursing to himself as he stumbled along the trail. He recognized the voice as that of Sergeant Regan.

Greatly relieved to hear his friend approaching, he took a few steps toward him, and just as he began to call out his name, a bright swath of a familiar color caught his attention off to his right. He squatted down by a fallen log and moved a branch slowly to the side. He could see Bonnie, in her bright turquoise blouse, seated on the tree stump, hand on the trigger, and waiting for Sergeant Regan to come into the open at the trail convergence.

Casey pulled the gun to a shooting position. Bonnie was already in a seated, combat stance, and Sergeant Regan was totally unprepared for the confrontation. Should he shout to save Regan, or take a chance and try to shoot Bonnie, an open target in front of him. They were outgunned, and he decided he better take the shot while it was open. He steadied the snub-nosed revolver, aimed just above the turquoise target and took a deep breath. She was 60-70 feet away, and under ideal conditions, the short gun was accurate for maybe 35 feet. Plus, this wasn't just a paper silhouette target, this was his mother!

Could he do it? Maybe he should just yell after all, and take their chances if she got away? His choice was quickly made for him as he heard Regan enter the clearing, and as he squinted, he could see Bonnie poised with her finger tight against the trigger.

He steadied his left hand against the log, cocked the revolver and peered down the short barrel until the front sight was again surrounded by turquoise. He held his breath and steadily squeezed the trigger until the gun fired. He heard Bonnie cry out in pain as the big gun fired in her hand, then she fell out of sight to the ground. He knew he had hit Bonnie, but he didn't know how well, because she was no longer in sight.

"Don, take cover," he yelled. "Are you okay? It's Bonnie. She's trying to kill us. Stay down."

Sergeant Regan was caught totally off guard by the explosions of the guns, first the pop of a .38, then the boom of the .44. The bullet had whizzed above his head, and he dove into the underbrush, and drew his own 9mm automatic. "I'm okay. Where is she?"

"Straight ahead up the trail in front of you. She's been hit. But I don't know how badly."

Steve Davis

After a few agonizing seconds of complete quiet, the men circled the location from which Bonnie had been laying in ambush. As they converged on the location, they could see a bright red stained turquoise body on the floor of the trail. Sergeant Regan approached the still form and declared that she was dead.

Sergeant Regan looked at Casey incredulously and said, "What the hell happened here, Casey?" But then he noticed for the first time that Casey had been shot. "Never mind for now. We've got to get you to the hospital, Casey. I'll get some units here to take it from here. You can tell me about it on the way up to the house."

Casey winced in pain, but only he knew the exact source of the hurt. "She shot me, Don. In cold blood. How could she do that to me, her own son?"

Regan shook his head back and forth slowly, "She had us all fooled, Casey."

Conclusion

The Next Day

"Ouch! Son of a Bitch!" Sergeant Regan grimaced in pain as he turned his ankle on a two-inch-thick branch that was lying across the trail, hidden by the leaves. He was still grumbling under his breath as he made his way up the last few yards to the clearing where the Plymouth sat. Alongside the old relic seated in an old lawn chair sat Casey, a beer in his left hand, his right arm in a huge cast on the arm rest, and his feet up on a stump, staring at Regan's arrival.

"Jesus, Don. Don't kill yourself."

Regan glanced to the rear of the Plymouth, where something new had been added; the freshly turned soil covered a small mound, upon which there was a pile of rocks and a crude cross. Motioning to the fresh grave,

Regan said, "That must have been tough, one-handed, with a cast. You should have asked. I'd have helped you."

"Naw. It needed to be just him and me."

"He was a good dog." Regan looked around at the dozen or so beer cans littering the ground, right where they had been thrown from the chair in all directions. "Everyone's been asking and worrying about you today. But I knew you'd be here."

"Good detective work, Detective Sergeant Regan. Keep it up and there might be a career opportunity for you." Casey's slurred speech told the story of his day.

Regan laughed at Casey's inebriation, a condition he'd never seen before. "You drink all those by yourself?"

"Hell, no. Dad drank most of them." His head rocked like a bobble head doll as he looked at the Plymouth and then around at the cans littering the clearing. "I've only have … had a couple."

"Any left for me?"

"Sure, there's the rest of the case in that backpack." As he tried to get his feet off the stump, he almost turned the lawn chair over.

"Easy, Casey. I'll get it." He opened the backpack and pulled a beer from the cold ice water of a plastic bag, and peeled back the top. "Celebrating?" he asked.

"Yeah, Don. I'm celebrating my independence. I used to have a father, and a mother, and a fiancée, and a faithful dog. I even had a normal life, once. But now that those burdens are gone, I'm pretty much a free man."

"I figured you could use some company." He took a long gulp from the can as he tried to figure out what to say to a friend whose father had been killed by his mother seventeen years ago, but he just figured it out, got shot for his efforts, lost his dog, and had to shoot his own mother to save a friend's life, ... and whose fiancée dumped him because her daddy told her to. "Wish I could say something profound, Casey, but I'm just not that creative at these things. All I can say is you still have a lifelong friend to commiserate with."

"Thanks, Don. I've been thinking. Maybe my purpose is finished here. Do you suppose if I quit being a cop, Andrea might let me back in her life?

"Nope. That ain't going to happen." Regan took another drink from the can.

"Well, thanks, friend. That's not exactly what I wanted to hear from you."

"The truth hurts. I know. Trust me. It ain't going to happen. It's too late."

"She might have a change of heart."

"Yeah, but you can't."

"What do you mean? I'm the one who's talking about it."

"Quit kidding yourself, Casey. This case just proved what we both already knew. You are a cop; a damn good one; it was meant to be, and you can never do anything else again. You are addicted. Just like me. It's too late." He accentuated the statement with a long drink from the can.

"So, what are you saying? I'm just going to be a lifetime loser like my new friend, Don?

Regan laughed at Casey's familiarity. Before, their 'friendship' had been purely professional, working on a big case together, but he knew that it had changed with the conclusion of the case. They would be close friends forever.

"You might not have to. Someone's been asking about you all day long."

"Really?" There was a long, confused pause. "Who?"

"Sally Perkins. She's been hanging around the office all day, asking why you haven't come in to the office today."

"Sally?" His voice changed as he mulled the thought in his mind. "What time is it?"

"Time for you to sober up and give her a call. Here's her phone number." Regan reached over and handed Casey a small scrap of paper with the number scrawled on it.

"Wow! You are a good friend."

"Yeah. But let's have another beer first." Gesturing toward the old Plymouth, he said, "The three of us just broke the biggest case of our careers, and we've got some celebrating to do."

THE END

WANT MORE ACTION FROM STEVE DAVIS?

'Perfect Alibis'
Novel – 395 pages

California Highway Patrol Lt. Ryan Foster glanced down at the smoking gun in his hand. This certainly wasn't the way he envisioned his life turning out. Yet here he was, standing among four dead young men in a dark New York alley; men he had just lured into an ambush and murdered in cold blood.

How could a highly regarded career CHP veteran turn into a cold-blooded murderer? He didn't even know their names. Men he'd never seen before tonight. He couldn't ponder the question for long, though, the sirens were getting closer, and he had to plan his next murder, in Florida.

Of course, the date his life went awry was very clear; that would be May 26, 2013; the day his seventeen-year-old daughter was murdered on a remote beach near Mendocino, California.

Author Steve Davis follows his first novel, "22E ... Officer Down!", with another thrilling suspense drama that takes Lt. Foster and his co-conspirators around the world in their quest for justice - street justice if necessary - while leaving perfect alibis and frustrated cops in their wake.

Their last escapade, an audaciously daring plot, thrusts them headlong into a trap set by the FBI and police from three states.

The ending is guaranteed to leave readers enthralled, while pondering the thin line between right and wrong, as they anxiously await the next novel by the author.

'Snap Judgement'
Novella - 72 pages

The first in a planned series of novellas (short novels) by Steve Davis, also under the pen name 'Lt. Steve Davis'. The series follows fictional California Highway Patrol Officer Corbin 'C. D.' Dixon as he investigates crimes originating from traffic accidents that don't pan out to be what they seem at first glance.

Here is the storyline of *'Snap Judgement'*:

Officer Dixon is assigned to investigate a hit-and-run accident near the mountain community of Cobb, in which the wife of a prominent defense attorney is killed.

As the clues reveal, the victim, a pedestrian on a deserted road, was actually struck by two vehicles, the first of which mortally injured her, and the second vehicle, which killed her outright. CD must find them both to unravel the case.

During the investigation, CD begins to suspect the first 'accident' may have been intentional, with the husband the prime suspect.

A carefully orchestrated of cat-and-mouse ensues, in which the husband uses the court system to destroy or exclude every piece of evidence until Casey is down to one final scrap of cloth upon which the entire case may hinge. When the court orders that scrap of cloth to be destroyed, the case appears lost.

Then CD devises a trick to save the evidence, but will it work? Just when it appears the trick may have worked, the case is blown wide open by the most unexpected game changing witness imaginable.

"22E ... Officer Down!" and *'Snap Judgement'*
are available at www.DavisMedia.com,
or on Amazon.com in paperback or Kindle E-book,
or may be ordered through any bookstore
using the ISBN# 9780991442003.

"22E … Officer Down!"

Steve Davis

93215314R00252

Made in the USA
Columbia, SC
09 April 2018